MUSCLE
AND OTHER STORIES

MUSCLE
AND OTHER STORIES

MATTHEW HUGHES

MUSCLE AND OTHER STORIES

Ebook ISBN: 978-1-927880-47-0

Paperback ISBN: 978-1-927880-49-4

FOREWORD

I always wanted to write fiction. In my teens, I vacillated between wanting to write historical novels and science fiction stories. In my twenties, I segued into wanting to write fantasy and even wrote an unpublishable post-apocalyptic novel about elves—the nasty kind—having come to North America to escape the Iron Age, only to have to hide themselves away in mountain fastnesses once the Europeans arrived with their deadly metal, then bursting out to rule once again when the iron-based civilization destroyed itself.

But by the time I was in my mid thirties, I had largely stopped reading science fiction and fantasy—except for Jack Vance—and was reading a lot of crime fiction: Elmore Leonard, Donald Westlake, Lawrence Block, Reginald Hill, and many more. It maybe came natural to me, because I come from a working-poor family that features a strong streak of criminality. Just within my close gene pool, I can think of instances of arson, thievery, dope-dealing of serious weight, fraud, and embezzlement. As a child, I often stole and shoplifted, and was never caught.

By my mid-forties, I was starting to become a crime writer. I had a suspense novel published by Doubleday Canada and won an award from the Crime Writers of Canada for the best short story of 1999. I had a New York agent shopping two suspense novels for me. I was selling crime stories to reputable magazines, like *Alfred Hitchcock's*.

And then flukes happened. The agent suffered a family tragedy and withdrew. Then an off-beat fantasy novel I'd had published years before, just in time for its publisher to be bought up and dissolved, was picked up by a major publisher and reissued with a sequel. The books were strongly influenced by all my Jack Vance reading, and suddenly I found myself being offered publishing contracts for more of the same. Before I knew it, I was a science fiction and fantasy author.

I went with the flow, but in the sneaky way of my family heritage, I wrote SFF about criminals and ne'er-do-wells, like the far-future master criminal Luff Imbry and Raffalon the thief in the Dying Earth.

So, I suppose I'm still a crime writer, albeit trapped in an SFF author's career. But in the back pastures of my hard drive are some of those stories from my early years, including the one that won the award. I've added a couple that were never published, and an off-beat novella that I put up on Amazon not too long ago, though it dates from the mid-eighties.

I hate to see the old stuff go to waste. I hope you enjoy the change of flavor.

STEPPING STONES

Way back in the late sixties, I read a magazine article about psychopaths, those amoral, narcissistic creatures who live among us as predatory lookalikes. As I read the descriptions of psychopathic behavior, I realized I had known some, even had some in my family. Since then, I've occasionally explored the way they operate.

This exploration originally appeared in the lost and lamented online magazine, Blue Murder.

I KNEW what Myrlene Buttle was the moment I saw her, bringing over the greasy paper sack that held the lunch I'd ordered from Herb Tetchley's Chikkin Shakk next door. She had a tumble of red hair, a face that could have shamed a Christmas angel, and the kind of body you find on glossy paper with a staple through the midriff. But she was trouble.

Normally, Calvin Feeblecorn would have brought my lunch order. He was the slow-blinking counterman with pimples and an Adam's apple that looked like he'd tried to swallow a hard-boiled egg unchewed. But Herb sent his new waitress instead, after first dressing her in a uniform a size too small, because that was his way of saying, *Check out what I'm gonna be gettin' some of.*

I didn't look up when I heard the street door chime because I was typing out a new listing—a piece of old orchard land that could be converted to a real sweet little money-maker of an industrial park, if somebody with cash was ready to move fast.

It had been a long dry spell since I'd seen the kind of commission that flows from a real estate deal like that.

By the time I noticed Myrlene, she'd already crossed the outer office and was leaning one rounded hip against the doorway of my half-glassed enclosure. Her eyes were blue. Most men would have found them as wide and innocent as a doll's, but they would have been reading into the frankness of her gaze a lot of things that would never be there.

That's because the girl was a full-blown psychopath. But don't get excited—there's nothing particularly startling about that. The movies and the newspapers make quite a fuss about psychopaths, real or imagined, so you'd think they must be some kind of supernatural bogeymen. But the truth is, they're not so special.

On the outside, they look like you. The difference is inside: you're a complex mix of shades and tints; a psychopath is just a few pure, primary colors. And there's plenty of them around— the condition is no more rare than left-handedness or a tendency to go bald.

I've made a study of them, and I've found that psychopaths come in two basic varieties: dumb and smart. Smart ones plan ahead, eyes on the prize. They dance you around and around, leading you on though you don't know it, until it's time to let loose. Then you go spinning off to anywhere, and they just smile and scoop up whatever it was you had that they wanted.

Dumb ones—and Myrlene was one of the dumb ones— they have no idea how to wait; an inability to defer gratification was how one of the books I read put it. They never learn how to counterfeit emotions like sympathy and compassion. Your dumb psychopath just walks up and hits you right away, hard and straight between the eyes, then strips you clean and moves on.

That's how Myrlene played men, and later that day that's how she would decide to play me.

But right now, she was glancing around the office, taking in the ten-year-old paint, the chipped desk and the dusty certificates on the wall. I watched her catalog me and everything I had in under two seconds. By the time she moved in and held out the sack, saying, "I'm supposed to bring you this," in a voice that sounded like there was honey in the back of her throat, I knew I'd been written off as not worth the trouble.

I said, "Thank you," and got a shrug in reply. Then she undulated back to the front door. I figured the movement was more from a habit she'd probably developed along with the hips than from any concern for how it might affect me.

The moment the latch clicked behind her, I heard the buzz start in the outer office. I employ two women of pretty advanced age, Miss Ellen and Miss Adie. A generation ago, before computers, there might have been enough secretarial work to justify their scant wages. Nowadays, I do most of the office chores myself, using a software package called Realty Prime. But I keep the old ladies on because, between the two of them, they're related to most of the town—including each other at some degree of second cousinhood once-removed. The ones they're not related to are old cronies from church socials or fellow coffee-klatchers at the Little Dixie cafe down the street.

There's very little that happens around here that Miss Ellen or Miss Adie don't know about within a day or so. And since death, desertion, divorce and drinking are known precursors of properties that arrive on the market, the information the two of them brought in—for free—more than compensated for the little I could afford to pay them.

Before the door tinkled closed behind Myrlene, the two old heads—Miss Ellen's a frosty blue, Miss Adie's a bright orange—were together. I heard the words, "trailer trash," and, for the first time outside an old movie, the expression, "no better than she should be."

I moved closer to the door and listened for a while. The Buttle girl, I learned, had come down from some little crossroads way up in the Smokies, after winning the heart of young Nestor Tollard. Nestor was one of the notorious pack of Tollards infesting the Rivertown district, which has more cars rusting in weedy front yards than moving on the potholed streets. He had met Myrlene while visiting a far flung branch of the Tollard tribe, staying long enough for Sheriff Abby Fellowes to lose interest in a recent string of gas station and liquor store stick-ups.

When the Tollards aren't relieving others of their surplus property, they hire out for yard work in the classier parts of town. They're capable workers, but they only take honest work to get a closer look at the locks and motion sensors of houses they plan on visiting in their other capacity.

Miss Adie told Miss Ellen that Nestor's only possessions were a hot-pepper temper and his daddy's old Smith and Wesson .38, each of which came with a hair trigger. Miss Ellen told Miss Adie that Herb Tetchley better put his brain into gear around that girl, because if he started thinking with any other part of his anatomy, Nestor was like to shoot it off.

I wasn't hearing anything that might lead to a listing or a buyer, so I went back to my chicken burger and shake, the Chikkin Shakk's Tuesday budget special. While I ate, I thought about Herb—specifically, I thought about the five fried chicken franchises he had acquired by marrying the former Evelyn Handefly, along with a block of downtown commercial property and a twelve-room colonial revival on Berkshire Crescent that had come to the happy couple, old Sam Handefly having died not long after their blessed union.

A lot of guys had taken a run at Evelyn. She wasn't pretty and she wasn't much fun to be around, but she'd been Sam's only child. I'd asked her out myself a time or two after high school, and tried to move things along. But it was plain that Evelyn was looking for someone who could carry on what her father had started. And I guess that's how Herb won the prize.

I'd sounded Herb on a couple of potential deals—the piece of old orchard land would be just right for him—because everything old Sam had left them was paid for and could have secured the financing for some solid plays. But, although Herb had always talked a good game, especially when he was courting Evelyn, once he was married his ambition veered well off the vertical.

Now all he wanted was to personally run the franchises, spending half a day a week in each one, and collect the rents from Sam's investments, which included the run-down office where I sat chewing his factory-processed chicken.

That left more time for his new interest, according to Miss Ellen and Miss Adie: corrupting the young women who came looking for minimum wage employment.

Miss Adie wondered why poor Evelyn didn't toss him out on his oversized ear. Miss Ellen was of the opinion that it was because the law now provided for an even division of assets, and Evelyn wouldn't part with a stepped-on bean.

After lunch, I drove out in my eight year old Honda to show a small farm to a middle-aged city couple hankering after bucolic paradise. The farm wasn't it. The place had been a hard scrabble even when it had first been cut from the virgin forest, more than a hundred years back. Now the thin soil was worn down to grit, and the only thing the land would raise was dust. I tap-danced my best about the view and the sense of history, but

I couldn't even get a "we'll see" out of the prospects, and drove back to the office once more with nothing to show for the day.

The Misses Ellen and Adie were locking up.

"That girl came by again," said one of them.

"Said Herb wants to see you before you go home," said the other.

I shrugged and went into the chicken place. It was too late for lunch and too early for supper, so the little open area with its few tables and chairs was empty. Myrlene was straightening up the condiments on the take-out counter.

"Herb looking for me?" I said.

"He'll be here directly," she said.

"Uh huh," I said. I doubted there was any profit in waiting around for Herb Tetchley. The lease was coming due, and he'd be looking to raise the rent. "I'll catch him tomorrow," I said and turned to leave.

She came around the counter fast. "No, please, he really wants to see you," she said, and put a hand on my arm. "Maybe I could get you a coffee?"

She was using her voice in a way that a lot of men would find compelling, and she left her fingers where they were. I could feel their warmth in the crook of my elbow. She was also trying to hold me with those big blue eyes. Something should have gone *ding* for me right there, but it doesn't always, does it?

"Okay," I said, "I take it black."

I sat down by the window. She brought me the coffee, then went back to the counter, and began rearranging the salt and pepper shakers. The coffee smelled like wet cigarette ash, and tasted thin and bitter. After a moment I said, "Wait a minute, isn't Herb always over in Bennettsville Tuesday afternoons?"

"I don't know," she said. She was looking past me, out into the street.

"Well, is Calvin here?" I said. "He'll know."

"He's gone home on his break." She craned her neck and

stretched over the counter a little, still looking out at the street. Then she turned without a word and went through the swinging doors behind her, into the kitchen.

I looked to the street, wondering if she'd spotted Herb's Lexus pulling into the alley that led to parking in the rear, and had gone to let him in—he was always forgetting his keys. But all I saw was a ten-year-old blue Lincoln making the turn.

"Mister," came Myrlene's voice from the kitchen. "Could you help me with something?"

"What?" I said.

"This thing," she said, "I can't do it on my own."

I went through into the back. She was standing at the stainless steel table where the fry cook would dip the chicken parts into premixed batter before dropping them into the deep fat. It was probably also where Herb dipped into the female staff, but I didn't care to think about that.

Her back was to me, the brown and yellow uniform's polyester stretched tight across her buttocks.

"What do you need?" I said, crossing the space between us and peering around to see what she had on the counter.

There was nothing there. "What's the deal . . . ?" I started to say, but then she turned full on to me and I saw that her uniform was unbuttoned to the waist. She wasn't wearing anything under it but skin that was mostly creamy white, except for two small pink spots.

She took my hand and pressed it to one of her breasts. I had time to register only warmth and softness, and the nubbin of her nipple against my palm, then the back door opened and a skinny young man with narrow eyes and a black tee-shirt walked in and froze.

Myrlene said, "Nestor! Thank God!" She stepped back and pulled things together. Nestor looked from her to me, and his jaw twitched sideways a couple of times. Then he spun on his boot heel and went down the three steps into Herb's parking lot. The girl followed him, and like a fool so did I. I wanted somebody to explain what was going on.

I was standing in the doorway when I heard Myrlene say, "He made me do it, I never wanted to," and saw her boyfriend reach through the open window of the blue Lincoln. He came up with a big hunk of black metal, and pointed it at me.

Luckily, from here on in, things started happening in slow motion. I had time to slam the door shut and throw myself sideways before a hole appeared in the painted wood. But that was just a little less time than I needed. Something with the force of a dinosaur-killing asteroid slammed into my left shoulder and set the inside of it on fire.

I went down. The tiled floor was a cold contrast to the blaze in my shoulder.

There was a sliding dead bolt on the bottom of the door, only two feet from my face. Without thinking, I reached and threw it closed. A half second later, Nestor hit the door from the outside. The next blow was from his boot, swung hard. Wood splintered, but the bolt held. I heard him swearing.

No more than thirty seconds had passed since I had come into the kitchen in response to Myrlene's call, but already I was putting things together, my head somehow rising cool and clear above the white fire of my wound and telling me, *She wants him to kill me.*

I got to my feet and headed for the front of the restaurant. Why she wanted him to put holes in me was a mystery I could leave until I had time to work on it. Right now, I needed to get out of the Chikkin Shakk and across the street to the red brick building with the sign that said "Sheriff" over the door. And I needed to do it quickly, before Nestor thought to come around to the front of the restaurant and finish what he'd started.

I was most of the way there, and getting ready to yell, "Abby, I'm shot!" at the big man in the tan uniform who was standing in the doorway with that big old heavyweight pistol in his hand, looking up and down the street. Then I saw his eyes go past me and focus.

"Down!" he said, and I let myself fall forward as his hand came up. The impact of the pavement against my outstretched hands sent a shockwave through the outraged flesh and bone of my shoulder. Then, for the second time in both my life and the last minute, I heard a shot fired in anger.

There was a big hole spreading itself beside me, inky black and bottomless. I wanted to let go and fall into it, away from the pain. Instead I rolled over onto my back and lifted my head up. Framed by my feet, I saw Abby Fellowes entering the alley next to Herb's restaurant where Nestor Tollard was sprawled face down. The young man wasn't dead; he began to push himself up on trembling, sinewy arms bent at the elbow, eyes casting around for the Smith and Wesson.

He located it a few feet in front of him. But just then the sheriff's size thirteen boot swung and kicked it way out of reach, then came around a second time to catch Nestor under the jaw and send him to the same black place that I could now let myself sink into.

I came to in the ambulance. A female paramedic was covering my nose and mouth with a plastic mask connected by a tube to an oxygen cylinder. On the other gurney, a second attendant was applying a tourniquet to Nestor's right leg. The pants of his jeans were soaked in bright red arterial blood. He was unconscious.

The paramedic lifted off the mask and asked me, "How you feeling?" *Damned mad*, I thought, but aloud I said, "I think I'm okay. How's he doing?"

"He'll live."

"Good," I said.

"Don't try to talk," she said.

She didn't have to tell me. I was already too busy thinking.

THE .38 SLUG they took out of my shoulder had been surprisingly cooperative. It had let the door absorb a lot of its force; once inside me, it just knocked a chip off the socket where my arm bone connected then tunneled most of the way through the muscle at the top of my shoulder. The ER doctor found it sitting under the skin like a kid hiding under the bedclothes, and sliced it out.

"You're going to have a small hole and a big bruise," he told me, then gave me a shot of Demerol that turned down the pain from high to simmer. "Lucky," he said.

I was out of emergency and into a regular ward by the time Abby Fellowes came to see me. "How's Nestor?" I said.

"They're doing an arterial graft." He pulled up a chair and sat on it carefully—men Abby's size don't automatically trust furniture to hold their weight—and said, "Why'd he shoot you?"

"I can only think it must've been an accident."

He stared at me and let the seconds go by. After a while, he said, "What were you doing in the kitchen?"

"Looking for Herb."

"On Tuesday afternoon."

"I forgot what day it was." Another wait. "What'd you want him for?"

"See if I could interest him in a real estate deal."

He looked at me even longer. "Where was the girl?"

"The waitress? Outside, I guess. I heard voices. Then *bang*! Bullet came right through the door."

Abby got up. "An accident?"

"That's what I'm saying."

"And Nestor was coming up that alley after you cause he was so worried for your health?"

I said nothing. After a while, he walked out.

THEY WHEELED Nestor in after supper. He didn't look too bad, but they'd wired up his broken jaw so he couldn't talk. That was okay with me; I just wanted him to listen.

I got out of bed and traipsed across the floor in the hospital gown and slippers, close enough for him to see me, but out of reach. He tried to sit up, making the kind of noise dogs make when their chains won't let them rip into something.

"I told Abby Fellowes it was an accident," I said.

He kept making the noise. "Shut up and think," I said. "I told Abby it was an accident."

This time he heard me.

"That's right," I said. "The most they could get you for is careless handling of a firearm. And, since Abby shot you without a warning, they'll probably just want to let the whole thing slide."

He made a noise that sounded like a question.

"Because you and me, we both been suckered," I said.

Nestor's gears moved slow, but they ground it out in the end. It took about ten seconds. Then the muscles at the hinges of his jaw bunched themselves up and his eyebrows joined themselves together.

I moved in and sat on the side of his bed. "That's right," I said. "I figure it's the two of them. They set us up."

That wasn't strictly true. Probably all Herb wanted was to lay Myrlene out on the stainless steel. I'd been shot because the girl saw Herb as the next stepping stone in her path, and getting Nestor sent up for murder was the quickest way to get rid of him, now that he'd served his purpose. Typical grab-it-quick thinking of your dumb psychopath.

But I didn't figure I owed Herb any consideration. On the contrary; he looked to be standing between me and something I had always wanted, and now might be able to get.

"Here's what we're going to do," I told Nestor.

I WAS BACK in the office in a few days, my left arm in a sling, still calling the whole thing an unfortunate accident. Myrlene, meanwhile, was making herself agreeable to Herb.

It was more than two weeks before Nestor was up and about again, while I waited patiently. The hospital released him on a Thursday, which conveniently coincided with Herb's regular stint at the counter next door, it being Calvin Feeblecorn's day off.

A little before five, I told Miss Ellen and Miss Adie they could go home and I'd lock up. I stood in the doorway to the street and watched them totter along to the Little Dixie. Standing where I was, I heard the click from next door as Herb locked the front entrance of the Chikkin Shakk from the inside.

I gave Herb and Myrlene a minute to get started, then I went into my office and dialed a number. It rang in a phone booth a couple of blocks away. I heard the sound of the receiver being lifted but no voice came down the line. "Oops," I said, "wrong number." And hung up.

A couple of minutes more, and Nestor's old Lincoln came down the street, turned into the alley beside the Chikkin Shakk and cut into the rear parking lot. That meant it was time for me to take my walk over to the sheriff's office.

"Some kind of funny noises coming from next door," I told Abby. "From around the back."

"What kind of noises?"

"Sounds like shouting, could be a fight."

He looked at me like he wanted to say something, then reached for his hat. I followed him out and stood on his front steps as he crossed the street. He tried the front door of the

Chikkin Shakk and found it locked, then went around to the back.

Abby was halfway down the alley when the sound of gunfire erupted from the back of the restaurant. I watched him draw his pistol and crouch as he peered around the corner then eased out of sight. I heard him shout, "Drop it!" Almost immediately, there was a shot.

I waited. A couple of minutes went by, then Abby came out the front door of the Chikkin Shakk. He crossed the street and stopped in front of me.

"Any idea how Nestor got a key to Herb's back door?" he said.

"You'd have to ask him," I said.

"I can't do that," he replied.

"Or the girl," I suggested.

"Her neither."

"Maybe Herb gave him..."

"Never mind," he said. "You still got that set of spares he gave you on account of he used to lock himself out?"

"I'm sure they're somewhere in the back of the safe. Want me to look?"

He just spat and walked away.

THE WHOLE TOWN turned out for Herb's funeral. I scraped up enough for a new suit and tie, to look good for the new widow.

I drove the Misses Ellen and Adie to the church in a rented luxury car—appearances count—then we joined the cortege out to the cemetery. The two elderly ladies sat in the back seat, and complimented me on being such a good chauffeur.

"Poor Herb," said Miss Ellen.

"But such a dignified service," said Miss Adie.

"Very," said Miss Ellen. "And isn't Evelyn holding up well."

"Poor dear," said Miss Adie, and then she wanted to know if Miss Ellen had noticed the good-looking man whose arm Evelyn had leaned on while they lowered the coffin into the ground. Miss Ellen said that she'd have had to be blind not to, and that she had heard the man was some kind of high-flying investment advisor the widow had been consulting.

Later, at the reception, I held onto Evelyn's hand as long as I could. "My deepest condolences," I said. "If there's anything I can do, any help I can offer."

She flicked her eyes over me the way she used to do back at those high school hops, when I'd ask for a dance but she'd be just too tuckered. Then she smiled that same little smile and said, "You've already done more than plenty. But you could talk to Tom Cromarty, here. He's my financial advisor now."

Cromarty's Armani suit was worth more than my car. He took my card and pocketed it without giving it a glance. Then he looked straight through me, and I saw the familiar blankness behind his eyes.

Later, I drove my secretaries home.

"It's funny how things will turn out," said Miss Ellen.

"Isn't it just," agreed Miss Adie. "I can't help thinking, if Evelyn hadn't hired Nestor Tollard to dig her new flower beds, Herb would never have seen that Buttle girl, and none of this would ever have happened."

"It's the hand of God at work," said Miss Ellen.

It was somebody's hand, all right. The same cool hand I'd now failed to win for the second time.

Like I say, we psychopaths come in two basic varieties: dumb and smart. I'd always figured myself to be one of the smart ones, but I guess I had to face the facts: smart comes in all different sizes, and I would never be playing in the same league as Evelyn Handefly and Tom Cromarty.

SOMETHING TO SELL

Somewhere back in the nineties, Mikey popped into the front part of my head. He was already formed, as so many of my characters are when I first encounter them: a small-time burglar with ambitions to rise in the world of crime. And he's smart; he comes up with some nifty ideas but, as so often with my characters, things don't go the way he planned.

I wrote three Mikey stories. The first one was sold to Alfred Hitchcock's Mystery Magazine, the other two to a great little online magazine, Blue Murder that was, unfortunately, a victim of the dot-com crash.

Too bad. Mikey's ambitions could have developed into an interesting basis for novels, but I was diverted into spec fic. I am sure he came back again as Raffalon.

Modern readers will have to make allowances for the Mikey stories' technology of thirty years ago.

WHEN HE SEES the piece in the morning paper, Mikey's own hand comes up and smacks his forehead medium hard, the sound like an echo of Ken Griffey's bat saying hello to a fast ball.

"Am I a dickhead?" he asks the flaking walls of his bare-bones studio in a rotting concrete high rise above English Bay. The last time the address was fashionable, so were wide-wale corduroy bell bottoms.

"I am a total dickhead. I been throwing away the jewels, selling the frigging boxes."

He cuts the item out of the tabloid and takes it over to East Vancouver to show Cheeks. His pee-o-ess Toyota pick-up with the cracked fiberglass canopy stalls on the off ramp of the Georgia Viaduct, then the battery dies before he can get it going again, so he has to give a cabbie his last twelve bucks for a jumpstart.

The fat man is in the back room, eating little cake donuts, one bite apiece, while his bratwurst fingers poke around in the guts of a Trinitron spread over the repair bench.

"You got something for me?" Cheeks says. He always looks first to see if there is anything in Mikey's hands before raising his beer-colored eyes to the burglar's face.

"I got opportunity, is what I got," says Mikey. "Check this out."

Cheeks reads the clipping, flakes of powdered sugar falling from silently moving, pink lips. Halfway through, he pushes the little square of newsprint away. "What is this crap? All I see, some broad is counting whales, somebody lifts her laptop, now she's crying about it."

"Go all the way to the end," Mikey says.

Cheeks sighs and rubs the roll of suet that is the nape of his neck, then works his way to the last paragraph. He reaches for another donut. "So?"

"You don't see it?" Mikey says. "It says five grand reward."

"So what? We ain't got what she's paying for."

Mikey wants to hit his forehead again. Instead, he spells it out for Cheeks. "Okay," he says, "the broad is a scientist, right, she's out looking at whales—what's it say there?—three years, making her notes, keeping track. All this work she puts into her laptop, which is this total junk Panasonic 386 that's worth, tops, ten bucks to some crackhead busts her car window and hustles it in the beer parlor."

CHEEKS DIGS around in his teeth for a glob of donut, sucks it off his finger. "I got stuff to do here," he says. "Whattaya trying to say?"

"I'm saying, the hardware is worth dick all. The information, man, that's gold."

Another donut. "When does this add up to something for me?"

Mikey walks him through it. Two years, he's been bringing Cheeks any computer hardware he picks up. The fence breaks up the desktop PCs, reformats the disks and sells them along with the CPUs and RAM chips on the gray market. Notebooks stay in one piece, passed on whole to a collector who ships them to eastern Europe.

"But some of these decks, man, they're full of information that's worth a whole lot to the schmuck that lost them. I mean, this babe with the whales, probably doesn't own one pair decent shoes, she's ready to drop five grand. So what's some suit gonna pay, we can give him his whole business back?"

Cheeks pulls something out of the Trinitron, looks at it and gropes around under the donut box, hunting up his multimeter. "The guy's gonna have back-ups, disks."

"Miss Whale Watcher got no back-ups."

"So she's stupid."

"People weren't stupid, how'd we make a living?" Mikey says. "Sides, half the time I'm in somebody's place, lifting a deck, the back-up disks are right there, on the shelf maybe, in the drawer."

Cheeks finds the multimeter, tests the component, puts it

back. He pulls at his nose, makes a horse noise with his lips, then says, "Nah. My business, I just want something to sell. What you're talking, you gotta make contact, stage a drop, use cut-outs. That's complications. One little thing goes wrong, bang, it's you in the jackpot."

"I already worked it out," Mikey says. "I got it covered, Cheeks."

"Uh, uh."

Mikey lets out his breath, then says, "Listen, you don't want in, fine. But how bout you front me maybe two, three grand to set it up? I'll give you payback outa the first score, plus, say, twenty points the first year, ten points the second."

"Gross or net?" Cheeks wants to know.

"Gross."

Cheeks considers it but shakes his head. After the last shake, his jowls are still moving. "Nah. People should be what they are. You're a pretty good burglar. I'm a good fence. Let's leave it like that. Bring me something I can sell."

"OKAY," says Mikey, talking to the Toyota's dashboard as he nurses it back to the West End, "the hard way."

He knows there are really two hard ways. But he's not going to take the one where he goes to Angie Tedesco and borrows at six for five. Cause, it might turn out, just maybe, he doesn't have it covered the way he was telling Cheeks.

"Then I'm screwed, blued, and tattooed," he says to the yuppie in the Saab who's nuzzling the pick-up's back bumper, itching to cut around and get downtown and make some more deals.

"I can't pay the vig, Angie seizes my collateral, then he twists them off."

The other hard way is one Mikey's been thinking about

since the time he was on probation and working as a window cleaner and got a look into the government office at lunchtime. He still has the big squeegee and the jumpsuit he kept when probation ended and he stopped coming in.

It's daylight work, scary. But he doesn't give himself time to think. A few minutes past noon, he walks into the Sinclair Center on West Hastings. The words E-Z Kleen are stitched across his back in faded blue thread and the squeegee sticks out of a gym bag stuffed with crumpled newspapers. Mikey moves against the flow of civil servants heading for the food fair or the up-market Italian restaurant. The commissionaire looks him over.

"How's it going?" Mikey says.

The face is familiar enough that the guard nods.

Six minutes, and Mikey's in the pick-up again, pulling away. Sweat sticks the coverall to his back, but the bag on the seat beside him now holds four good notebooks, retail eight to ten grand apiece, that would not be waiting on their owners' desks after lunch.

Cheeks pays seven-fifty each for the decks. "You get more, I'll take 'em," he says. "These I can sell."

Mikey buys phoney IDs from the guy at the photocopy store, then spends a couple of days opening bank accounts, fifty or sixty bucks each, at branches all over the city, under all different names. Each account gets him an over-the-counter ATM card. He has the banks send the PIN numbers to a post office box he rents at a no-questions place on West Broadway.

From a guy he knows is okay he buys a cloned cell phone, good for a month, until the citizen paying for all the calls sees his bill. Last, he goes to an Internet cafe, where anybody can log-on for two bucks an hour, and a white-faced kid with round glasses and chin stubble shows him how to do what he needs to do.

Now he has to wait a week for the PINs to come through. He

spends the time scoping out targets. First he thinks it through, working out the profile of a soft hit. From the yellow pages he makes a list of one-man chartered accountant and tax consulting firms with office addresses in the better suburbs. Then he cruises the prospects, looking for ground floor locations, alleys he can park in, windows he can break. Alarms don't worry him: police response time is fifteen minutes on a slow night; he means to be faster than that.

Mikey finds three he likes, two accountants and a tax consultant. After the PINs come, he does them—one, two, three —between ten and eleven the same night. His method of operation is the same for each job: he puts the Toyota under a window, climbs up and smashes in with an arm-long crowbar. Inside, he locates the computer, pulls its leads free or snips them with wire cutters if they're screwed in. He pries open drawers and cupboards, loads any disks he finds into the gym bag, and carries it all to the window.

He's quick and efficient. His slowest on-the-job time this night is under three minutes: there are two desktop decks to cut free and bring to the window, but he saves time on the back-up disks, neatly boxed in the accountant's bottom drawer.

Mikey's home before midnight, too wired to sleep. One by one, he connects the decks to a monitor lifted from one of the offices, powers them up and scans the hard drives. Each one is loaded with data, a lot of the files hidden behind passwords.

"Password, my ass," he tells the monitor screen.

Mikey waits until a quarter to noon before calling the first hit —he figures it's easier to negotiate with a guy whose belly is thinking about a Big Mac. It's a dud. When the tax consultant hears Mikey's proposition, he says, "Shove the disks up your ass. My whole operation's backed up on a notebook at home. You didn't even break my stride, prick!"

Mikey shrugs and dials the second one. He tells the girl who answers he needs to speak to the boss.

"I got your stuff," he tells the accountant.

The guy is slow. "What?"

"You didn't notice something was missing this morning. I got it."

There's a short silence. "You're the burglar?"

"Ding," says Mikey.

"What do you want?"

"I wanna sell you your back-up disks."

The man tells Mikey to do something anatomically inappropriate.

"Okay." But Mikey doesn't hit the cell's off button.

"No, wait!" the accountant says, and Mikey can see him now, chewing his lip, thinking about it. "How much we talking about?"

Go high, Mikey says to himself. "Ten," he tells the voice on the phone.

"Ten what? Ten thousand? You're outta your goddamn mind!"

"Yeah?" Mikey comes back. "So whatta you offering?"

Another silence, then, "I'll go two."

Mikey laughs. "If you're going two, then it's worth ten."

The accountant doesn't know many swear words. In only ten seconds, he's repeating himself.

Mikey cuts in. "Hey! Any more this abuse, the price goes up. Or maybe you never see your files again."

The man on the phone is choking it down. "Okay," he says, "ten. What do we do?"

"We stop thinking about calling the cops in and phone traces and all that TV crap. I'm on a cell clone, you know what that means?"

"I know."

"Good. You got a cell?"

"Yeah."

"Gimme the number." Mikey writes it on a pad. "Okay, go get the ten grand, fifties and hundreds. I'll call you back, one hour."

"Wait! How do I know you've got my files? Maybe you just read in the paper about the break-in and you're gonna try and rip me off."

Mikey is ready for the question. He reads off the names of a couple of files.

"Okay," says the accountant, "one hour."

While he's waiting, Mikey phones the third opportunity. The man is a recent immigrant. His thick Chinese accent gives Mikey a little trouble, but it doesn't take too long to make an arrangement. Mikey settles for five, and arranges to call back. It's embarrassing because the guy is crying and talking about his children.

"Man's either a great negotiator or a frigging great actor," he says to the parking lot where he stopped to make the calls.

At one o'clock, he calls the cell phone of the accountant with the ten thousand, tells him to put two grand in a certain account at the TD bank at Forty-First and Boulevard.

"How do I know you're going to come across with the files?" the man wants to know.

"If I rip you off, you'll tell your friends. Then how'm I going to do business with the next guy?"

"That's bull."

"Then you just gotta trust me," Mikey says. "Put the money in."

Mikey waits by an ATM on Commercial Drive, sitting on the Toyota's hood, kicking a front tire with his heel. He give it twenty minutes, then puts his card in and checks the balance of the TD account. The screen says the balance is $2,050.

The bank card will only let him withdraw a thousand a day. He takes half of the two thousand, then tells the bank to transfer the remaining money to another of his accounts. Then he uses the second account's card to withdraw the other grand.

"Hoo, hoo," Mikey says, and dials the accountant's cell again. This time, he wants four grand in a Bank of Montreal account on Oak Street. While the accountant is traveling, Mikey heads to another ATM.

He takes the thousand the machine will give him, then moves the other three grand to other accounts and drains them. Then he sends the accountant to another bank to drop the last installment of the ten thousand, and it works again.

"Smooth," Mikey says. The ten thousand goes into a safe deposit box at a bank where he does no other business. Then he drives out to an Internet cafe in the yuppie stronghold of Kitsilano. He calls the accountant one last time and gets the man's modem number, dials it up, and uploads the twelve data disks through the big funnel of the cafe's 56 modem.

"You seeing it come through?" he asks the accountant.

"Yeah," comes the answer.

"Here comes the last one. Nice doing business with you."

"Bite me."

Mikey laughs and heads out the door to his pick-up. As he walks, he dials the Chinese accountant's cell. The man is blubbering again, but he's ready with the five. "Okay, stop making all the damn noise," Mikey says. "I'm trying to tell you what you gotta do."

He gives instructions, then hangs up. He thinks about the man scurrying around to get him some money. "This is how it feels," he tells the guy with the grin in his rear-view mirror, "this is how it feels to be like Angie T. This is how it feels to be. . . more."

"YOU SHOULDA COME IN WITH ME," Mikey says.

"Gimme them pan-fried noodles," Cheeks says.

Mikey passes the dish. He's just picking at the ginger beef and shrimp chow yoke, a little steamed rice in a bowl. There are three more heaping piles of Chinese food on the table, and Cheeks is eating from every one, using the serving spoon that came with the rice.

The proprietor brings over a platter of garlic prawns, then goes into the kitchen, starts yelling something in Chinese. There's nobody else in the place.

"You're lucky you can eat like that," Mikey says. "A burglar, you don't keep the weight down, some night you get stuck in a narrow window. The cops come, they're all laughing at you, or maybe it's the guy owns the place, finds you, gets himself a two-by-four."

Cheeks grunts.

"What I'm doing now, it's better," Mikey says. He fingers his shirt. "Silk. You shoulda come in with me. I got six guys working that I trained myself. We're grossing ten, fifteen grand a night. I been clearing forty a week for six months, not counting what I get from you for the decks."

Cheeks stops eating for a moment. "You got anything for me now?"

"I got eight desktops, three notebooks."

"I'll take 'em," Cheeks says. "Something I can sell."

"They're in the truck. See that nice little Subaru out there? The weekend, I got a Porsche."

Cheeks doesn't bother to turn and look. "Yeah, nice."

Mikey leans back in the chair. "So, Cheeks, why you call me? You don't want to get in on my thing, now the money's flowing?"

Cheeks's small teeth crunch through crisp batter and into a prawn. "Nah. I just sell what people want to buy."

"I don't get it," Mikey says. "You want to sell me something?"

Cheeks says nothing. Now, Mikey notices that the only sound he's hearing is what's coming from the lips and nose of the fence as he's eating. There's not even any noise from the kitchen.

Mikey gets up, but so does Cheeks. His speed is surprising for a fat man, and he's wider than the front door.

Mikey backs a step away, turns toward the back, and freezes. He swallows and says, "Hi, Angie, how's it going?"

Angie Tedesco comes out of the kitchen, a compact man with hands too big for comfort. The guy behind him, about the size of the Marine Building but made of harder stuff, has an aluminum softball bat. He's rolling the wide rack of his shoulders to loosen them up.

"We need to talk about this new line of business you been starting," Angie says, then adds, ". . . for us."

Mikey turns to the fat man. "Jesus, Cheeks. . ."

The fence shrugs. "Mikey, you bring me something I can sell, you think I'm not gonna sell it?"

-

NUMBER CRUNCH

The second Mikey story. It ran in Blue Murder.

OVER A MUG of Labatt's draft, Mikey tells Terry Denning he'll murder Andy Clay, Terry's embezzling partner, for ten grand.

Terry says, "Murder, my ass," and laughs all the way down to the other end of the bar, where he pours refills for the two lawyers who must've won their case, because they keep ordering Glenlivets and clicking their glasses together.

The place is called T&A's and it's otherwise empty at three-thirty on a Wednesday afternoon, the lunch crowd long since gone. Before five the after-work crew will be trickling in, the serious drinkers coming early to get a jump on the amateurs.

Mikey knows the restaurant has got to be pulling in good money. It's in a choice location on Howe Street, about midway between the Law Courts and the Vancouver Stock Exchange, and the steaks and prime rib draw the brokers and lawyers pretty evenly.

Which ought to make Terry a happy man, and Terry would be if his diminutive partner wasn't stealing him into bankruptcy to please a nutcase girlfriend.

Mikey has heard all about Andy's girlfriend from Ellbee, the sharp-faced relief bartender with whom he has had an intermittent professional relationship. Ellbee sometimes asks Mikey to seek out a particular piece of merchandise—a notebook computer or a stereo TV—which Mikey then looks for and finds in some place where the owner hasn't invested in a first-rate security system.

"She's a Kabalarian," Ellbee tells Mikey. They're shooting pool in a place just off Commercial Drive.

"What's that, one of them new countries used to be part of Russia?"

"No, it's some kind of cult," says Ellbee, lining up a drop-dead easy corner shot. "They got this thing about numbers. Like, you change the way you spell your name, cause each letter's got a certain number attached to it, and if they all add up right, you're golden."

"This is like a lucky number?" Mike says, watching Ellbee blow the easy shot. He's the only guy Mikey knows who plays consistently lousier than he does.

"Yeah, except it's more. You get in tune with all these major cosmic forces. Like, her name's Linda, I mean that's how it sounds, but she spells it L-Y-N-E-D-A-H. Supposed to add up to her special perfect number. But, you ask me, the only number she's really clocked onto is Andy's bank balance, which is winding down at a pretty radical rate of descent, you know what I mean."

"She's sucking him dry?" Mikey asks. He runs the table fast, the balls finding the pockets as if they lived there.

"It ain't going to take much longer."

"Andy doesn't figure this out? He never looked like a dummy to me."

"Short-man syndrome," Ellbee explains. "Andy's what, five-five on tip-toe? She's got to clear six foot. He sees her, he just wants to get into his climbing gear—like the guy with the credit card, 'Because it's there, man.' Anything else, he don't think about it."

Ellbee figures Andy has been stealing from the business, maybe three, four months, skimming from the receipts when he's working the till. "A little bit at first, buy her a bracelet or something, but now it's getting serious. One time, he erases the name on a check Terry's written to a supplier, puts in his own name and cashes it."

"Dumb," says Mikey.

"Yeah, but she ain't. She sees me make a little mistake on a bar bill one time, and bang! she totes up the right answer faster'n I could punch it into the register."

"Little mistake, huh?" says Mikey.

"Do I comment on how you make a living?" says Ellbee.

"Looks like I just made some of it off you," says Mikey, dropping the last ball into a side pocket.

Ellbee reaches into his jeans. "What do I owe you, ten?"

"Fifteen," says Mikey, "but you can keep it, you do me a favor."

Which is how Ellbee comes to take a look through the office, when he's in the restaurant alone, it being Terry's night off and Clay having left early with Lynedah.

"It's pretty bad," he reports back to Mikey. "They got a note at the bank, one-fifty k, and they're tapdancing, at least a couple payments behind. Few more weeks, the place is padlocked."

He also tells Mikey one more thing: the bank loan is insured—if either partner dies, the note gets paid out in full by the insurance company.

That's how Mikey comes to be in the restaurant on a slow Wednesday afternoon. "You wanna laugh, laugh," he tells Terry when he comes back from lubricating the lawyers, "but I got this thing sussed."

Terry comes around the bar, says, "Get off the stool a

minute." He runs his hands over Mikey's chest and back, feels in his pockets.

"You think I'm wearing a wire, I'm not," Mikey says.

Terry goes back behind the bar, looks to see that the two lawyers are happy with their scotches, and leans in close so he can talk softly. "Ellbee tells me you're a burglar. You're telling me you're a contract killer?"

"I'm always interested in moving up," says Mikey.

"Okay," Terry says, "I'm not saying I'm interested in your career plans, but—just for fun—run it by me."

"Better, I'll show you," says Mikey, taking a folded newspaper clipping from his shirt pocket. "I been saving this till I find the right opportunity."

Terry reads the item. It's by a Vancouver Sun columnist, about a drunk driver who killed three young men who were heading up the Sea-to-Sky Highway for a little skiing at Whistler. The drunk veered across two lanes and drove his pick-up head-on into their VW Rabbit, then walked away unhurt. The judge gave him a "conditional sentence"—a five-year license suspension and community service hours—but no jail time. The guy's lawyer bitched that now his client would have to catch a 5:40 a.m. bus to get to work on time.

"So?" says Terry.

"So," says Mikey, "I know guys would put up with that kind of cruel and unusual punishment, there was a couple grand in it for them."

Terry is working it through. "Suppose—and I'm just talking here—but suppose, afterwards, they want more than a couple, or they go to the cops?"

Mikey has already been there. "They go to the cops, they're not going to get away with community hours. Contract killing, that's first degree—they're away for twenty-five minimum. Even if they plead down to second degree, it's ten years mandatory."

"I got to think about it," Terry says.

"Sure," says Mikey, "take all the time you want."

THE HIT IS SET for a Thursday night outside the Red Barrel cabaret on Edmonds Street, a busy arterial, deep in the suburbs. The club is in the middle of the first block east of Kingsway, with nowhere near enough parking in the little lot next door. Most customers leave their cars in the big super-market lot across the street and jaywalk to the front door, instead of detouring to the lights on the corner.

Terry has told Andy they need to talk, cards on the table, someplace they won't run into people who shouldn't know their business.

At nine forty-five, Mikey will call Terry's cell number from a pay phone, and say "Oops, wrong number." That will tell Terry that Mikey is ready. He should wait ten minutes, then lead his partner out of the Red Barrel.

"I'm at the curb, up the street," is how Mikey has explained it. "You see him step off the sidewalk, you drop your wallet. Soon as I see you bend down to pick it up, I'm on the gas. Five seconds, it's over. My friend moves into the driver's seat, you pay me what you owe, and I split. Then you wait for the cops, tell them the tale."

"What about this guy, your friend?"

"He'll be so wasted he won't know his ass from the man in the moon."

Mikey's friend is Grady Konigsberg. Twenty-years back, Grady was a master plasterer, drinking Canadian Club and driving a new Buick every other year. Now he drives a nineteen-year-old Plymouth Volare and drinks anything he can get.

Mikey hasn't told Terry that the original plan has mutated in a way that leaves Grady out of the money. "I'm looking out for the old drunk," Mikey tells the back of the seat in front of him, as he rides the Sky Train elevated transit line from East Vancouver down to Grady's basement room in a New Westminster boarding house. "Two grand's worth of alcohol'll kill him ten times over."

He's told Grady he wants to use his car a couple hours. Grady can even come along for the ride, and Mikey will give him fifty plus a full bottle of medium-good rye.

By nine-forty, they're parked out front of a 7-11, a mile from the Red Barrel. Mikey has already checked to make sure the pay phone works.

"Want a drink?" Grady says, but he doesn't let the bottle get more than an inch closer to Mikey. Two-thirds of its original contents are already gone.

"No, man," says Mikey. "All yours."

Grady tilts the bottle, and his Adam's apple plays elevator. "Thanks," he says. "Good stuff."

"Knock yourself out," Mikey says. He sneak-checks the unshaven man in the passenger seat. Grady's eyes are losing focus, and he's breathing with his mouth open. From time to time, he hums an unrecognizable tune.

At nine forty-five, Mikey is at the pay phone. Terry answers on the first ring.

"Oops, wrong. . . " Mikey says, but Terry cuts in, his voice a little panicky, "It's off!"

"What?"

"It's off," Terry says again. "She's here with him."

Mikey's brain goes clickety-click. "Where are you? Can you talk?"

"Washroom."

"Are they suspicious?"

"I don't think so. She's just protecting her interest, giving me this line about him buying me out—like she's got backers, which is total crap. Andy just sits there nodding. Man, I never seen a guy so whipped."

Mikey makes up his mind. This is where he moves out of nickel-dime B&E, into that place where people have to look at him with respect. "We're doing it," he says, "just like we planned. I'll try and get 'em both. No extra charge."

"Too dangerous!" says Terry.

"We're doing it," says Mikey.

"I don't think so."

"You're not going to get another chance. She won't let him out of her sight."

"Then forget it."

"Forget nothing! This is not your decision anymore. Andy steps off the sidewalk, I'm nailing him." He hangs up.

There's less than two fingers of rye left in Grady's bottle. The song he's humming is louder now, but still not recognizable. His eyes are closed.

Mikey takes the car carefully down Edmonds, puts it against the curb about fifty feet from the Red Barrel's door. He slides the stick shift into neutral, but keeps his foot on the gas, keeping up the revs on the classic slant six Plymouth engine. He takes a deep breath, and it comes out slow and trembly. He takes another.

He turns the mirror. "We're doing it," he says to his own eyes. "We're doing it."

Grady is mumbling something, but Mikey tunes him out. Because now the cabaret door is opening, and there's Andy, with Terry right behind him, so the woman must be the Kabalarian, and boy, Ellbee's right, she really is a big one.

Here they come, heading for the curb. Why are they moving in slow motion, like a movie? At least Andy is out in front. Now he's stopping, cause the woman is saying something to Terry. The hell's Terry doing? Digging around in his wallet. Oh, good acting, Terry, I don't think.

Mikey's knuckles whiten on the gear shift, his eyes locked on the group. The words, *Any second now, any second now,* are circling through his mind like the horses on a speeded up carousel.

Beside him, Grady stops humming, belches a glottal stream of garbled syllables, and opens the passenger door. Mikey flicks his head to the side—any second now—sees the drunk stooped over, hands on knees, hosing down the sidewalk with twenty bucks' worth of recently used, medium-good rye.

Mikey's eyes snap back to the front. No time to get Grady back in the car. Andy is stepping into the street. Lynedah is still on the sidewalk, looking even more statuesque because the height of the curb adds to the six inches she must already have on her pint-sized embezzling boyfriend, even in flat shoes.

Now Terry throws his wallet down then bends, with amazing slowness, to pick it up. His eyes are bugged out, locked on the car revving at the curb.

Forget Grady. Now, now, now, chants the voice in Mikey's head. His foot goes down and his hand yanks the shift into the low gears. Rubber squeals. *We're doing it!*

Andy and his big girlfriend have seen the vomiting drunk and instantly look away. But now the tall woman's head snaps around as she hears the shriek of overheated rubber.

Mikey's hands squeeze the wheel. The Volare's screaming rear tires dig into the asphalt and throw the car forward on twin spirals of blue smoke.

Andy freezes in the headlights. His thin, weaselly shoulders pull closer together, like they're trying to make him an even smaller target.

But then the big woman with the name that's spelled funny moves! Her hands go into the back of her boyfriend's pants, she grabs his belt, and then she pivots on her low heels and flings her meal ticket back up onto the sidewalk.

Mikey has seen the movement somewhere before, and his speeded-up brain decides to tell him where: TV sports shows, where oversized Scotsmen in kilts whip around and hurl a chained iron ball off to the edge of the world. The inane recognition occupies the front of Mikey's mind as Andy practically completes a full orbit before the little man crashes into Terry's ass, which is Mikey's client's most prominent feature, being as he's still bent over, clutching his wallet.

The impact drives Terry into the street just as the Volare arrives. Terry disappears below the line of the hood, but Mikey hears the thud, then feels both sets of wheels clump-clumping over the body. He stomps the brake and jumps out, but he already knows it's too late.

Andy is sitting on the sidewalk, gazing blankly at the tumbled heap that the Plymouth has left in the gutter. Then he looks up, and a puzzled expression works its way through the shock. "Mikey?" he says.

Lynedah puts it together as quickly as adding up a bar bill. There's an envelope poking out of the mess in Terry's suit jacket. She bends and retrieves it, opens it and a moment later says, "Ten thousand. This was for you?"

Mikey says nothing.

She puts the envelope in her purse. Mikey says, "Whoa!"

She looks down at him, then at Terry. Her gaze reminds him of a time he once saw a crow eyeing a baby robin that had fallen out of the nest. Not a whole lot of sympathy.

"You want to tell the cops I took your money?" she says.

But Mikey's head can work fast, too. "Sure, then maybe I tell them you hired me to do Terry?"

Little lines appear at the corners of her eyes. Mikey sees her upper teeth.

"On the other hand," Mikey says, "I keep my mouth shut, you got the whole business now, debt free. These two insured each other."

The lines clear, the lips close. She looks up the street at Grady, then back to Mikey. "And he drove the car?"

"Call it a hit and stagger," Mikey says. "He won't remember."

Andy is getting to his feet, a worried look now joining the puzzlement. "Wait a minute," he says, but they both ignore him.

"Fifty-fifty," Lynedah says. "You got to admit, on job performance you weren't too smooth."

Mikey shrugs. "It's my first time. I'll get better."

She gives him a different look for a moment, then her eyes slide briefly to Andy Clay and back to Mikey. She counts out five thousand. Mikey puts it in his jeans pocket.

He can hear a siren coming down Kingsway. He turns to walk away, but she stops him with one cool finger on his arm, hands him a card and says, "Why don't you take my number?"

WIPE OUT

The third and final outing for Mikey. This appeared in Blue Murder.

MIKEY WAITS by the elevators until the receptionist comes out and heads for the washroom, then he walks into the law firm's offices. He tilts back the baseball cap with the Purolator logo, and says, "Here for a pick-up?"

Several women are in a corral of desks behind the receptionist's empty seat. One of them looks up briefly from her computer screen, says, "Should be right there somewhere."

Mikey makes a show of looking on the chest-high counter that separates the receptionist from whatever drifts in the door. "Nothing here," he says.

"Kay-Lynne'll be right back," says the woman. Her fingers don't stop rattling the keyboard in front of her.

"Sure," says Mikey. His eyes haven't stopped moving since he came in. He's making a list: good quality motion detectors, positioned right where they need to be; a hemisphere of dark glass on the ceiling by the back wall almost certainly houses a video camera; a wire running under the carpet beneath his feet

—*pressure plate*, he thinks, *and better than even money they got laser trip-wires and maybe even thermal sensors in the walls.*

The receptionist comes back in. "Pick-up for Purolator?" Mikey says.

That makes the girl look puzzled, so Mikey gives her a show of him checking his clipboard, then puts on his *I'm so dumb* face and says, "Sorry. Wrong floor."

Two minutes later, he's in the underground parking garage. He dumps the Purolator hat and clipboard on the passenger seat of the Toyota pick-up and heads up the exit ramp.

"No way to go in and out of that place, nobody sees it," he tells the steering wheel. The thought of giving Angie T the bad news sends an involuntary shiver through his back muscles.

The mid-afternoon traffic around Georgia and Granville is just as crazy as you'd expect in a major city with neither a downtown freeway nor a decent transit system, where the city council has decided to dig up major streets to lay down an earthquake-proof water system. Mikey finally makes enough right turns to add up to a left and gets onto the Viaduct heading for East Vancouver.

He decides he's not going to tell the client the job can't be done. "I gotta think about this," he says to the windshield.

MIKE FINDS Angie Tedesco sipping murderous black coffee in the bare back room of a *trattoria* on Commercial Drive near East First Avenue, a neighborhood they used to call Little Italy before everything got multicultural, though it's still at least as easy to find pasta as Thai noodles.

Angie T is a short, balding loan shark and money mover with a little black moustache and a lank comb-over. The hands that cradle the diminutive espresso cup are big enough to conceal a bocce ball. Mikey has heard that those hands have done things nobody's hands should do.

Sitting next to Angie is Carmine Zuccaro, who would need only a ten per cent increase in body hair to qualify as Bigfoot. Angie keeps Carmine around for when he has to rearrange somebody's agenda.

"You shouldn't deal with this guy," Carmine says, when Mikey sits down across from his boss. "He's a mook."

"Did I ask you your opinion?" Angie says, and looks at Carmine until the big man looks away. Then he asks Mikey, "Well?"

"I guess I got good news and bad news," Mikey says.

Angie turns and gives Carmine a different look. Carmine reaches over and puts a hand on Mikey's shoulder, then somehow manages to insert a thumb between muscle and bone in a way that makes the arm feel like it's coming off.

"Jesus, Carmine!" Mikey says, squirming.

The giant's expression never changes. He keeps up the pressure a few more seconds, until Angie wriggles his thick eyebrows. Mikey rubs the spot where the thumb was, trying to get the blood moving again.

"I'm waiting here, you're gonna come tell me jokes?" Angie says.

"I was just trying to put it in perspective for you, Angie," Mikey says.

"For perspective, I don't hire a burglar. I hire a . . . " Angie can't think of anybody he would hire for that purpose. "Just tell me how does it look."

Mikey takes a breath. "Okay. How it looks is there's no way I go into that place and nobody knows it. They got the whole catalog, all top of the line. You just walk by thinking about going in, they probably got something reads your mind and speed-dials the cops."

Angie says a short word, then slams down the little coffee

cup and says it again. He looks at Mikey, and his face works its way into an expression the burglar has never seen on the man before—kind of *help me, I'm sinking*, Mikey thinks—as Angie says, "Suppose somebody, maybe a security guard, was to cut the power?"

Mikey shakes his head. "I'm figuring battery back-up, hundred per cent sure."

His client lets his hands lie flat on the chipped Formica tabletop. He looks down at them as if they could give him the answer to his problem, and Mikey is thinking those hands have probably solved most of the problems Angie T has bumped into over the years.

"What did we say, two Cs?" Angie says, without looking up.

"Yeah, but . . ." Mikey says.

"I don't wanna hear no buts," the loan shark says. Still looking at his hands, he tells Carmine, "Pay him."

Mikey takes the two bills and puts them in his shirt pocket. "I said there was good news."

Angie T looks up. This is where it all happens, Mikey knows. A mouse pulls a thorn out of a lion's paw, it can do the mouse some serious good. But if the mouse messes up, maybe drives the point in deeper, the last thing the mouse is going to know is how it feels to be ripped apart. Mikey swallows.

"You were saying," Angie says.

"You asked me to look over this lawyer's set up," Mikey says.

"I know what I asked you."

Mikey keeps on. "You wanted to know could I go in, get a package out of the safe, nobody knows it's gone. And you said the package was like so big." Mikey holds his hands as if they were molded around a pound of butter.

Angie's jaw moves sideways like a lizard chewing a beetle. A joint under one ear creaks. "I'm not hearing any good news," he says.

Now Mikey goes for broke. "Well, that size," he says, "I'm thinking computer diskettes."

There is a silence in the little room, a stillness so profound that Mikey can almost hear individual dust motes rubbing together in the shaft of light that slides in from the curtained window.

Angie T's brown eyes stay on Mikey. They don't blink or shift their focus by a hairsbreadth. Mikey finds it hard to breathe.

"You don't got to tell me what's on the disks," the burglar says, the words tumbling into each other like falling dominoes in a commercial. "But if that's what's in the package, I can solve the problem."

Angie blinks. His eyes flick toward Carmine. He says, "Carmine, whyncha go put a dollar in the meter?"

The giant's face shifts its placid expression toward a question, an uncomfortable transition, like a man trying on a coat that's too tight in the shoulders.

"Just go and do it," Angie says. Carmine's features reset to blank. He rises from the little square table like a big old moon rocket inching up off the launch pad.

When he's gone, Angie turns back to Mikey. "I know you, what? six, seven years, right?"

Mikey nods.

"I see you're always trying to get out of this nickel-dime B&E crap."

"I got a brain, Angie," Mikey says. "I see angles, opportunities."

Angie's short laugh has no humor in it. "The thing is this," the loan shark says, "the stuff you do, you screw up, you get six months, maybe a year. The stuff I'm into, a guy screws up and pffft! he's dead."

Mikey nods again.

"Don't sit there nodding at me," Angie says. "I'm telling you something you don't know. This business, it's got floors and it's got ceilings. To you, me and Carmine, we're the ceiling. But there's guys look at us, we're just the floor."

"I get it," Mikey says.

The loan shark looks at the table, looks up at the burglar again. "You better get it. I'm gonna offer you something now. You take it, you take it all the way. What I'm gonna tell you, it can get *me* whacked, somebody hears about it. You, they step on like a bug."

Mikey's mind shows him a picture of a dark forest, bad things shifting and lurking behind black trees. Somewhere down the trail, made faint and misty by distance, is the golden light he's always wanted to get to. *Whatever it is*, he tells himself, *I can do it*.

"I get it."

Angie T looks over his shoulder, although he knows the room is empty. He lowers his voice. "It's this asshole, Terry Alizotto, married my Angelina. For her sake, I give him some things to do, but every time he makes a godawful mess. I mean, forget about it—there's guys passed out in alleys, you wake em up they gonna do better work.

"So, I tell him, Terry, this life ain't for you, and I get him a straight job hauling stuff off building sites. Two grand a week, all he's gotta do is show up, sign in now and then."

"He didn't go for that?" says Mikey.

Angie T rolls his eyes. "He gets my own daughter bitching at me. Then they come for dinner, and while he's in my house he goes into my den, copies some stuff off my computer, gives it to this lawyer to hold. Then he says, 'Put me back on the count, or I start showing your business around.'"

"Sheesh," says Mikey.

"Sheesh, my ass," says Angie T. "It's not just *my* business on those disks. There's things I'm doing for other people, you know what I'm saying?"

Mikey knows, and now he has an inkling just how bad the beasts in the dark forest might be. But what Angie T is telling him brings the warm golden light a lot clearer and closer.

"I can fix this," he says. "If it's just disks, I can fix it."

"You fix this, I'll give you the opportunities I gave Alizotto. But it's gotta be quick—I got till the weekend to fix him up with what he likes, or he's back at the lawyer's Monday to collect the disks." Angie looks out into the *trattoria*'s main room, where Carmine is coming back in from the street. "The meantime, any of this gets to the wrong people, all bets are off, you know what I'm saying."

Mikey checks his watch. "It's noon. I can put something together this afternoon, then forty-eight hours and you're clear. You want me to tell you what I'm gonna do?"

Angie looks to see if Carmine is coming back. "No," he says, "Just do it."

"I'm going to need a couple of grand for supplies."

The loan shark reaches for his roll. He peels off twenty hundreds and passes them across the table. Mikey puts them with the other two. "I gotta hurry," he says, and starts to rise.

Angie reaches over and puts a big hand on Mikey's arm. "Stay in touch," he says.

Carmine is outside on the sidewalk. "What's that all about?" he wants to know.

"I can't tell you."

Carmine's face never shows much, but then it never has to. People study it closely, because it can be directly relevant to them to know what Carmine's about to do.

Mikey doesn't like what he sees in the big man's face. "He told me I can't tell nobody," he says.

One of Carmine's hands reaches for the burglar. Mikey says, "You got me scared, Carmine. But he's got me more scared."

Carmine puts his hand down.

"I'm just looking to move up," Mikey says.

"Everybody's looking to move up," Carmine says. But now there is an identifiable expression on his face. Somewhere inside Carmine's head, ponderous wheels are turning. He watches Mikey walk away, then goes back into the *trattoria*.

MIKEY GOES four blocks down Commercial to an electrical supply place he almost hit once, when he had a potential buyer for big spools of copper wire, but the guy changed his mind. Now he goes in and buys the materials he needs for under fifty dollars. The rest of Angie's two grand he spends at a coin shop, buying silver in dollars and ten-ounce ingots, along with a couple of commemorative sets from the Montreal Olympics.

He takes it all back to his one-room apartment in a crumbling high rise overlooking English Bay, and spends an hour at his kitchen table, winding thin copper wire around a flat piece of iron, then connecting it through a timer switch to a compact, heavy-duty battery. He sets the timer for ten seconds and watches to see if the switch will open. There is a faint hum, and a pair of needle-nose pliers slides across the table and sticks to the home-made electromagnet.

Now he puts a formatted blank disk into his computer's floppy drive and copies onto it a few files chosen at random. He pops the disk out of the drive and lays it on top of the magnet, waits a minute then puts it back in the drive. *Disk error. Disk not formatted*, appears on the monitor. Mikey repeats the experiment with another disk, this time letting it sit for ten minutes a foot away from the electromagnet. When he puts the plastic square into the floppy drive, the computer tells him it, too, is unreadable.

Mikey kills the current to the electromagnet and resets the timer switch to reactivate it at nine o'clock that night. He figures the battery is juiced enough to keep it running for an hour.

Then he packs it into the bottom of a wooden box that once held a bottle of premium Okanagan wine, covers it with a page torn from the newspaper, and fills the box with the silver.

Kay-Lynne doesn't recognize him in a suit and without the Purolator hat. When Mikey tells her his name is Ron Fenshaw and he wants to see a lawyer, she takes him to an office that has the name William Takashita on the door.

Mikey explains that he is holding a box full of silver as security in a business deal and wants somewhere safe to keep it overnight. He opens the lid of the box and shows the lawyer the heaped coins and ingots.

"Cost you fifty," says Takashita. Mikey pays cash and accepts a receipt. The lawyer has him sign Ron Fenshaw on a gummed label that he then pastes over the box's side and lid so it can't be opened without breaking the seal. Mikey asks to see the box put in the safe. The lawyer shields the combination lock while he spins the tumblers, but when the thick door opens, Mikey sees the package Angie T described. The lawyer slides the box in next to it.

He tells the lawyer he'll be back in the morning, then goes downstairs to the shopping mall and phones Angie T. "It's in place," he says. "Ten o'clock tomorrow, I'll go in again, see if it worked."

"Let me know, soon as," Angie says. For the first time, Mikey hears in the loan shark's voice the kind of shake that Angie T must have heard a thousand times. He wonders if his client is as good at bearing pressure as he is at applying it.

MIKEY IS at the lawyer's a little before ten. There's a small crowd in the reception area: a silver-haired guy in a hand-made suit that might as well have "senior partner" stitched across the back, and a couple of other guys who don't need to have "cop"

stenciled on their off-the-racks. The big lawyer scans a blue
piece of court paper, then kneels to open the safe.

William Takashita is off to the side, with Kay-Lynne and the
women who do the word processing. Mikey puts himself beside
the lawyer. "I come for my package," he says.

Takashita keeps his eyes on the cops and talks out of the
side of his mouth like he's auditioning for an old-time gangster
movie. "It'll be a minute."

"What's up?"

"Search warrant," the lawyer says. "Evidence in a homicide,
they're saying."

The kneeling lawyer straightens up and hands one of the
cops Terry Alizotto's package of disks. The cop tucks it under
his arm like he's a running back with a touchdown in his
future, then he and his partner are out the door.

Takashita stoops and gets Mikey's box before the senior
man closes the safe and hands it to him. "Homicide, eh?" Mikey
says. "They say who it was?"

The lawyer has spent his career doing wills and real estate,
Mikey figures, or he wouldn't be so excited about what he has
been seeing. "It was on the warrant. A client of Mr. Plimley's,
guy named Alizotto."

As he boots the Toyota back to Commercial Drive, Mikey is
struggling to see the golden glow somewhere up ahead. Black
shapes are moving around the edges, shading the light, trying
to compress it to a pinpoint and smother it. The closest parking
spot to the *trattoria* is almost a block way, and he leaves the
pick-up and legs it fast down the sidewalk. But halfway there,
Carmine Zuccaro is standing in a doorway. The giant steps out
and puts a hand like a grizzly's paw on Mikey's shoulder. Mikey
stops.

"It worked, Carmine. It's totally cool. Just let me go tell the
man."

Carmine says, "Forget about it." He is between Mikey and

the restaurant, standing sideways to watch the *trattoria*'s front door.

"That thing he was worried about. Man, I fixed it."

Carmine shakes his head, still looking the other way. "We've moved on."

The restaurant door opens. A knot of men in suits comes out, swarming around Angie T. like Secret Service agents around the President, hustling him to a car at the curb. For a second, Mikey sees the loan shark's eyes, wide and flicking around like a cow's when it's being pushed into the slaughter-house, then somebody puts a meaty, pinky-ringed hand on Angie's head and pushes him down and into the back seat. The car pulls away.

"But he's clear," Mikey tells Carmine. "The disks, they're wiped."

"Don't know about no disks," the big man says. He looks at Mikey. "You're smart, you don't know nothing neither."

"We had a deal, Angie and me," Mikey says.

"Angie don't make deals now," Carmine says. "I do. And I got no business with you." He sniffs and moves his neck like he needs to rearrange its position inside his shirt collar, then heads down to the *trattoria*. There's a difference in the way he walks. One of the guys out front opens the door for him.

Mikey watches the car carrying Angie T. dwindle in size as it goes down Commercial Drive. A gleam of sunlight reflects from the chrome trim above the rear window. Mikey watches the glimmering spark grow smaller and smaller, until the car turns the corner on East First Avenue and the light is gone for good.

MEAN MR. MUSTARD

With the 1997 release of my novel, Downshift, *I acquired a fan in the form of Melanie Fogle, editor of a neat little magazine called Storyteller. She asked me for a story. I had recently read a diatribe by some comfortable middle-class bloviator who thought the poor had it too easy. I decided to take my revenge.*

THE ROOM WAS small and simple but neatly kept and warmed by the early summer sun. There was a narrow bed with a clean but well-worn quilt, a wooden table and chair, and a chest of drawers. No one piece matched any of the others; it was a room furnished from the Goodwill store.

"Very nice," said Anthony Mostardi. It was not his first lie of the day. He put his suitcase on the faded throw rug and limped to the window. "That's a good-looking vegetable garden. Must be rich soil."

"A lot depends on what you plant," said Mrs. Strang from the doorway. "You got a farming background?"

"No, I just don't think I've ever seen a cabbage quite that size."

"Too bad. I always appreciate good gardening advice, and

my tomatoes could use some help." She crossed the room, glanced at the rows of plants and shook her head. Then she sat down at the table, a little fireplug of a woman with tiny, dark eyes and bristly hair that was just a shade too red for human. She crossed her stubby arms. "I like to know who I'm opening my home to," she said. "You won't mind me asking a few questions."

Mostardi sat on the edge of the bed, extending his right leg slightly so that the frayed cuff rode up and exposed the bottom of the steel brace. "Fire away," he said.

The interrogation lasted less than three minutes. She asked most of the questions he had thought an experienced boarding house owner might ask, and he told her the plausible false-hoods he had carefully rehearsed.

"That's fine," she said, letting her arms unfold. "There's just a couple of forms you can fill in after you get yourself settled." She stood and moved to the door with a rolling, muscular gait that reminded Mostardi of the prize-winning bulldog bitch that belonged to his neighbor on the quiet, leafy street in the up-market Shaughnessy district, where he really lived.

He clumped downstairs five minutes later and found her in the big, old-fashioned kitchen. The house was three stories, wood framed, dating from the twenties, and probably purpose-built to be a boarding house. It was one of a row of four similar piles of post-and-siding on East Eleventh Avenue out near the rim of Vancouver, in an area that had never been anything but blue collar.

She gave him a standard form provided by the Ministry of Social Services which authorized the government to send the rent portion of his monthly disability money straight to Mrs. Strang. He signed it and she handed him another.

"If you don't have a bank account," she said, "you'll have to cash your check at the Money Mart. Which means they'll hold back five per cent. Or you can sign this and authorize me to cash it for you, and I'll do it for free."

This is her insurance that she'll get her board money too, he thought, *preventing it from becoming confused and disoriented in some place where they serve alcohol, and never making it home at all.* Out loud, he said, "That's very good of you," and signed the paper.

"This is the last one," she said. "Tells me who to notify in case of emergency."

"There's nobody," Mostardi lied.

She put the completed forms in the top drawer of an old sideboard, then picked up a tray loaded with a pitcher and glasses. "Would you like some lemonade?" she said, assembling a smile. "Homemade."

Mostardi liked his beverages poured from bottles with labels he had to blow the dust off. "Maybe later," he said, getting up. "I like to walk most afternoons. Keeps the leg from paining me come evening."

"I serve supper at six," she said. "No later."

"I'll be here."

Walking the two blocks east to Commercial Drive, he realized he'd never been on foot in such a neighborhood before. He was glad when he reached the Saab in the parking lot behind the low-rise medical-dental building. Before he got in, Mostardi unclipped the brace and laid it on the passenger seat.

Fifteen minutes later, he was in his half-glassed office on the periphery of the *Vancouver News Herald* newsroom, his fingers skittering over the keyboard. So far, it was just notes, but he couldn't resist writing up what he knew would be the lead para.

They live better than the kings of old, the exposé would begin. *They can flick a switch for light and heat, get hot water from a tap and free books from the library. They have a warm place in which to sit and do what the mighty Charlemagne had to accomplish over the edge of a drafty battlement.*

MOSTARDI KNEW the liberals and left-wingers in the newsroom called him "Mean Mr. Mustard" behind his back. He didn't care. Right was right, and it was his calling to sweep away the cobwebs of pap and pop psychology, to lay bare some home truths about human nature.

"It's not as easy as you think," said the paper's chief bleeding heart, an editorial writer who wore her hair just a little longer than shaved and favored black sweaters and tights. "You try living on a disability allowance."

I will, said Mostardi, but only to himself. *And I expect to enjoy it.*

In truth, he knew that nobody on the public dole was living as well as he was. He had a tasteful house, a wine cellar that would be truly worth crowing about in another three or four years, money in the bank and an investment portfolio that would comfortably see him through to the grave. His wife had moved on to a man with lower standards, leaving him more than content.

"But if life has dealt you low cards, you can still live a decent existence," he would say. "Beethoven is on the radio for free. Dickens will tell you the same tale whether you picked him up for a dollar in the second-hand store or paid ten thousand at a rare book auction."

"Things always look simple to the simple-minded," said the editorial writer. "The rich and the poor live on different planets. For the rich it's a pleasure garden; for the poor it's a jungle."

Mostardi had given her one of the sniffs that he'd decided to establish as his trademark.

A bottle of single-malt scotch had secured the aid of the

paper's senior crime-beat reporter. The columnist was vouched for to a little man who had an office in the back room of a printer's shop in suburban Burnaby. For less than the scotch had cost, Mostardi was fitted out with a complete set of suitably tattered identification, including a note on a physician's letterhead that said he suffered from a disability with a long Latin name, and was permanently unemployable.

It cost him more scotch—but this was taken by the glass in the comfortable bar of the Meridien Hotel on Burrard Street—to have his lawyer assure him that his imposture would not be a criminal act, so long as he made full restitution of any moneys received from the government.

"Most people don't know," said the counselor, a plump, soft-looking man with a mind that could cut glass, "that you can open bank accounts under false names, tell outrageous lies about your accomplishments, and grant yourself a string of phony degrees—so long as you're not doing it for fraudulent gain." The lawyer noticed that his glass had become empty and rattled its half-melted ice to summon a fresh supply from the waiter. "Just make sure you keep meticulous records and repay every penny before you publish."

Mostardi swore the crime reporter and his lawyer to secrecy and prepared his plans. The next Monday, he asked for and received a three-week leave of absence. On Tuesday morning, he got in line at the welfare office on East Hastings Street, inching forward to the glass booth with a grilled hole in it, behind which stood a semi-somnolent clerk. By early afternoon, working from a list of addresses provided by the Ministry of Social Services, he had located Mrs. Strang's boarding house and been found acceptable.

AFTER MAKING his notes at the office, Mostardi drove home and parked the Saab in the garage, fed the goldfish and asked the bulldog fancier to keep an eye on the place.

"Going away?" asked the neighbor.

"For a while."

Mostardi took a cab to Commercial and East Broadway, put his brace back on and walked the two blocks to the boarding house, arriving a little after five.

Mrs. Strang stuck her head and shoulders out of the kitchen as he came through the front door. She was wearing an apron smeared with flour, and white flecks were caught in the fine hairs that covered her forearms. "Supper in a little while," she said. "How about some of that lemonade, now?"

"No, thank you," Mostardi said. "Lemons are too acidy for my stomach."

She stared at him as if he was a puzzle she was working out.

The house was very quiet. He could hear the rush of traffic a block away on East Twelfth. "Is anybody else around?" he asked. "I'd like to meet some of the other boarders."

"You'll be joining them directly," she said. "Do you drink coffee? Tea? I have some iced tea."

Offering beverages seems to be important to her, he thought, *but I guess a decent wine's out of the question.* "Iced tea would be fine, thank you," he said.

She smiled then, a quick flash of uneven teeth. "Why don't you sit in the parlor, and I'll fetch you a glass," she said.

The room had an unlived-in feel, the mismatched armchairs and couch slumped around the 1960s vintage console TV like depressed old men. The curtains were drawn against the late afternoon sun. Mostardi turned the set on and sat in the chair that looked the least unhappy.

It took all of thirty seconds for the picture to resolve itself. Before the image cleared, a refined female voice said something about "the miniature monsters that stalk and rend each other unnoticed beneath our feet." Then the screen showed a trapdoor spider popping out of its hidey hole to drag a cricket down to doom.

Mrs. Strang came in with what looked to be the same pitcher and glasses from which she had offered him lemonade. She poured two glasses and handed him one, then sat on the couch. "I put in plenty of sugar to sweeten it up for you," she said.

Mostardi wondered if, by the time he wrote his article, he would have any palate left. But he smiled, lifted the glass to her and drained half of it in three big gulps.

"Interesting aftertaste," he said. "It reminds me of. . . " but before he could finish, the glass slid from his hand. His face took on an expression it had never worn before, while his body straightened wherever it had been bent—he was no longer a man sitting in the chair but had become a rigid man-shaped object leaning against it. His heels juddered a brief tattoo on the carpet, then the room was still.

Mrs. Strang got up, poured her untouched glass of tea back into the pitcher and collected Mostardi's glass. Miraculously, it had landed on its base and had not tipped over, so there would be no mess to clean up this time.

A WEEK after his leave of absence expired, people started to wonder about Mostardi's whereabouts, but it was almost a month more before it could be said that anybody was actually worried. It was still longer before the crime reporter and the lawyer were convinced they ought to break their oaths of confidentiality, and even then the investigation almost hit a dead end because the little forger in Burnaby couldn't remember which false name he'd put on the papers.

It was still nothing more than a missing person case, so it

was almost Labor Day before a police constable, checking out a list of disability claimants culled from Ministry files, climbed Mrs. Strang's front steps and asked her about the man whose twice-monthly checks she'd been cashing since June.

Mrs. Strang said she believed he was out walking, for the benefit of his bad leg, but would be back real soon. She asked the policeman to step inside for a glass of cold lemonade, the day being unusually warm. A few minutes later, she left the house carrying a suitcase and a metal strongbox. She scuttled down to the street, put the luggage into the trunk of her car and drove away.

She regretted leaving her garden unharvested, especially now that Mr. Mostardi was bringing her tomatoes to perfection.

MUSCLE

This one ran in Alfred Hitchcock's Mystery Magazine. *When I wrote it, I had developed a liking for the cinematic work of Emma Thompson and I imagined her in the lead role. I think it would make a good premise for a light action-comedy movie.*

CYNTHIA MAIDSTONE HAD NEVER BEFORE SEEN a man writhing on the floor, clutching his testicles with both hands and moaning inarticulate syllables of rage and pain. Over her fifty-two years, she was fairly sure she'd encountered it in movies and television, and she was vaguely aware that it was a staple of those repetitious home-video programs, whose studio audiences automatically greeted the accidental occurrence of such injury with barks of laughter.

She doubted that Gerald Mallanger was finding anything to laugh about, curled fetally on the carpet of the Fairlawn Country Club's smaller boardroom. Cynthia almost felt sympathy for the man, but the sentiment merely glided by without pausing to touch down. She set her still firm jaw, drew a long breath through her well-turned nose, put her fists on hips that also remained nicely proportioned, and waited for her best friend's estranged husband to cease making such an unmitigated fuss. After all, the pain couldn't be much compared to childbirth, and it was certainly a lot briefer.

Dodi Mallanger, a plump woman who had come through more than five decades wearing a perpetual expression of mild surprise at whatever life contrived to do to her, was now registering pure astonishment. She gazed down at her spouse, and her eyes and mouth made three circles of the exact same size. Their twenty-eight years of marriage had presented Gerald to her in many positions and aspects that Cynthia had mercifully been spared, but clearly this was a new one.

The fourth person in the room, Marion Caouette, whose broad knee had done the damage, stood with beefy arms folded across an overstuffed chest and regarded the squirming man with equanimity. She nodded, as if he had confirmed some opinion which she had long held and which he had finally brought to an empirical test.

Gerald now let go of his injured parts and made it to his knees. His overfed face was almost crimson, the clipped white moustache standing out like a noncom's stripe on a red serge mess jacket. There was a bruise on his right cheek bone, and a slight trickle of blood from his lip, where Cynthia had punched him twice before Marion had stepped in with her conclusive blow.

He looked up at the three women and collectively called them a four-letter word which Cynthia had read in *Lady Chatterly's Lover*, but which she had never actually heard spoken aloud.

"I'll kill you!" he ground out, his voice pitched low, to keep the sound from carrying beyond the closed door where it might be heard over the buzz of conversation and the clink of ice against glass, out in the Club's main salon. It was the height of the season, and the upper reaches of Oakleigh Park's social order were simultaneously smiling into each other's faces and slipping daggers of gossip into any exposed back.

"I rather think not," said Cynthia. "Instead, you'll write Dodi a check for what she's entitled to."

"The hell I will!"

Marion unfolded her arms and took a step forward. Gerald began to struggle to his feet, fists balled and lower lip stuck out like a schoolboy. That's what Cynthia thought he'd probably been the last time he'd hit anybody who was likely to hit him back—which, of course, did not include Dodi.

"Enough!" Cynthia said, putting out a hand to stay Marion. "Time you started thinking, Gerald!"

He made a noise that originated somewhere between his chest and his mouth. Dodi took an involuntary step back, but Cynthia bored straight in.

"On the other side of that door is everybody whose opinion matters to you, Gerald Mallanger. And if you don't write that check, Dodi and Marion and I are going to walk out into their midst and tell them exactly what we've just done to you. You can kiss a fond fare-thee-well to any hope of becoming the chair of the membership committee."

Now Gerald was making a different noise. Cynthia wouldn't have thought that the color in his face could have deepened, but a decidedly dangerous shade of purple now crept beneath the crimson. He craved the chairmanship with a hunger that would not have disgraced a great white shark.

"If you think you can avoid writing the check by having a stroke instead, we'll still tell them. Then you'll have to sit there, propped up in a hospital bed, while they trail through your room to express their condolences and giggle in the hallway."

She stepped closer, almost nose to nose now, and dropped her voice to the soft purr that she used when coaxing a nervous thoroughbred through its first baby-sized jumps. "But if you do right by Dodi, then what happened here will never leave this room. Isn't that so, ladies?"

She said it without looking around, knowing that Dodi would be nodding her head like one of the little plastic dogs that some people, somehow, find to be just the perfect touch for the rear window of a car, and that Marion would be twisting her mouth into a wry shape that signified her concurrence.

"I'll get you for this," Gerald whispered. His back was against the door. His breath carried a mingled reek of good whiskey and sour bile.

"Write the check, Gerald," Cynthia said. "It's by far the smartest thing you can do."

And he did. Then he straightened his clothing, wiped his lip with a silk handkerchief, and ran manicured fingers through his silver mane—"A weave," Dodi had long ago confided to Cynthia. Without a backward glance, he opened the door and became one with the crowd.

The check lay on the polished maplewood table that dominated the boardroom. Dodi picked it up with both hands, and her eyes grew even wider. "My God," she said. "We did it."

OF COURSE, they hadn't meant it to happen that way.

Dodi had only been looking for moral support when she'd driven up to Cynthia's acreage in the canyons, where Marion's teenage daughter, Misty, was practicing for her first regional show jumping competition. Three decades before, Cynthia had been a candidate for the national team, and might have made it if her horse had had as much presence of mind as she did.

She dropped jumping after she married Victor Maidstone and the boys had come along. Now Vic was five years in the ground. Her sons were young men, pursuing their own lives in other places, with other people. A year after the funeral, she sold the townhouse, bought a nicely sited riding stable close to the better suburbs, and began to teach others who wanted to go further than she had.

Misty's horse, Philemon, a deep chested seven-year-old gray gelding, was boarding at Cynthia's stable while she tried to make a jumper out of him. Lately, with Cynthia on his back, it had finally begun to sink into his equine brain that jumping too soon would mean crashing into the second or third fence of the triple oxer.

Cynthia had already taken him around the course laid out in the south field once this afternoon. Now she and Marion watched the teenager canter the horse into position and prepare to dig in her heels.

"Looking better," Marion said.

"I don't know," said Cynthia. "I never saw a horse more likely to bolt." It was not quite true, but Cynthia didn't like to think about long-since-dead Pescator, the four-legged scatter-brain that had ruined her one big chance. She signaled the girl to go, then quietly held her breath as Philemon rollicked up to and over the three fences. The rails were set low at this stage, when timing was all that counted, and Cynthia had to admit, the girl's timing was not so bad.

She heard the rattle of tires on gravel behind her, but didn't take her eyes off the horse until it was safely over the last bar. Then she turned to find Dodi, distraught and almost disheveled, getting out of her green Cherokee, a piece of paper in her hand.

"Oh, Cyn, he's. . . ," Dodi said, struggling to get it out, "he's just. . . *screwing* me! That's what he's doing, screwing me, like some competitor he was beating out of a deal." She tried to hand the paper to Cynthia, but her friend declined to take it.

"Wait until Misty's finished," she said, and they did, Dodi fretting almost audibly, as the girl turned the gray and took it once more, a little more smoothly this time, over the triple jump. When Misty trotted the animal over and dismounted, a broad smile brought a glow to her usually low-wattage features.

Cynthia put down a tiny surge of envy and gave the girl an encouraging smile. "Put him away," she said, and turned to take the paper from Dodi.

It was a report from Dodi's lawyers—Cynthia's, originally— to whom the plump woman had gone, bewildered, the month before. Gerald had summarily announced that he wanted a divorce so he could marry the younger, slimmer, altogether more stylish woman he'd apparently been seeing on the side for more than a year. The lawyers were reporting that the Mallanger family assets had been very skillfully slid from view over the past few months, and were now hidden behind impenetrable barriers of Channel Island trusts and offshore bank accounts. It looked as if Dodi might have to settle for the relative pittance her soon-to-be-former husband had flung in her direction.

Cynthia finished reading and handed the letter to Marion, who scanned it quickly, then made a face that left no doubts as to her opinion of Dodi's husband.

"What am I going to do?" Dodi wailed.

"Talk to him directly," Cynthia said. "Threaten to make a stink at the Club."

"I did. He just laughed. He said most of them had already done what he was doing. Dumping the old bag for a trophy wife is apparently all the rage."

She started to cry. Cynthia put an arm around her shoulders. "Now, now," she said, "maybe what he says and what he'll do if he's pressed are two different things. Vic used to say Gerald was always ready to bluff on a weak hand."

Marion said, "We'll go with you, back you up."

THEY'D ALL BEEN PLANNING to be at the Fairlawn Club that night, anyway. The main salon was the venue for the Cowper Foundation's scholarship presentations, an annual exercise in *noblesse oblige* whereby the tip of Oakleigh's social pyramid dispensed tokens of grace and favor to a few young but deserving denizens of its lower tiers.

Cynthia was on the Foundation's selection committee. Marion's husband, Gil, was a benefactor, although education had played no part in his rise to wealth: he had sold the family sawmills back east at a time when their timber holdings were at a premium, then used the proceeds to get into and out of sunbelt real estate at precisely the right times. The impetus to back the scholarship fund came from Marion. Three generations of her family had been hands in Caouette mills, and her father had scraped to send her to college, so she would not end up working for a wage.

Dodi had planned to attend the reception—"Just to show the flag," was how she put it—but the letter from the lawyers had undercut her confidence. "I don't think I could bear it," she now told Cynthia and Marion, "everybody speaking to me in careful tones, as if I were crystal that might suddenly shatter."

"Or a bomb that might suddenly explode," Marion said.

"I'm sure Gerald can be brought to see reason," Cynthia said. "All this,"—she indicated the letter—"may be just male menopausal bravado."

"Will you come with me?" Dodi said.

"Of course I will," said Cynthia.

"Me too," said Marion.

Although, strictly speaking, Dodi hadn't included her in the invitation, Cynthia was glad to think of her standing close by when she called Gerald's bluff. She found Marion Caouette somehow quietly reassuring, like a well laid floor.

The three arrived at the gala when the salon was already full and the noise was approaching that level where individual conversations dissolve into a general blare. Dodi and Marion went into the small boardroom, while Cynthia crossed to a corner where Gerald Mallanger stood with his fellow silverbacks, each accoutered with whiskey and cigar, and all centered around the Club's president, Taylor Finshaw.

Finshaw was, as always, delivering one of his interminable golf stories. And, as ever, the tale reflected the maximum credit on their teller, while placing some absent golfing partner in a less than favorable light. Acknowledged as the wealthiest and most influential man in Oakleigh, Finshaw had inherited a fortune in his twenties, which he had since quadrupled, by dint of a moderately cunning brain, abetted by an entirely ruthless character.

Somewhere in the room, surrounded by her own clique of hangers-on, would be Taylor's wife, Carmen Finshaw. Although less thin than an Italian stiletto, she was just as polished and easily more dangerous.

Once, and briefly, Cynthia had tried to teach the rudiments of horsewomanship to the Finshaws' teenage daughter, a vicious little bundle of pouts and sneers named Frisia. The one and only lesson had apparently marked the girl's first experience of not being allowed to do whatsoever she pleased. Frisia had also not enjoyed being told that the next time she struck one of Cynthia's horses, she would learn first-hand how it felt to have a braided leather quirt—the one Taylor Finshaw had given her for her birthday—applied to her backside.

Since then, the Finshaws had not deigned to notice Cynthia's existence. The continuing snub did not, however, prevent the male half of Oakleigh's social pinnacle from sliding his eyes over her, from ankles to neck, as she approached and took Dodi's husband's arm.

"Gerald, I wonder if I might have a word," she said, "in private?"

He allowed himself to be led away, with one wink over his

shoulder to encourage the raised eyebrows and nudging elbows with which the others were marking his being cut from the herd by the Maidstone woman, who was to many of them an arrangement of female flesh still worth considering.

Gerald's smirk sagged into a frown the moment Cynthia led him through the door and into an encounter with his estranged wife.

Dodi began badly, stumbling over the words she had prepared to say. Cynthia stepped in and picked up the fumbled ball. "It won't do, Gerald. You can't treat your wife this way. People won't stand for it."

But it turned out that Gerald thought he could treat Dodi any way he chose. He drained his whiskey and set the glass on the maplewood, then proceeded to give them a cigar-enhanced display of egotism that made Cynthia blink. With the Havana Churchill clamped between his square incisors, he sneered and shrugged, dared Dodi to do the worst her lawyers could come up with, and ended by inviting them all to kiss a part of him that Cynthia, by now, would have enjoyed kicking.

He stubbed out the cigar in the whiskey glass in cold contempt, and strode to the door. Dodi, stammering, tears darkly streaking her cheeks, reached for his arm to pull him around. Gerald spun, covered her face with one fleshy hand, and pushed her backward so that the broadest part of her crashed painfully against the big table.

Cynthia thought she was about to say something dreadful, something ruinously cutting, to this contemptible man. It took her by surprise, therefore, to find that she was instead stepping toward him and that her right fist was delivering two quick blows to his sneer. She struck him the way she would have struck a horse that was trying the sly stable trick of pushing her up against the side of a stall: short, hard impacts that drove his head back and drew blood from his lip.

Gerald slid out the tip of his pale tongue to taste the blood.

"You bitch!" he said, and drew back his own larger and more experienced fist.

It was then that Marion Caouette drove the heel of her pump into his left shin and brought up the hard knee that ended matters.

"Arrogant bastard," Marion said, when Gerald had left the room.

"Oh my God," Dodi repeated.

"Never mind," said Cynthia, still wondering from what unknown part of her had come the impulse to strike the man. "It's all done and best forgotten. But not a word to anyone." She had no doubt that what she had seen in Gerald Mallanger's eyes as he had knelt in pain and humiliation was murderous rage, barely controlled. "This didn't happen, and we'll never speak of it again."

CYNTHIA DID SPEAK of it to herself, though. She was accustomed to pursue her thoughts through the medium of internal conversations, dividing her psyche into two sides of a debate, the better to mull things over. She came to the conclusion that what she had done to Gerald was what her Vic, or any other right-thinking man, would have done under the circumstances. He was a bully who deserved to have his tail lowered, especially if it served the purpose of seeing her friend properly provided for.

"But the fact was, we committed a crime," one side of her said. "Assault, possibly aggravated assault, compounded by extortion. And yet we fully expect to get away with it."

"People of our circle," countered her other side—though she winced at the superiority implicit in the phrase—"often commit crimes and get away with them. Perhaps not murder and mayhem," —although she remembered some celebrated trials that sometimes had her believing that a sufficiently well-paid battery of lawyers could blunt any prosecution—"but certainly many malfeasances go unpunished. One of our men can get away with financial skullduggery in the millions, and be admired for it by his peers. Yet if some bookkeeper in an off-the-rack suit did much the same thing for five thousand, he'd be jailed for fraud."

In the end she judged that she'd done wrong in a right cause. But the truth she dared not admit to herself was that the few seconds of physical conflict had brought her back to a quality of experience she had thought to have abandoned in some turn of the road behind her, left with her youth.

It had been wonderful to hit Gerald Mallanger, to surrender completely to sudden rage. She had not felt so much alive, not since the last time she had set a spirited horse at an eight-foot-high wall, with glory or ignominy on the other side, feeling the animal's hindquarters bunch and its front hooves leave the turf, the leap begun and nothing to do but ride it to the end.

In the weeks that followed, she would think of Gerald's preposterous face looming like a harvest moon tethered to the horizon, and her fist flashing toward it, and she would sigh.

She didn't speak of it to anyone else, and as far as she knew, neither did the other two women. But somehow it became known, as these things do, that Dodi had won a better settlement from Gerald than had first been offered, and that her friends Cynthia Maidstone and Marion Caouette—with whom both Cynthia and Dodi now found themselves spending more time than before—had had a hand in it.

So Cynthia might have expected, might even—without admitting it—have quietly hoped, that eventually some other friend or acquaintance would sidle up to her and shyly broach the subject. But she wouldn't have thought the shy sidler would be Madelaine Shaftesbury , whose skeletal thinness and social rank almost rivaled that of her closest crony, Carmen Finshaw.

"It's my babies," Madelaine said, her long, narrow face as full of despair as a Münch portrait. She brushed past Cynthia's attempted denials. "He's taking my babies."

So, of course, Cynthia had to agree to hear her out, standing at the buffet line between the curried shrimp and the vegan quiche, while pent-up demand began to build in the other members of the Oakleigh Women's Literacy Movement queued up behind them.

"There's a table in the far corner," Cynthia said. She caught Dodi's and Marion's collective eye across the room, and gestured them to join her and Madelaine there.

The "he" in question was, as Cynthia had expected, Pemberton Shaftesbury , to whom Madelaine had been wed the summer after she—and the Edsel—had come out. The marriage had lasted longer than the auto, but without engendering an equivalent ardor. Now it was reaching its climactic, courtesy of Pem's suddenly renewed interest in firm female flesh, of which his skeletal wife had little remaining. She was as thin and tall as a woman could safely be without invoking thoughts of carnival sideshows. Her features fell sharply back from the blade-like prominence of her nose, around which, Cynthia suspected, her countersunk eyes must have had trouble focusing on anything that loomed too close.

"Your babies?" Cynthia said, when the four women were seated at the table, heads leaning toward each other in a group pose that recreated the lines of the once space-age terminal building at Los Angeles International Airport. She could recall no second generation of Shaftesburys. "What babies?" she asked.

"I've collected them since I was a girl," Madelaine said. "I couldn't part with a single one, and now Pem says he's taking half of them. That's the law, he says. I could *kill* him."

Dodi caught it then. Gerald, in his hunger for social

advancement, had once gotten the Mallangers invited to a Shaftesbury dinner party. "You mean your glass!" Dodi said.

"My babies," Madelaine nodded. "My poor babies."

Cynthia remembered now that the woman had accumulated an uncommon collection of glassware—bowls, vases, knickknacks, sculpture—over more than five decades. Some were pieces of great price, Lalique or antique Venetian; others were of only sentimental value, but that value was monumental to Madelaine Shaftesbury.

Her departing husband, whose powers of imagination were in inverse proportion to the size of his inherited fortune, had seized, with an unshakeable grip that pit bulls might envy, upon the notion of an equal division of property. He was resolved to apportion everything fifty-fifty, including his wife's glass collection. And nothing, neither tears, nor logic, nor lawyers' letters, would sway him from his aim.

"The Shaftesburys are known for their single-mindedness," Madelaine said.

Comes from having only one brain cell between them, Cynthia said to herself, while aloud she said, "But what do you think we can do about it?"

Madelaine shrugged and looked away. "Just come with me while I try to reason with him one last time."

"You just want us there for moral support?" Dodi put in.

"Well. . . ," said Madelaine, examining the design on the club's cutlery.

The main part of Cynthia was hoping that Marion would say no. That would end the discussion, the way her knee had ended the confrontation with Gerald. Instead, her newfound friend quirked her eyebrows and moved her mouth in a sideways twist that said, "What the hell?"

"I suppose it would be the right thing to do," Cynthia said. She did not want to look inward at that moment, because she would have seen the recently rediscovered part of her, a small but rapidly growing part, rising up and putting a fist into the air.

They drove to the Shaftesbury house after eight in Dodi's Jeep. Madelaine let them in herself, explaining that she had given the housekeeper an unexpected evening off. "I thought that would be best," she said. "Pem's right through here."

She led them into the library, where Pemberton Shaftesbury sat primly erect in a wing chair, unruffled in muted tones and gentle fabrics, pursuing his customary after-dinner enjoyment of the newspaper crossword. He prided himself on knowing his way around an acrostic.

"Don't get up," Cynthia was about to say, before realizing that the man's habit of ignoring his wife now extended to her guests.

Madelaine stood in front of her husband's chair, and waved the three visitors to range themselves behind her.

"Pemberton," she said, quietly but firmly, "I want all of my babies."

He looked up, blinked rapidly a few times, then refocused his gaze on the puzzle. A slight smile crossed his lips as he filled in a couple of vacant squares.

"I said," Madelaine repeated, in exactly the same tone, "I want all of my babies."

There was no answer. They all waited in a silence broken only by the scratch of Pemberton Shaftesbury 's pen across the newsprint. Then Madelaine smoothly stooped and seized the front legs of the wing chair. Lifting with her legs, and not her back, she just as smoothly but quite suddenly stood up, so that the chair tipped over backwards, taking her husband with it.

Pemberton emitted a squawk that might have been the precursor of a full sentence, but before any more sounds came out of him, Madelaine stalked around the chair, knelt beside him, and began an endless rain of blows on his upturned face, her long, thin arms rising and falling like the parts of some antiquated machine. Each impact was accompanied by one of the syllables from her chanting, mantra-like, "All of them, all of them, all of them. . . " in the same restrained but steadfast tone.

It was only seconds before Cynthia and Marion moved to pull the woman away. Dodi, again, merely watched with wide eyes and parted lips.

Pemberton, his face blotchy red from his wife's attentions, a slight rivulet of blood running from his swelling nose and across his upper lip, lay looking up at them, breathing hard.

Finally, he swallowed and said, "Madelaine, you've gone quite mad."

"Not *quite*," she answered, still calm. "But if you don't give up your ridiculous claim to my babies, I will go into whatever territory lies beyond mad. And then we will all do to you exactly what was done to Gerald Mallanger."

She made as if to pull free of the other women's hands and commit further outrages. Pemberton raised his hands to shield his face, making a noise like a duck with a sore throat. "All right!" he said. "The glass is yours!"

They left him there, still tipped over, one knuckle nudging gently at his bleeding nostril, and went into what Madelaine called "the parlor." Cynthia had been in houses that were scarcely larger than this one vast room. The far wall was done in shelves of polished dark wood, on which the "babies" glistened and shone under carefully arranged lighting. Madelaine walked to the end of the room, raised her arms to the shelves like Nixon waving his final goodbye, and let go a grand sigh.

"Madelaine," said Cynthia, "what on earth did you mean about doing to Pemberton 'what was done to Gerald Mallanger?'"

The woman turned and came back to them. She narrowed her eyes, somehow making her face even thinner and sharper than its usual axe-edge proportions. "Women like you," she said, her eyes moving to take in Dodi and Marion as well, "women like you, who go to university and run businesses, you think that women like me are a lot of empty-headed ninnies."

Cynthia was about to make the obligatory denial—although the description was not wholly inaccurate—but Madelaine shushed her with a wave of an attenuated hand, and went on, "Just because we went to finishing school and learned which fork to use and how to say *chacun à son goût*, does not mean that we put away our brains with our trousseaux the moment we were tied to some man. Women like me were running great houses and great families, even great countries, before women like you were ever invented."

"I assure you. . . " Cynthia began, but Madelaine raised an imperious finger.

"I saw Gerald follow you into a room, and I saw him come out not three minutes later. I saw how he looked going in, and I saw how he walked coming out. And I drew the appropriate conclusions. So did quite a few of the people who were there, I'm sure."

"We promised we wouldn't tell," said Dodi.

"And you haven't. Because you needn't."

"But Gerald might not realize that," Cynthia said. "There could be a problem if he thinks we did."

Madelaine sniffed. "Leave Gerald Mallanger to me. The silly little man positively drools to be membership chairman. If he has that, it will be enough to keep him happy. I'll have Pem say a word to Ollie and Porter, and all will be well in the garden." She let her eyes drift to her babies. "I suppose it's the least I can do, after using you in such a calculating manner."

"Do you think your husband will cooperate?" Cynthia asked her. "I mean, after. . . "

"He'll be delighted."

"NEXT TIME SOMEONE asks whatever happened to Lucrezia Borgia, I'll know the answer," said Cynthia, as they pulled out of the long drive that led to the Shaftesbury house.

"I need a drink," Marion said.

"That's what we pay dues for," said Dodi, swinging the wheel. Ten minutes later, they were at a corner table in the lounge that had been, in the original arrangement of the Fairlawn, the "Ladies' Retreat," and which somehow still seemed to offer a more hospitable ambience for female members than any other room at the Club.

The steward knew their tastes, and responded to Marion's wave by bringing them two gins-and-tonics and a bourbon on ice. The reached for the drinks the moment they touched the table, and each took more than a sip. Marion put the whisky glass to her forehead, closed her eyes, and said, "My babies." Then she had to bite her lip.

The other two women both spoke at once.

"What have we got ourselves into?" Cynthia said.

"My God, wasn't that just the best thing ever?" said Dodi, and giggled.

Marion stared at Dodi, her usually loquacious features held rigid. But then, piece by piece, the rigor broke down—first around the eyes, then at the corners of the mouth, then spreading to her whole stocky torso, which began to shake with silent laughter.

"Did you see him lying there?" she spluttered, two red spots rising on her cheeks. "His little feet, up and down like a tantrum. And all the time, Madelaine's beating the other end like a tin drum."

"Wait a minute," Cynthia began.

"Hey, Pem, what's a five-letter word for whup-your-ass?" Dodi said, her voice breaking on the last syllable.

"Guys," Cynthia tried again. "Come on."

"*You've gone quite mad, my dear,*" Marion mimicked, then her fists beat a rapid tattoo on the table top. She and Dodi collapsed into fits of giggles and snorts, covering their mouths with their hands, tears squeezing from the corners of their eyes.

"It's not funny," Cynthia managed to get out, but then the contagion caught her. She put her palms flat on the table top and lowered her forehead to her knuckles, while her sides shook and long, rolling peals of laughter bubbled up from some subbasement she'd forgotten was ever there.

"This is getting out of hand," Cynthia said, when she could breathe again.

"My side hurts," Dodi said.

Marion drummed on the table, which set them off again.

"Ow," said Dodi, one hand holding her ribs.

"No, really," said Cynthia. "This is not good."

"Worried?" said Marion.

"No," said Cynthia, then corrected herself. "Well, maybe a little. You know, we were just accessories to an assault. Pemberton would have the law on his side."

"He was more concerned about having Madelaine all over his noggin," Dodi said, then had to hold her side again.

"I'm just afraid we're getting into something we can't control. I mean, what do we think we're doing?"

"Having fun," said Dodi, "for a change."

"And doing a little good," Marion put in.

"Well, that's true," Cynthia had to agree. "But although the ends are right, the means are out of line."

"So what?" said Marion. "Look, this Club is full of men who think they can do whatever the hell they want. They've got money and power, most of it handed down to them by their daddies, and they use them both any old way they choose. We're just giving the worst of them a taste of their own medicine."

"Besides," said Dodi, "we haven't robbed them or anything.

And we didn't do it for money, so it's not like we're hired muscle."

"Hired muscle?" Cynthia said. "You've been reading too many mysteries."

Dodi stuck out her tongue, and for a moment Cynthia remembered the girl her friend had been, way back when the world was made of simpler shapes painted in brighter colors.

"Admit it, Cyn," Marion said. "You liked it, too. They had it coming and it was fun being the good guys."

Cynthia hung her head just a little. "All right, I admit it. We're the Three Musketeers. We're Robin Hood's merry sisters, righting wrongs and raising hell in a genteel way. Just let's not go looking for trouble."

"I don't think we'll have to," said Marion, inclining her head toward the imposing woman in a designer original who had just appeared in the lounge's doorway.

"Isn't that Allison Moberley?" said Dodi, "the woman who owns the *Exotique* chain?"

"And a prime member of Madelaine Shaftesbury 's clique," said Cynthia, her insides suddenly bubbling with a mix of excitement and apprehension. "I have a feeling that in Madelaine's definition of keeping a secret, telling your friends doesn't count."

"That's our definition, too," said Dodi.

"Here she comes," said Marion, folding her arms across her chest.

TEDDY SHANKHILL SAW the plump woman in the pale silk suit bending over the engine compartment of the green Grand Cherokee as soon as he got off the elevator in the second-to-top floor of the downtown parking garage. He couldn't have missed her, since the Jeep was parked in the space next to his J-series Jag.

When she heard his footsteps, she withdrew her head from under the raised hood and say, "Could you please help me? I don't know anything about cars."

He was about to walk by, leaving only a flippant remark, but something about the woman's vulnerability nudged the avarice that was never dormant in him. Female helplessness, in Teddy's experience, was a reliable starting point for an increase in his net worth. He gave her a quick but expert appraisal as he approached, totting up the combined worth of the Dior suit, the double strand of pearls and the wink of diamonds from the wedding set on her left hand, and decided his afternoon massage could wait while he explored her potential for his gain.

He gave her his boyish smile, and saw it smooth most of the anxiety from her once pretty face. "What seems to be the trouble?"

"I think there's a loose wire," the woman said.

He glanced at the engine, about which he knew little more than she did. "Where?" he said.

"Down there in the back." She pointed at a piece of curved plastic. "Behind that round black thing. But I can't reach it."

Teddy stooped over the Jeep's innards.

"I don't see. . . " he said, but the rest of his response was superseded by the thump of the Cherokee's hood against the crown of his head. The sheet of steel was propelled downward by Marion and Cynthia, who had been waiting, crouched behind the car, for Dodi to signal that the mouse was in the trap.

"The handcuffs!" said Cynthia.

"Oh, yes, sorry!" said Dodi, reaching into the pocket of her jacket for the restraints. Cynthia pulled the dazed man's arms together behind his back and Dodi slipped the cuffs on.

Marion knelt and cinched his ankles together with a broad leather belt. Then, just as they had practiced it, they lifted the hood, caught Teddy as he sagged toward the floor, and stood him more or less upright. His eyes were unfocused. Dodi slapped a strip of duct tape across his mouth and put a pillow-case over his head. A minute later, he was under a blanket in the Cherokee's rear compartment, and they were rolling out the exit ramp.

Teddy regained full consciousness before they made it back to the woods above the stables, a spot chosen for its isolation and rarity of passersby. He began to push his knees into the back of the rear seat, causing Dodi some discomfort.

"Don't fuss, dear," she said. "We don't want to have to hit you on the head again."

Teddy settled down.

They parked in a small stand of maples and rolled the man out of the vehicle. "Who's got the scissors?" Cynthia said, at which Teddy curled up into a ball and began to make muffled noises under the pillowcase.

"We're just going to cut your clothes off," Dodi said. "We need you naked, you see, and we can't risk untying you."

Teddy twitched once or twice, when the steel touched his skin, but it wasn't long before the tattered pieces of his Versace suit and Alfred Sung shirt were scattered around.

"Shoes off or on?" Marion asked.

"Off, I think," Cynthia said. "He looks silly wearing just socks and shoes."

"Thought that was the point."

"Off," Cynthia repeated.

When he was stretched on the ground, naked except for the restraints and the pillowcase, Cynthia bent over him. "I suppose you're wondering why we've done this?" she asked.

The pillowcase nodded vigorously.

"I should think you'd be more interested in knowing what

we're going to do next." She clicked the scissors so he could hear the noise they made.

Teddy froze.

"Well," said Cynthia, "we thought that first we'd give you an injection of a rather strong animal tranquilizer, then we'd paint your private parts some interesting colors, and finally we'd release you naked outside that oyster bar which seems to be your favorite place to meet friends."

"What about the daffodil?" Dodi said.

"Oh, yes," Cynthia said. "One of us wants to stick a daffodil. . . well, I'm sure you get the picture."

"Worth a try," said Marion.

"Can't hurt," said Dodi. Then she giggled. "At least, it can't hurt *us*."

By now, Teddy was moving again. Marion put a foot on his chest, and he stopped.

Cynthia said, "But let's get back to your original question: why are we doing this?"

The pillowcase now seemed very alert for a pillowcase.

"You have some photographs," Cynthia went on. "We'd like to have them, and the negatives."

Teddy began to thrash again. "Tell him about the Crazy Glue," Dodi said.

Teddy lay still.

"Oh, yes. One of my friends thinks that glue is better than paint. We're having trouble making up our minds. Perhaps you have an opinion."

Muffled sounds came from under the pillowcase. Cynthia reached in and stripped away the tape without uncovering the man's eyes.

"Which photos did you want?" said Teddy.

"You mean there's more than one set? That hadn't occurred to us," Cynthia said. She thought for a moment, then said, "We'd better have them all."

Teddy said some things that none of them wanted to take personally.

"You know," said Dodi, "the daffodil would probably stay put if we used the Crazy Glue on it."

"That's true," said Cynthia.

"All right," said Teddy. "How do we do this?"

They had that all worked out as well. Within an hour, they had retrieved the photos and negatives from the cache Teddy had created beneath the floorboards of his beach-front condo. They left him handcuffed under the blanket in a disused gravel pit several miles away. Nearby, they piled some jeans, a sweatshirt and a pair of flip-flop thongs that would probably fit, along with the handcuff key. By the time Teddy got the pillowcase off, the Cherokee was long gone.

For a while afterwards, he told himself that wished he had memorized the license plate. But eventually, he could admit to himself that he would just as soon never run into those terrifying women again.

Cynthia, Dodi and Marion found some of Teddy's photo collection surprising, but most of them were only sad. They gave Allison Moberley the ones that he had used to blackmail her with, declining her offer to pick anything they wanted from her stores. The rest of the pictures they burned in Cynthia's fireplace.

"Well, that was fun," said Dodi, watching the flames. "So what's next?"

"Nothing, for God's sake!" Cynthia said. "We've got to stop it before we get into trouble. Suppose that man had had a gun?"

"We'd have glued it to him," Marion said.

"No," said Cynthia. "No more. It's been fun. It's been exciting. But I can't help thinking we've been dancing blindfolded on the edge of a cliff. Let's just get back to normal, before somebody gets hurt."

THE FAIRLAWN'S annual election of officers was held on an autumn Saturday. The occasion marked the first visit the three friends had made to the club in some weeks, they having thought it wise to let time build up some insulation between them and their newfound notoriety. Cynthia and Dodi came together, choosing seats in a rear row of the ranked chairs where they were less likely to be noticed and where they could catch Marion's attention when she arrived a little later, after dropping Misty off somewhere in town.

But they had scarcely sat down before they realized that the smiles and beckoning gestures coming from Madelaine Shaftesbury and Allison Moberley, in the places at the front of the room to which their rank entitled them, were directed at them.

"So much for back to normal," said Cynthia.

"Oh, my God," whispered Dodi, as they made their way forward. All around them, she saw eyebrows rise, heads incline together and the beginnings of whispered conversations throughout the room.

"We'd prefer not to draw attention to ourselves, Madelaine," Cynthia said when they arrived at the front of the room.

"Nonsense," was the reply. "Let them look. Let them prattle. One is who one is."

A few moments later, with the meeting about to begin, Marion Caouette arrived. It was an event which should have been noted by few. Instead, it drew the eyes and comments of all, because in the crook of Marion's arm rested the whip thin limb of Carmen Finshaw.

The queen of Oakleigh society ignored the murmurs and stares, sweeping Marion to the elite clique in the first row. She declared that she had encountered the millworker's daughter in the parking lot and "begged her to lead me to the other two musketeers." Dodi smothered a laugh. Cynthia drew her lips into a tight line and said nothing.

"It's all right, dear," Carmen went on, "I know what you've been doing, and I heartily approve."

Those close enough to hear Carmen's public blessing passed it in murmurs and whispers through the rest of the seated crowd. Clearly, everyone else in the room knew what they'd been up to.

Madelaine Shaftesbury was looking languidly about, rather like a long-necked wading bird seeking a frog to spear. "Is Taylor not to be with us?" she said.

Carmen Finshaw's frosted head moved briefly on the svelte cords of her neck. "He said something, a meeting of one of his boards, I gathered."

"Not like him to miss the election of officers," Allison said. "He is president, after all."

"He'll arrive eventually, I'm sure," said Carmen and changed the subject.

As vice president, Pemberton Shaftesbury rapped his gavel on the felt-covered head table to open the meeting in Taylor Finshaw's absence. Officers read their reports, then the meeting proceeded to elections. Gerald Mallanger's name was placed in unopposed nomination for chairman of the membership committee, and he was duly voted in. He advanced to the head table and made some remarks, his hands gripping the small podium as if it contained the keys to heaven, and his dull eyes brushing over the membership like a prince taking obligatory note of his courtiers.

Dodi dropped her eyes, but Cynthia nodded cordially as her gaze met Gerald's. She was rewarded with a sudden flash of the same lethal rage that had leaped at her as he had kneeled in the small boardroom. It was quickly suppressed, and his eyes moved on, but the flare of murderous hate had been as clear as the flash from a lighthouse across a dark channel. An involuntary shiver raced up her spine and shook itself free from her shoulders.

"I'm sorry," she said to Carmen Finshaw. The woman had just said something. "I was listening to Gerald."

"Can't think why," was the response. "Such a curious mixture of fawning gratitude and preening egotism. But I was saying that I'm sure our Frisia could benefit from a return to your tutelage. Would Thursday afternoon be convenient?"

Cynthia knew there was no point in starting something that would not be finished. "She would need to be more. . . receptive to my suggestions," she said. "The last time. . . "

Carmen cut her off. "I wouldn't worry about that, my dear. I've already spoken to her. She knows you are not a woman to be trifled with." She looked to the rear of the room. "Ah, there's Taylor now."

The man who occupied Oakleigh's social pinnacle made his usual sedate progress to the head table, as Gerald Mallanger was taking his long-sought seat. Finshaw paused to nod—it was almost a bow—to his wife and her companions in the first row of seats. It was only then that he noticed Cynthia and her two friends.

Cynthia looked up to see a series of expressions pass in rapid succession across his self-satisfied face. First came his usual blank indifference to all others, a product of inborn arrogance. There followed a sudden flash of recognition, which immediately gave way to a pale wash of fear behind his eyes, before being just as quickly buried beneath a conscious redrawing of his habitual uninterested stare. He rounded the table and stepped to the podium, and took charge of the rest of the meeting.

In the little more than a second that it had taken Taylor Finshaw to react to finding her and her friends in the company of his wife, Cynthia had grasped exactly why the three off them had been so precipitously promoted to the social vanguard. They were to be cocked and aimed at a new target.

Less than half an hour later, the members having discussed and voted on the Fairlawn's plans for the year, the annual general meeting wound down to Taylor's final gaveling of the felt-covered table. Club staff opened the room-high doors to the adjacent reception room. The members rose and waited for the Finshaws to lead them to the refreshments. Despite imperiously summoning looks from Madelaine Shaftesbury and Allison Moberley, who fell in with their husbands in the second rank, Cynthia held Dodi and Marion back.

"I'm leaving," she said. "You should too."

"What?" said Marion, at the same time as Dodi said, "Why?"

"Carmen wants us to do something to Taylor."

Dodi's eyes expanded. "Did she tell you that?"

"No," Cynthia said, "he did. He was trying not to, but it was written on his face."

"Wow," said Dodi, while Marion frowned in a way that somehow caused the cords in her neck to pop out.

"We don't need this," Cynthia said, and her friends agreed.

"Guys like Pem and Gerald are one thing," Marion said. "When we say they act like they can get away with murder, that's just talk. Taylor Finshaw's the kind who might just give it a try."

"I wouldn't be surprised if he already has," Dodi said, and shuddered.

"I don't know what he's done to Carmen, or what she thinks we're going to do for her," Cynthia said, "and I don't care. I'm out of the hired muscle business."

"Me too."

"Oh, my God."

"We'd better make sure Taylor knows that," Cynthia said. "Wait here."

She went into the reception room, where the Fairlawn's various cliques had already sorted themselves into nodes and satellites, with uniformed waiters whisking trays of champagne and delicacies through the intervening spaces. She spotted Taylor in the power center of the room, Gerald and Pemberton at his elbows, while other silverbacks clustered close, leaning in as if E.F. Hutton, the Wall Street brokerage made famous in an old advertising campaign, was about to say the sooth.

Cynthia felt the crowd's attention swing toward her as she crossed the floor, inserted herself into the group and touched Taylor's elbow. "Taylor," she said, "I wonder if I might have a word?"

There was an instant hush, the constant clink of glasses borne on elevated trays now sounding as loud as an advancing panzer division. Every eye in the room was fixed upon Cynthia Maidstone and Taylor Finshaw — every eye except the six owned by his wife and her two cronies, who were studiously examining the brocade of the cloth covering the buffet table, which they had seen and ignored a hundred times before.

Taylor looked first at Cynthia's fingertips where they touched his sleeve, then at her serious face, then over at Dodi and Marion, visible through the open doors that connected to the meeting room. A jovial expression remained painted on his countenance, but the skin that was its canvas paled noticeably. He took a breath and said, "Perhaps later."

Oh my, thought Cynthia, *that was the wrong approach.* Aloud, pitching her voice to carry throughout the hushed room, she said, "There has been a mistake, Taylor. Whatever Carmen has told you, it's not going to happen. Nothing's going to happen."

Taylor raised his glass and sipped champagne. Cynthia had to admire the lack of tremor in his hand. "I have no idea what you're talking about," he said.

"Fine," she answered. "Let's leave it like that."

She turned on her heel, collected Dodi and Marion, and the three friends went out into the autumn air. The muted rumble and buzz of voices from the reception room followed their footsteps until the front doors swung closed behind them.

"I've had enough of this place," Marion said. "Whatta you say we start our own club?"

THE CLOCK RADIO'S LED read 2:40 a.m., more than three hours before its alarm would tell Cynthia to get up and get the day started. She focused sleepy eyes on the red digits, separated by a flashing colon. She'd been having the dream about riding Pescator again, on that awful day, her knees urging him up to the water barrier, feeling the tension building in him, knowing that he was going to balk, just as he always balked whenever she had the dream. If she didn't wake up, she'd be tossed over his head, and he'd be running off around the course, kicking his heels, while the commentators made sympathetic noises, and all her dreams faded to black.

But it hadn't been the dream that woke her—she knew that somehow. She rolled onto her back and wondered what was wrong. That was when she heard the horses screaming.

She threw back the covers and was at the window in a second, yanking the curtains out of the way to look down into the stable yard. Nothing. Doors closed, lights on, no lurking figures. Yet she could hear Philemon and Packy and Buck, the terrible, shrill scream of panicked horses, the metal-shod hooves crashing against the floorboards and the sides of their stalls.

She flung herself downstairs, wrapping her robe around her. Out the side door and across the stone flags to the stables, grab the steel handle of the big door. Now she could smell the smoke, sweet and sharp, the acrid bite of burning hay.

She prepared to slam the door sideways, knowing that pulling it might be the last thing she ever did. If the hay was smoldering, throwing open the door would let in a sudden gush of flame-feeding oxygen. Then she would be hit by a blast of superheated air that would cook the inside of her lungs while it tossed her across the yard like a puppet with its strings cut. But she couldn't stand there and listen to the animals scream.

She took a deep breath, then yanked the door aside. There was no explosion. Her eyes went first to the hay bales stacked at the rear of the stable, but she saw no flames, no tell-tale glow of embers. There was smoke in the air, quite a lot of it, but she couldn't see where it was coming from. Then she realized that all of the inside lights were off.

Electrical? she asked herself. But it was burning hay she was smelling, she was sure of that. And the outside lights were working, though they were all on the same circuit.

"What the hell?" Cynthia said, took a deep breath, and went into the stable. She'd get the horses out and wait to find out what was going on.

Two steps inside, the smoke stung her eyes and she could feel heat on her face. There *was* a fire, and it was close. She moved forward, gingerly, eyes streaming, hands extended. She felt her way to it through the smoky darkness, her palms guiding her as if they were playing a real-life version of the old "hot-and-cold" game she'd played with her boys when they were children.

Fifteen feet into the smoky blackness, she found the source of the heat. Through streaming eyes, she saw red beneath the pall of smoke, down low. She nudged a toe forward, and connected with the old steel wash tub that should have been hanging on the wall near the cupboard that held farrier's tools. Instead, here it was in the middle of the wide central aisle between the stalls. *What the hell is this doing here?* she wondered. *And why is it full of burning hay?*

She'd leave the questions till later. If that was all the fire amounted to, she'd douse it now, before it could spread, then get the horses into the fresh air.

"If this is somebody's idea of a joke," she said aloud, groping toward the fire extinguisher that should be hanging on a post between two empty stalls. Talking was a mistake. The biting fumes rasped the lining of her airway, and she coughed. Clamping her lips closed, trying to ignore the unbearable tickle in her chest, she finally found the upright timber, then the metal cylinder. She pulled it free from its steel bracket, and turned back to the burning hay.

The need to cough became overwhelming, triggering a spasm that almost doubled her over. Stooped, she felt a rush of air as something passed through the space where her head had just been and smashed into the post.

Cynthia spun around and flung the extinguisher at the smoky darkness. She heard it hit something softer than the wall. There was a whining, guttural growl, oddly muffled, and she knew that all she had done was to make her assailant even more angry.

She threw herself backwards, but not quite quickly enough. Whatever had been swung at her before now came back for a second blow. Something hard and heavy, a club with a sharp edge was the image that popped into her mind, grazed the muscle between her left shoulder and neck.

Even the glancing blow, softened by the thick fabric of her robe, was enough to numb her left arm. *If that hits me in the head, I'm done for*, said a part of her that had coolly detached itself from the fear and confusion, while she backpedaled through the choking blackness of the stable.

The smoke was getting thicker, but she could sense more than see a grayness to her left—the door to the light-filled stable yard. She needed to get out there, away from whoever was stalking her, whoever had set the fire as bait to draw her into this trap.

Gerald? inquired her internal commentator. *Taylor Finshaw? Maybe even that Teddy, if he found out. . .* The thought ended in another fit of coughing. She wiped her eyes and headed for the open door, close enough now to see it as a dim oblong.

Then she saw the shape pass between her and the gray light, too indistinct to identify. *That's where he'll be waiting.* Coughing, she backed away.

There was another door, human sized, beyond the hay store. But whoever had trapped her would have blocked it, she was sure. *Time to think, before you suffocate.*

She crouched to the floor. The smoke was thinner here. She could see all the way to the door, to the pair of legs between her and the light.

The horses were still shrieking. Misty's high-strung Philemon was making a lot of the noise, but her own buckskin quarter horse, appropriately named Buck, was adding plenty to the din. Big Packy—short for pachyderm because she walked as slowly as an elephant—was rumbling and whickering, like an outraged dowager demanding an explanation.

That's it, half of Cynthia's mind told the other. *Cavalry charge.* She scrambled on hands and knees to Packy's stall, stood upright and felt her way along a wall to the head of the enclosure where, the oversized horse's halter was tethered to an iron ring. She slipped the rope loose, talking and patting and stroking, and backed the big mare out of the stall.

That brought Packy's nose closer to the source of the smoke, and she stamped and pulled toward the doorway.

"No, wait, there's a baby, good girl," Cynthia whispered, as she snugged the lead rope through an iron bracket bolted to the post where the fire extinguisher had been. "Let me get Buck."

She crawled to the quarter horse's stall. The buckskin

calmed a little when she ran a hand over his nose and let him smell her, all the time talking in his ear to soothe and gentle him out of panic.

She got him out of the stall and tried to pull him over to where she had left Packy. Her plan was to position herself between the two horses, holding on to their halters—she'd seen it in a movie, somewhere—then charge out of the stable hanging between them. It would take a lot more than a lurker armed with a club to stop their progress, once they got going.

But Buck had had enough of smoke and darkness. He wanted *out*. When Cynthia tried to pull him sideways toward Packy, the gelding tossed his head so hard and sudden that she was almost jerked off her feet. The coarse sisal rope burned her palm and she involuntarily released it. Buck's hooves thumped on the floorboards, and he was gone.

Damn horses, said the cool part of her. *Always let you down when you need them.* But she could still do it with Packy. She crawled to the big horse, stood up to untie her from the post, then took a good grip on the halter strap. "Okay," she said, "let's go!"

But now there was nowhere to go. The gray oblong was shrinking. She heard the rumbling sound of the big door closing. The attacker was shutting them in.

Cynthia swore again, the same word Vic would use when he hit his thumb with a hammer. She got down on her hands and knees again, breathing the cooler, cleaner air on the floor.

Now what? she asked herself, but this time the answer didn't come from the calm, rational corner of her inner household. This time, the response rattled up from the part of her that had stepped forward and punched Gerald Mallanger, the angry part of her that she had kept hidden, even from herself, like a dangerously deranged auntie locked in the basement for too many years.

A welling, rising, towering *rage* roared straight up out of the core of Cynthia Maidstone, filling her with a cold, crackling energy so intense she felt that she could point her fingers and chill lighting would coruscate from their tips.

A part of her was asking, *Where did this come from?* but all of her knew the answer: it came from the damned horse that balked at the water jump in the national try-outs; from the damned sweet husband who'd died and left her with all this life yet to live; from her damned sweet sons who'd wandered off into the world with scarcely a backward glance; from the talent-less teenagers she had to teach; from rubbing up against the Mallangers and Finshaws and all the other well-fed barracudas that continually circled the Fairlawn Country Club, ready to tear into any tiny wound that leaked a smell of weakness into the social pond.

She should have recognized the signs when she'd popped Gerald in the nose, or when she'd gone along with playing at being hired muscle. Somewhere down inside her, sealed away, was one hell of a sense of grievance. She'd been standing on its head for a long, long time, and now it wanted out, just the way Buck had wanted out of the stable. It wanted someone to take it all out on, someone to hit back at, someone who could be made to pay for what life had done to Cynthia Maidstone.

And somewhere in this dark, stinking stable, armed with a mere club, was the son of a bitch who had volunteered for the position.

"All right, then," she whispered, already crawling to the empty stall where she'd thrown the fire extinguisher. She felt around and found the cylinder, then dragged it back to the wash tub. A few seconds of chilled carbon dioxide, and the fire was out, though the smoke was just as dense.

She crawled to Philemon's stall, a plan putting itself together as she moved. The part of her that reflected on her thoughts commented on the iciness of her rage, but the rest of her was too busy to discuss it.

The attacker had been in the thick of the smoke before Cynthia arrived, yet she hadn't heard a cough. *Gas mask,* she thought. *That means I can't find him by listening, the way he can find me, so I'll have to bring him to me.*

She felt her way along the trembling length of Philemon. The thoroughbred was making less noise now—not because he was calmer, but because he had entered the stock-still, quivering-all-over stage of horse panic, his entire weight hauling backwards against the rope and the iron ring that tied him to the wall.

He wasn't going to calm down soon, Cynthia knew. That was all right. She didn't want him calm.

She took hold of the end of the tethering rope. It hung loose from the ring, tied in a quick-release knot that would come open if she yanked down suddenly. She squatted down in a corner of the stall and listened. She heard only the stamping of Packy's giant hooves on the floorboards by the big door and the snuffling of her breathing. The big mare must have found a gap between the door and the jamb, and was sucking fresh air through the opening.

Cynthia could hear no sound from the attacker, but she knew he was there, waiting for her to move to one of the doors. Or for a cough that would tell him where she was hiding.

The smoke was thinner now. There were vents in the roof peaks that would let it dissipate. If it got any thinner, the attacker could find her just by turning the lights back on and looking around. It was time to act.

Squatting in the corner, Cynthia spoke firmly into the darkness. "Police," she said, then counted five seconds before she continued, "This is Cynthia Maidstone, 1204 Argyle Road. There's a man trying to kill me and burn down my stable. Send the fire department, too."

She waited another couple of seconds then called out, "I've

called 911. The police are on their way. If you're going to run, now's the time to do it."

But the observer part of her knew she didn't want the attacker to run, didn't care whether or not he believed she had a cellular phone. She wanted him to follow the sound of her voice, to come sneaking through the blackness.

"I'm not kidding," she said, and listened. And heard what she'd been listening for. The sound was faint, a tiny creak that was almost smothered by Packy's snorts and the air whistling through Philemon's distended nostrils. But she heard it again, a shrilly complaining floorboard, in just the right place.

She yanked down sharply down on the gelding's tether and immediately let go. The rope unknotted from around the iron ring, and the tall thoroughbred stumbled backwards into the aisle between the stalls.

Cynthia heard a gasp and a whine as Misty Caouette's high-strung jumper blundered around in the darkness, desperate for a way out. But those were not horse noises. They came from the person who had been standing immediately behind Philemon when Cynthia loosed the terrified animal like a bolt from a catapult, the person who was now down on the floor getting a thorough acquaintance with the gelding's hooves.

Cynthia didn't wait to assess the damage. Ducking low, she scuttled to the big door, worked the handle and threw it wide, then got out of the way as Packy and Philemon made their clattering exit. The horses ran to join Buck in the south field, while the woman took only twelve strides to reach the door of the house.

She slammed it closed behind her, grabbed the portable phone from beside the kitchen door and locked herself in the downstairs bathroom. There, crouched in the bath tub, the shower curtain drawn, she dialed 911 and repeated to the police operator who answered what she had said to the darkness of the stable.

One of the advantages of living on the right side of town was the rapid response time of the Oakleigh police department. In less than five minutes, Cynthia saw blue light strobing through the bathroom window. She made her way to the side door and looked out to see two police cars in the yard, and four uniformed officers with guns drawn edging toward the stable door.

A gray Mercedes came up the driveway. Cynthia saw two of the cops turn and put their guns on its driver. Taylor Finshaw got out with both hands raised, his face contriving an expression of jovial disbelief at the idea that anyone could think him a criminal.

He gave his name and said, "I live nearby. I was on my way home and saw the commotion. Everything all right with Cynthia?"

"Just fine," said Cynthia, stepping onto the porch, in a voice that sounded steadier than she felt. She watched him react, then saw him cover up that first reaction. She knew that his arrival was no coincidence. Whoever was in the barn had been sent by Taylor Finshaw. Unable to resist a chance to gloat, he had come to see Cynthia carried off to the hospital, perhaps to the morgue.

But now he didn't know how this was going to turn out at all, and from the way he clenched his fists behind his back, she knew that there was a growing worry behind the facade of neighborly concern.

The police returned their attention to the stable. One of them shouted into the smoky darkness, "Come on out of there! Hands where we can see them!"

The response from inside was muffled. Cynthia couldn't make out words, but the pain and panic in the voice were real. She saw Taylor swallow, and now there was sweat on his forehead, even in the coolness of a September night.

Two police officers went into the stable. Seconds, later, one of them came out with his gun holstered. "We're clear," he said. "You two help get the perp outta there. I'm calling the paramedics."

In his hand he held a wooden mallet, two-foot long, with a steel horseshoe nailed to the business end. He set it on the passenger seat of one of the police cars, and leaned into the open door for the radio mike.

Now the pieces were falling into place for Cynthia. It was not hard to see how this was supposed to have gone: the mallet was intended to make her look like a stable owner who had been kicked and trampled unconscious while rescuing horses from a fire. And maybe she'd have been left to burn.

She crossed the yard to where Finshaw still stood, tying to see into the stable. "You bastard," she said.

"I didn't know anything," he answered, not taking his eyes off the darkened doorway. Then he swallowed and said, "It was all her own idea."

His last words stopped the tirade that had been lining up in Cynthia's speech center. "*Her* idea?" she said. She followed his gaze. Limping into the stable yard, borne between two police officers the way Cynthia had meant to hang between her horses, was a slim figure in jeans and a leather jacket, head bowed in pain. The third policeman came behind, carrying a military surplus gas mask.

"Looks like just a busted leg and maybe a couple ribs," said the policeman who had radioed for an ambulance. He got out his notebook and approached Taylor Finshaw. "Are you acquainted with the suspect?" he asked.

"She's my daughter, Frisia."

"My God," said Cynthia. "You would use your own daughter? She could have been killed! How do people like you manage to live with themselves?"

The officer looked at her, but spoke to Finshaw, "When you

say, 'It was all her own idea,' does that mean you were aware of her intentions in coming here tonight?"

Taylor Finshaw pulled at least some of his customary poise back into position. "That's ridiculous," he declared.

The policeman had an undeveloped sense of the ridiculous. He took a small card from his breast pocket and began to read from it, "You have the right to remain silent."

FRISIA FINSHAW TOLD the judge it was all her own idea. She said it several times, elaborating on how she hadn't wanted to take riding lessons from Cynthia, who'd once threatened her with violence. She'd only wanted to scare her, she said, and now she was so very sorry things had got out of hand.

She pled guilty to assault and mischief, and was put on probation.

A few days later, it was her father's turn. The prosecutor drew what Cynthia found to be a convincing picture of a nasty, frightened man who enlisted his own daughter to commit serious crimes. But by the time the rich-voiced silverback from the Finshaw family's law firm was finished, Taylor had metamorphosed into a deeply concerned parent who, worried that his excitable, horse-shy daughter might be about to do something rash, had come looking for her at Cynthia's place—regrettably arriving just a little too late to prevent the girl from acting out her teenage fantasies.

"My God," whispered Dodi Mallanger at the back of the courtroom, when the judge dismissed the charges on the grounds of insufficient evidence. "He let his own daughter take the fall."

"Take the fall?" said Cynthia. "You're still reading too many mysteries, Dode."

Marion Caouette moved her lips into an arrangement that

made a silent but eloquent commentary on the blindness of justice. Misty had already reported that, as soon as the cast came off, Frisia would be departing on a six-month tour of Europe, her parents having recently reversed a long-standing refusal to let the girl roam the Old World unattended.

"They really could get away with murder," Dodi said.

"Come on," said Cynthia. They went out into the hallway, accompanied by four other members of the new club that the three friends had organized since leaving the Fairlawn. In total, there were now more than two dozen women in MUSCL, the Mutual Support Club. None had been chosen for her social prominence, but all had been selected for their robust constitutions and for favoring a direct approach to resolving some of life's inequalities.

The seven women walked a few yards to a small room where lawyers could meet privately with their clients. They already knew it was soundproofed and could be locked from the inside.

"Someone lower the blinds," Cynthia said, when they had entered and made sure the room was still free. She turned to Dodi. "Do you have the daffodil?"

"And the glue," her best friend confirmed.

Marion held up a Polaroid camera and smiled.

"Here he comes," said one of the new recruits, who had been keeping an eye on the hallway.

Cynthia took a deep breath, reached into that once hidden part of herself that she was now increasingly more comfortable with, and said, "All right, ladies. One, two, three—just the way we practiced it."

Together, they stepped into the hallway. Finshaw blinked as they smoothly surrounded him and diverted his course.

"Taylor," Cynthia said, as they hustled him out of sight, "I wonder if I might have a word."

SEALED WITH A KISS

A fellow Canadian who was putting together an anthology of crime fiction asked me for a story. I sent him this one. The anthology was never produced because the editor was based in Fort McMurray, which was largely wiped out by a forest fire. I sent it to a couple of places, but it didn't click, and then I forgot about it.

SHE KEPT SAYING it all was the priest's fault. Father Brosz had made a move on her. Then her pathologically jealous husband had shown up and it all went to hell from there.

She sat in the small interview room on the third floor of the station, telling her story for the third time. Detective Nick Parma could see that the shock was wearing off now. He led her through the sequence of events again and noticed that the words she used didn't vary. It was the same phrases he'd jotted down in his notebook: "He said he wanted to pull over and talk; we're sitting there and suddenly he's all over me; I look through the window and see Arnulfo coming across the street; I get out of the car and run."

HER NAME WAS ROSARIA ARENAL. She was 37 and had come to the attention of Parma's house twice before: the first time when the downstairs neighbours had called in about a fight in her apartment; the second when the ER attending at St. Mary's wouldn't believe that she had sustained a split lip and a fractured cheekbone tripping over a loose rug. Both times, Mrs. Arenal had refused to say the words that would have let Parma put her husband away.

"For how long?" she had asked him when they had sat in this same interview room eight months ago. "A week? Two weeks? Then where are you, Mister Policeman, when he gets out and comes home with a pistol?"

PARMA HAD A VERY good picture of what had happened inside and outside Hoolie's. There were plenty of eyewitnesses and they were all cops. Hoolie's was where half the cops downtown went after shift.

Rosaria Arenal had come into Hoolie's fast and scared, a compact little woman, eyes and mouth so wide open they made three perfect circles in a triangle. One of the eight-to-four traffic guys said they reminded him of the holes in a bowling ball, if the ball was bloodless pale except for a smear of lipstick across one white cheek. She slammed the door behind her, rattling the heavy smoked glass, and croaked, "He's going to kill him!"

There were maybe twenty off-duty cops distributed between the long bar and the red leatherette booths along the other side. In the booth nearest to the door were four guys from traffic who'd been putting away shot-and-a-beer combos since they'd clocked off three hours ago. At her end of the bar were a couple of detectives from the squad over at another house who came to Hoolie's because they had a history with the ex-cop who tended bar.

Every face in the place turned to her, every voice stilled except for one of the detectives who said, "Whoa, lady. Who's gonna..."

That was when the three shots came from outside: *pop, pop, pop,* so fast together that the third had already come and gone before anybody heard the tinkle of brass hitting asphalt.

The detectives drew their guns and stood up. The one who'd spoken to her was Chisholm, a lean, balding man with a thin and crooked nose. A good cop, Parma knew. He put his hand on the woman's shoulder to move her aside. But by then the four hotshots from traffic already had the door open and were crowding out in a testosterone- and-booze-fueled clutch of profanity and drawn nine-millimetres.

Parma read Chisholm's statement. He'd heard a chorus of "Freeze! Drop it! On the ground!" followed almost instantly by enough gunfire to pacify Kandahar. Chisholm and his short, stubby partner were in the doorway, looking out and screaming, "Hold your fire! There's people in those buildings!"

The bartender's statement said that after everyone else had rushed outside, Rosaria Arenal stood leaning her forearms on the bar, her sides heaving as if she'd run a quarter mile. She didn't turn her head to see what was going on outside but lowered her brow until it touched the gouged wood and its ring-stains and cigarette burns.

"Oh, god," she said.

"HERE'S THE THING," Parma said, when she'd run through the story for the third time, the lines coming out just the same as the other two tellings. "Father Brosz is driving you home. You've been going to him for what, three months, right?"

"He was counseling me."

"Yeah, you said."

She'd been picking at the chipped Formica on the table top with one lacquered fingernail. Now her head came up and she looked at him. He saw it then, because he'd taken the training and was watching for the micro-expression that flickered across her eyes in less than a second: a flash of wariness and calculation. Then she looked back down at the Formica and her fingers went back to work.

"So, he's driving and you're talking and suddenly he wants to pull over and then he's grabbing and kissing."

"That's how it happened."

"Yeah," said Parma. "But in the middle of all this, you put on fresh lipstick.'

This time she didn't look up. Parma waited, letting the room fill with silence except for the hum of the fluorescents and the *pick, pick, pick* of her fingernail.

"How come?" he said.

THE TROUBLE with Rosaria Arenal's story was that Parma had known Father Brosz for fifteen years, ever since he came out of the seminary as a beardless twenty-one-year-old and started at St. Jude's. Cops get to know priests because their jobs often intersect—sometimes over a body that's breathing its last while the holy man applies the oil of extreme unction; sometimes over attempts to get kids off the street corners where crime breeds and into a program that just might offer them a glimpse of a better life.

Beyond the contacts that came with work, Parma and Father Brosz had been friends—not beer-and poker-every-Tuesday-night friends, but they would always stop and talk for a few minutes if they ran into each other on the street. Over a decade and a half, the detective had seen the priest in all kinds of situations, seen him under pressure and at his ease.

He'd also seen him around women, seen the way he looked at them. Parma thought he might have been one of those men who flee to the priesthood as a refuge from homosexuality. Brosz had not been the kind of priest who would do what Rosaria Arenal said he did: seduce her when she came to him for help with her crazy husband, carry on a clandestine affair for three months, then grab her for one last smooch when she told him she was breaking it off.

"Is there anybody who can confirm this relationship?" Parma asked.

Her head came up again, defiant this time. "You think I went around telling people I was . . . you know, with a priest? I was ashamed. I just wanted it to stop."

"Did your husband know?"

"He knew I was seeing Father Brosz for counseling. He wouldn't come."

"Why did he follow you?"

She looked away. "I don't know. Maybe something made him suspicious. Anything could get him going."

"But you didn't know he was behind you when Father Brosz pulled the car over."

"First I knew was when I saw him coming across the street with the gun."

AFTER HE HAD her tell it all again for the fourth time, same words, same hand gestures even, Parma knew she had rehearsed this performance. When she finished, he closed his notebook and just looked at her until she fidgeted a little in the interview chair. It had a hard seat, and the front legs were cut a little shorter than the back. Sitting in it for a long time was meant to be uncomfortable.

After a while she said, "So can I go now?"

"No."

"Am I under arrest?"

"No."

"Then I can go." She started to rise.

"You're being held as a material witness."

"Then I want a lawyer."

"You're not entitled to a lawyer when you're just a witness."

"Why can't I go?"

He laid it out for her, watching her as he built the thing from the ground up. "You had a crazy-jealous husband who beat you up and would have killed you if you'd tried to leave him.

"The only place he'd let you go alone was the church. So, you went to John Brosz for counselling and somewhere along the way you hatched this plan. You'd seen there were always cops at Hoolie's after their shifts—it's on the route between the church and your apartment.

"You left some kind of little clues to make your husband suspicious, make him follow you. Maybe you called a couple of times from the church and hung up when he answered. That would have done it.

"So tonight, after your counseling, you ask Father Brosz to drive you home then you get him to pull over just in front of Hoolie's. You know your husband is tailing you. You wait until you're sure Arnulfo can see you, then you grab the priest and kiss him. You've got fresh lipstick on so it will leave a smear on his face—that's your evidence.

"You see your husband coming with his gun. You know what's going to happen and you run into the bar full of armed cops who've had a few drinks.

"Bang, bang, your husband's dead and you've got away with murder-by-cops. Maybe there's even insurance."

HE LEFT her in the locked room to think about it. Sometimes, when you came back they were ready to confess; sometimes, they'd got hard. Rosaria Arenal had got hard.

"He seduced me. He made me do it in the vestry, six times since April."

"I don't believe you. Father Brosz was pure priest, all the way down. He never wanted anything but to be a priest. He told me that and I believed him. So, I don't believe he was capable of doing what you said he did, maybe not even physically capable."

Her mouth turned down at the corners. "Oh, he was physically capable," she said. "Priest or no priest, he was still a man. He had what every man has."

"No."

"You think, under their cassocks, priests aren't men?"

"Some priests, sure," Parma said. "Not Brosz."

"Prove it."

Not defiance now, but victory. She wasn't even trying to hide it. Parma wondered if life with Arnulfo Arenal had chilled her this hard, or if she had been cold to begin with and her husband's fists had just polished it to a high gloss.

"Did you have relations tonight?" If so there would be traces.

"No," she said. "I told him I wouldn't do it anymore. I said I'd tell the bishop."

It was plain to Parma: she didn't care if he believed her or not.

"I want to go now," she said.

"Not yet." Parma wanted to keep her as long as he could, see if something would crack her shell. But he suspected that all those sparring sessions with Arnulfo Arenal had built up a layer of emotional scar tissue he could never penetrate.

The door opened and a uniform came in, handed Parma a

sheet of paper. The medical examiner had phoned in a prelimi-
nary on the priest and the desk sergeant had jotted it down.
Parma glanced at the point-form notes—gunshots to head and
thorax, time of death—then stopped at the last line. The
sergeant had underlined it.

He stared at the paper for a long beat, knowing she would
have seen this kind of situation on television cop shows. The
TV detectives would often pretend to have new evidence so
they could fool a suspect into changing her story. Then they
would pounce on any discrepancy.

He continued to rest his eyes on the note, letting her get
ready. Then he looked at her over the top of the paper.

"Six times since April?" he said.

"I can show you the dates on my calendar. The same dates
will be in his appointment book."

"Each time, it was all the way?" He made a ring with the
fingers and thumb of one hand then pushed the other hand's
index finger through it in an unmistakable motion.

Her chin came up. "He was an all-the-way kind of man."

Parma thought about John Brosz, about how becoming a
priest had been everything to him, his whole life. Then he laid
the ME's notes on the chipped table. He stood her up and put
the cuffs on her. "Rosaria Arenal, I am arresting you on suspicion of murder. You have the right to retain and instruct
counsel . . . "

She swore at him, but he kept right on through to the end.
When he had finished, he told her, "Father Brosz was an all-
the-way kind of priest. It was the only thing he ever wanted to
be, and he would not have let anything come between him and
his vocation.

"He wasn't your lover. You never saw what was underneath
the cassock. If you had, you'd have known the secret he must
have carried all the way through the seminary and fifteen years
at St. Jude's."

He showed her the note on the ME's report, drew her attention to the bottom line. "John Brosz," he said, "was a woman."

ONE MORE KILL

This story ran in Blue Murder. *It won me the Arthur Ellis Award from the Crime Writers of Canada for best story of 1999. Later, I expanded it into a novel with the same title, published by PS Publishing.*

"So how many would you say you've killed?" Dr. Anselm asked.

"I wouldn't say," was my first response. "It's not something I talk about."

He leaned forward and poured another inch from the decanter. It was the kind of bourbon that even the best liquor stores keep on the highest shelf, smooth and dark, like the leather upholstery we were settled into, and as soft as the old Persian carpet that covered the floor of the doctor's study. The light was mellow from parchment shaded lamps.

"Nice den," I said, to change the subject.

"My private turf," Anselm said. "The wife decorated the rest of the house."

I hadn't met his wife, but I gathered that her taste dominated every part of the mansion except for Anselm's private corner. So far, I'd seen only a spacious foyer and a short hallway that led to the den: Mrs. Anselm's preferences ran to track lighting, rose marble walls and dark tiled floors. The tiles were interrupted by monochromatic rugs with starkly geometric designs, the walls by niches that held angular bronze sculptures, all triangles and thin struts that might have been crafted by talented social insects. The doctor's lair was from another century: shelved in mahogany and unjacketed books, with a carved sideboard displaying antique medical instruments.

I sipped more bourbon. "Should I be drinking this?" I asked. "I mean, my condition. . . "

"Won't make any difference," he answered, bluntly.

"I guess you're right." I emptied the glass.

Even when you know that, one day, life intends to yank the rug out from under your feet, it's a shock to find out that *one day* has actually become *today*. For eight years, I'd known that I suffered from a low-grade form of leukemia that would eventually move to the front burner and kill me fast.

Two weeks ago, my GP had reviewed my monthly blood count and sent me to Anselm. The specialist had drawn a red bead from my fingertip, smeared it on a slide and crouched over a microscope lit by the April sunlight that flooded his office. I stood beside him and looked out at Central Park, ten stories below. There were kids on the playground and boats on the lake.

"Your chart says you were a professional soldier," Anselm said, without looking up from the eyepiece.

"I made major in the Rangers," I said, "until the leukemia. I've run a little travel agency since '96."

He straightened and looked at me. "Then I'll give it to you straight."

"How long do I have?"

"All I can give you is an 'at least' and an 'at most.'"

"All right."

"At least two months, at most five."

So there it was. Somewhere in the next two to five months, my red blood cell count would take a drastic, permanent slide, and I would ride it down to oblivion.

"Anything I can do?" I said, "to make it more likely it's the five instead of the two?"

"Nothing but the obvious," he said. "Don't go on a bender or play chicken with a Mack truck."

I ATE lunch in a little place in the mid-fifties then called the office and said I was taking the rest of the day off. I walked up Central Park West to the natural history museum and took a look at the dinosaurs.

"Pretty soon," I told the T Rex, "you and I are going to have something in common." Trying it out, just to see if it would kick something over inside, pull up some kind of reaction. But nothing came: I wasn't mad, I wasn't sad, I wasn't scared.

Gotta be shock, I said to myself. *Couple days to sink in, then we'll see.*

Two days later, I *was* hit by a wave of emotion, but the stimulus came from the outside. My office manager put her head into my cubicle to tell me there was a Dr. Anselm on line two.

It hit me then, when I looked at the phone's blinking light. Each time it flashed a new thought shot through my mind: *he made a mistake, I'm not going to die; no, it's worse, I've only got weeks; what if there's a new treatment, maybe a cure? or he just wants to put me in a study.*

And each little shunting thought came towing its own little tender full of emotion—hope, despair, surging optimism, deflated resignation—until I pushed the hold button just to stop the bouncing.

Anselm's news was no news. He wondered if I would come

out to his house. He wanted to talk, a non-medical matter was how he put it.

So here I was in Warren, Connecticut, drinking fine bourbon in the blood doctor's anomalous, anachronistic study, and again he wanted to know how many kills I had made. "I'm not asking out of morbid curiosity," he said.

"I can't tell you," I said, at last. "The ones close up, I know about. A lot of the others were two hundred yards deep in the Nicaraguan jungle, and we got the hell outta there without collecting souvenirs. Every enemy I saw in Desert Storm was either already in pieces or surrendering."

That was all I was going to say. I was starting not to like the doctor. He had a soft sleekness about him. "So, how many have you killed?" I said.

He kept his face still while he poured some more. "Take a look at this," he said.

It was a manila folder full of photocopied newspaper clippings. They went back several years and the datelines were from different parts of the country, but they all had one thing in common: each reported a violent death.

The phrases, "police baffled" or "no leads or suspects" cropped up more than a few times. Most of the victims were linked to organized crime, including a prominent attorney who had just been acquitted of jury tampering when an unknown gunman had walked up to him in his driveway and blown his brains all over the roof of his BMW. I remembered that one, plus maybe a couple of the others.

I closed the file and said, "So?"

He looked at me over the rim of his glass. "So, now I put my life in your hands," he said. If he was waiting for a response, I wasn't prepared to give it. I hadn't warmed to him, and I had more important things to think about than his amateur theatrics.

He put the glass down and touched the file. "All of these

people had done a lot of harm, and would have done more. They thought they were shielded from justice—by money and by influence."

I waited.

"Well, it turned out they were only shielded from the law. Justice came for them after all."

"And you had something to do with that?" I asked.

"A little," he said. "Mostly, though, it was people like you."

That took me by surprise. I had thought he would tell me he'd been playing Masked Avenger—old radio-serial melodramatics would have suited the atmosphere of his den—but my growing irritation must have gotten through to him, because now he laid it out for me quickly and efficiently.

For several years, he said, he had been enlisting the aid of "terminals" like me to kill criminals who'd been able to thumb their noses at the law. He said that four of his patients had accounted for eleven of them. None had ever been caught, or even suspected.

"The most difficult killing to solve is the killing by a stranger who has no discernible motive."

"You're telling me you've arranged the murders of eleven people?" I said.

"The executions of eleven vicious criminals."

"Whatever. What's to stop me from going to the police?"

He poured us more whiskey. "I'll deny everything, and say you're out to punish me because I'm the one who gave you the bad news about your condition."

I lifted my glass. "You're nuts," I said.

"That's just what your four predecessors said. Until they thought it over." He drank. "Why don't you think it over?"

I didn't feel like thinking. I put down my glass and stood up. "No thanks," I said.

He rose with me. "It's just one more kill," he said. "And in a good cause. Besides, what else have you got to do?"

And there I had to admit he was right. Didn't want to. Didn't like the smugness that peeked out from behind his question. But there was no doubt I had nothing on my agenda. I'd head back to my tidy apartment on West Fifty-Fourth. My apartment that was always completely empty when I wasn't there, and only a little less empty when I was.

I could go home and inventory my belongings—mostly books and maps and a few medals—and wonder who on earth I might leave them to. I was an orphan. The army had been my life before the leukemia; there had never seemed much point in building anything afterwards.

Until I got sick, I could say I was serving my country, maybe not always liking it, but doing my duty. After I left the army, I'd become like the man in the old Ian Tyson song: just getting up every day and walking around. I'd meant to do a lot of things— go back to school, read some good literature, maybe learn to play music—but I'd done none of them.

"Good-bye," I said. I got up and crossed Anselm's den. It had lost all its coziness.

"Just think about it," he said, following me across the Persian carpet.

I put my hand on the door knob and said, "Sure," just saying it to be out of there.

But even as I opened the door, I felt some subtle balance shifting. Now that I was truly dying, I discovered a perverse need for something to live for. I wasn't going to acknowledge that the doctor had figured me out—I was liking him less with each moment—but I didn't go out into the marble hall.

We stood together in the doorway. He handed me another folder. "Here," he said, "it might be easier if we don't leave it in the abstract."

This file was thinner. There were some sheets of paper dense with single-spaced typing, and a newspaper photograph of a jowly man with thick eyebrows who was giving the camera the finger and a sneer.

"That's Torres," I said. Anybody who owned a TV or read the tabloids knew about Little Tony Torres. His pre-trial maneuverings had been a six-week wonder, until the narcotics importing charges had suddenly been dropped for lack of evidence. Despite police protection, the witnesses who were supposed to connect the New York underboss to a container load of cocaine seized on the docks had all ended up dead. There were rumors the executioners might have been cops themselves.

"You've got to be kidding," I said. "He has bodyguards, an armored limo."

"Does that mean we're past the moral question and into the logistics?" Anselm asked.

That stopped me. Again, he was right. The balance had definitely shifted, sliding me all the way across to the doctor's side without my noticing. I looked into myself and had to admit that I had killed people who had more right to live than Little Tony. I had no moral objection to relieving the world of the stain of his presence, if I could do it without getting caught or killed.

"Lay it out for me," I said.

He started to speak, but just then we heard the front door open and close, a clicking of heels on marble, and a woman's voice softly la-la-ing a song that I vaguely remembered hearing sung on TV by the world's three most overexposed tenors.

"My wife," said Anselm. He drew me back inside the den and shut the door.

THE CLINIC WAS in an exclusive neighborhood on the upper east side, with a doorman behind the thick glass doors. But in the alley behind the building was an unattended entrance whose lock opened to any plastic card with the right data encoded into its magnetic strip. Anselm consulted at the clinic from time to time. He'd lifted a spare key card from the security desk.

Torres came in once a month to be attached to a machine that helped undo some of the damage that booze and a boyhood fondness for amphetamines had done to his liver. He lay on a gurney in a locked room while the equipment gurgled next to him. His bodyguard hung around drinking coffee and hitting on the nurses.

I went in by the back door at 10:30 a.m., a half hour before Torres's scheduled appointment. A pass key let me into a base-ment storage room, where I found a pair of latex gloves and a .45 caliber Colt automatic pistol in a carton whose markings said it contained tongue depressors.

I put on the gloves, then field-stripped the weapon and reassembled it. It was used but in good order, a dependable design that had only recently been decommissioned from US military services after decades of effective use. I had shot this model thousands of times, and had killed with it.

I checked the loads: highly engineered slugs that would expand into razor-edged, hooked shrapnel once they pene-trated flesh. I'd never used such rounds before: there was a Geneva Convention banning them from warfare, but they could be bought in gun shops or by mail order.

Satisfied, I worked the slide and eased a round into the chamber, put on the safety catch then slid the pistol through the belt at the small of my back. I slipped into a white jacket that was hooked on the back of the door. There was a stetho-scope in the tongue depressor box; I hung it around my neck.

At 11:10, I climbed the fire stairs and stepped into a hallway at the rear of the first floor. The pass key let me into a consulting office that connected to the treatment room where Torres should be lying. I cracked the connecting door and peeked through. The mobster was face up on a padded gurney, his gut making a mound under a hospital blanket. Clear plastic tubes connected him to a machine mounted on a wheeled cart. Blood flowed through the tubes, while the machine whirred like a blender on low. He was snoring.

I opened the door a few inches. Anselm had oiled the hinges; they made no sound. The room was empty except for Torres. I drew the .45 and thumbed off the safety, then picked up a spare blanket from a shelf by the door and loosely wrapped it around the weapon.

Torres's feet rested on a pillow at the end of the gurney. I yanked it out from under him, and his heels hit the padded surface with a thump. He snorted and started to sit up, but I shoved the pillow into his face and pushed him back down. Then I put the muzzle of the Colt against the pillow and fired four shots through it. The blanket and the pillow muffled the gunshots thoroughly. Little white feathers floated in the air, some of them smoldering.

I left the Colt, still wrapped in its blanket, on the gurney and went back through the connecting door, I locked it behind me, then crossed the consulting room and went out the way I'd come in. A heavy-shouldered, balding man in a shiny suit was standing in a doorway a few feet up the hall, a Styrofoam cup in his hand. He was looking toward the door of the treatment room, a puzzled expression on his face.

I smiled, turned and went through the fire door and down the steps. A few seconds later, the lab coat and stethoscope were in a heap by the clinic's back door, and I was out of the alley behind the clinic and onto a tree-lined side street, weaving between the clumps of window shoppers who eddied past the up-market stores. When I heard a shout from around the corner behind me, I stepped into a coffee bar, sat down at a table by the window and picked up a discarded newspaper. A moment after, Torres's bodyguard was outside the window, pushing aside pedestrians, his head swiveling to scan up and down the street. He didn't look puzzled anymore—just desperate.

"So, how's it feel? No guilt, I bet."

I grunted. I'd met men like Anselm before: it wasn't enough to know he was right; he had to hear someone else confirm it. I would have thought that anyone that smart—especially a doctor who dealt with terminal patients—would be more empathetic.

"No," I said, "no guilt. Pretty good." Better, in fact, than I'd felt most days during the long years since the army doctors had started my countdown ticking. Taking Torres out had been like the deep recon missions I'd led against Sandinista bases over the Honduran border, the ones that officially never happened. It was playing a game that was way off the edge of the board, with everything on the line. I'd almost forgotten how *alive* I'd felt every time I'd gone into harm's way and come out the other side all in one piece.

"Well, it's normal to feel like that," Anselm was saying. "It's just how the others reacted."

I grunted again. I didn't want his soft, white fingers on my private feelings. It was the day after Torres, and we were in a bar not far from my office. "Should we be meeting like this?" I said, mostly to get him off the subject.

"Why not?" He signaled the waitress for another round. "You see the papers this morning? The cops think one of Torres's competitors decided to retire him and take his business. Now they'll wait and see who inherits his territory, then try and build a case in that direction." He sipped his fresh drink. "But, mostly, they don't give a rat's hind end."

I shrugged. I couldn't think of anything I wanted to say to

this man. He didn't notice, because he was busy hauling a brief-case from the floor to his lap and rooting around inside it. He pulled out another manila folder and leaned across the table but then he hesitated about handing it over. "This one might be too much for you," he said, his voice low. "Have you ever killed a woman?"

I remembered checking the bodies of a Sandinista patrol for documents, fat drops of jungle rain soaking the living and the dead, suppressing the reek of blood and emptied bowels. I rolled over a fatigues-clad form, and long dark hair spilled from under a canvas cap, framing a face that mostly wasn't there anymore. "Yeah," I said. "One time."

He handed me the file. "You might have heard of this one, too."

She was Deborah Curtis. A TV newsmagazine had done a piece on her a few months ago. She'd built up a leisure clothing empire on the sweat of southeast Asian kids who slaved four-teen-hour days in sweltering sheds of corrugated steel for barely enough to keep them in rice and rags. The reporter said that after some of the workers spoke to him and his camera crew, they'd been shipped to a Bangkok brothel.

A newspaper clipping in the file described a fire in a Burmese shirt factory that Curtis was believed to control through a front company: dozens burned alive because the emergency exits were wired shut. I remembered the newspaper photo: the charred bodies of girls and women heaped against a door like smothered chickens stampeded by a dog in a hen house.

"There's no picture of her," I said.

"She makes sure of that," Anselm said. "She's paid paparazzi big bucks to hand over film, or take a beating from her bodyguard."

"Where and when?" I said. I kept my face deadpan and my voice was mild, but I was already starting to feel it again. There was no doubt the Curtis woman deserved what she was going to get, but I could admit to myself that my motives were all about me. I wouldn't be alive for long, but I would be fully alive for as long as I could manage it.

"She has a boyfriend. He's married, so they meet twice a week at a hotel in midtown. The chauffeur-bodyguard stays with the car. They always take the same suite on the top floor. I've booked you a room down the hall for Thursday."

"You were pretty sure I'd do it."

He shrugged. The gesture did nothing to endear him to me.

"What about the boyfriend?" I said. "I'm not doing bystanders."

"She always gets there first, maybe a half-hour before he does. She orders champagne and hors d'oeuvres from room service. That's your opportunity."

I thought about it, then said, "How do you know all this? Did you hire a detective to tail her? That's a lead the police might follow to you, and then to me."

"I did the surveillance myself," he said. "She's not hard to find if you know what she looks like. Remember what that old writer said: the rich are different. Only a few places are good enough for them. Narrows the search considerably."

"So what do you expect me to do?" I asked.

He leaned even closer and told me.

I knocked on the door of room 2404. A voice said "Yes?"

"Room service." I rattled the little cart so the flute glasses tinkled against each other.

The door opened. She was tall and honey-haired, and if the color was out of a bottle it was a better piece of craftsmanship than I'd ever see through. Her perfume was how the clouds probably smell on a good day in heaven. Anselm was right: the rich are different.

"Over by the window, please," she said. I pushed the cart across the room. It had been easy to get: I'd just checked in an hour earlier under an assumed name and ordered it up from room service. The waiter's jacket had come from a uniform supply place.

The window was open more than a foot, soft spring air idling into the room as if it had no place special to go and no hurry to get there. I raised the sash a little more and looked down at the street—a long way, but there was a substantial marquee sheltering the sidewalk. There was no danger of crushing some hapless pedestrian.

The plan was simple. When Deborah Curtis bent to sign the room service chit, I would step behind her, apply the right grip and break her neck. I'd never done it for real, but I had been trained by experts, and the night before, I'd studied my old unarmed combat manual.

When she was dead, I would throw her body through the window, push the room service cart back to my room, and wait until the police had come and gone. In a hotel of this quality, the fuss would be minimal.

I folded out the wings of the cart to make a table, then opened the leather folder with the room service bill inside and produced a ballpoint pen, thoughtfully clicking it into readiness.

"Thanks," she said, and gave me a smile that looked real. She leaned over the table. I stepped back and sideways, and put out my hands. She was humming something as I reached for her.

THE SUN WAS POURING into Anselm's examining room again. He was pacing behind his desk. "How did it go?" he said.

I sat down in the patient's chair. It was less than an hour since I'd knocked on the door of room 2404.

"Fine," I said.

"Did she say anything? Did she scream? What was it like?"

His hands were shaky. His face kept twitching as if some wild expression was barely confined beneath the surface, and would jump out and crazily contort his features if he lost control for even a second.

"No, she didn't say anything," I said.

"Good," he said, and turned to look out the window. His shoulders were rigid under the lab coat. "There's a new treatment I want to try," he said, without looking at me. "Experimental, but very promising."

"A cure?" I said.

He must have caught my skepticism. "No, no, not a cure," he was quick to say. "It's, uh, a kind of immune system booster. Keep you going longer, put off the. . . well, it could give you another six months, maybe more."

"Really?" I said.

"It's right here," he said, turning around and showing me a hypodermic full of clear fluid. "Just roll up your sleeve."

"Sure."

He came around the corner of the desk, moving jerkily, as if his legs were stiff. His trembling fingers made a jet of liquid arc from the needle's tip. As he bent over me, I stood up and hit him very hard in the solar plexus. The wind puffed out of him like air from a split beach ball, and he sank to the carpet.

The hypodermic fell from his hand. I picked it up. "What does it really do?" I said.

He was having trouble getting enough breath to speak. "Nothing," he finally got out. "Just tune you up."

"Then you won't mind going first." I jabbed the spike into

his left arm just below the shoulder and pressed the plunger all the way.

He tried to scoot away, one hand clawing for the phone on top of the desk. I pounded my fist on his fingers. He yelped and pulled them back and tucked them into an armpit. He was turning an interesting shade of purple from the neck up.

"There were no others, were there?" I said.

He spluttered something that sounded like a denial.

"If you're straight with me, I might get you some help," I said.

"Please," he said. He swallowed, then opened his mouth as if something was stuck in his throat. Out came a wheeze. "Okay, you were the only one. I thought you'd be more agreeable if you were one in a series. Now call 911."

"Nope," I said. "The whole truth. Last chance."

"Only got a few minutes," he said. "Please. . . 911."

"How about I tell it, and you just nod during the pauses?" I said. "First of all, the Torres hit was just what you said it was. You set it up for me to kill a dopester."

He nodded.

"But today was something else. That wasn't a tycoon holding thousands of Third World kids in slavery. That was just a doctor's wife whose marriage was heading for break-up."

I stopped and waited for him to respond, but he was busy tearing at his collar, so I went on, "But then her husband said he wanted to reconcile, asked her to meet him in a hotel room. A little champagne, some oysters, and maybe they could rekindle the old feelings, avoid a messy divorce. That was pretty nice of her, wasn't it, Doc? Considering—and I'm really just guessing here—but I'll bet the money was all hers and he had signed a prenuptial agreement that would have left him nothing but a handful of old medical instruments."

He shook his head and gasped out something that might have been "No."

"Except hubby wasn't going to show, was he?" I said. "Instead, a big dumb lunk would come in, break the lady's neck and throw her out the window."

Anselm was spluttering. I ignored him.

"And it almost worked. I would have done her just like Torres, then come back here to let you shoot me up with whatever's killing you now. There'd be no autopsy. I'm a terminal patient, and you would have signed the death certificate yourself."

I wasn't sure whether he was hearing me now, but I continued. "Yeah, it almost worked. If something hadn't made me hesitate, long enough to see the name she wrote on the room service bill."

His eyelids were fluttering, but the rest of him was still now. I picked him up and sat him in his chair, then I put on a pair of latex gloves before carefully wiping the hypodermic clean. I pressed his fingertips onto the barrel and plunger, then left it in his limp right hand.

There was a rattling now from the bottom of his throat. I knew that sound. I peeled off the gloves and threw them in the biowaste container, waited until the noises stopped, then went in search of the nurse.

No doubt Elizabeth Anselm was confused when room service sent up a second order of champagne and goodies. And she was probably disappointed when her husband failed to show. But I figured she'd get over it. It wouldn't be hard to find a better man.

After I talked to the police—"Yes, he seemed despondent, rambled on about his marriage,"—I went downstairs and out into the last April I'd ever see. On the way back to my office, I passed a store that sold classical music.

"Do you know what this song is?" I asked the clerk, and repeated the few notes the doctor's wife had hummed in the hotel room. The same sad, triumphant melody she'd been singing in her tastefully decorated house while her husband was recruiting me to kill her.

"*Nessun Dorma*," said the clerk. "From Puccini's opera, *Turandot*. We have it on a Pavarotti disk."

I bought it, along with a couple more. I wouldn't have a lot of time to develop an appreciation for opera, but I'd try to get as far as I could.

BUBBLE UP

I was in the kitchen of a house my wife and I were looking after. I was chopping vegetables for a stew when this story popped into my head. I wrote it in one sitting but never made a real effort to place it anywhere. So, consider it pristine.

THE FIRST TIME Dalton saw himself stabbing Claudia with the Henckel chef's knife he was cutting up carrots for a beef stew. The water was almost boiling and he had already added a small onion cut into quarters. The new potatoes sat in their bag beside the wooden cutting board and beside them the celery, all waiting their turns to be sliced then slid from the wood into the water. The beef was already in the frying pan, being seared and sealed in garlic-flavored oil.

It wasn't so much a thought of stabbing her as it was an actual image of the deed. He saw himself turning with the chef's knife and plunging it into her belly, one straight thrust, no complications.

There was nothing more to the vision: no blood, no screams, not even the withdrawal of the blade. Just the turn and the thrust. But it was a very real image; it lingered on the screen in his mind for a second or two. Then he blinked and looked up from the little rounds of orange-colored root and saw his own face reflected in the glass-fronted cupboard above the counter.

He saw on his own face an expression he had never seen it wear before. He supposed, thinking about it later, that he had never seen his nondescript features take on that particular arrangement before because he had never been suddenly surprised by a mirror.

But he saw it now: his eyes and mouth forming a triangle of three perfect circles. Then the look of shock was gone, replaced by down-drawn brows and a firming of his lips as he said to himself, in the privacy of his mind, *No.*

He finished cutting up the carrots, thinking to himself, *Now, where did that come from?*

He knew, of course, that was the wrong question. He knew the murderous image had come bubbling up from one of the varied fragments of his psyche that formed a crowd within his head. It was generally an amiable, cooperative assemblage of splinters, none of them the full-blown "multiple personalities" that featured in films but were, in real life, so rare as to be almost non-existent. The splinters didn't have names.

But Dalton had known since before adolescence that there were different parts of him chambered together in his skull. The first he'd identified was the one who conducted his school-yard fistfights for him, methodically punching and shifting his feet while Dalton stood to one side watching the performance. Then there was the one who played the piano while Dalton thought about other things.

And, of course, there was the one who wrote speeches and op-ed pieces for senior corporate executives, feeding the words and phrases to Dalton as he typed and polished the texts, hearing them via his well-attuned inner ear in the voice of the client who would deliver them.

And then there was the fragment that occasionally sent a

picture bubbling up from the murkiest depths: the horrified queue at the bus stop turning to look as Dalton's car mounted the sidewalk and charged toward them; the flailing arms of some astonished passenger suddenly finding himself plunging from the ferry deck toward the foaming wake; or the real old one where he tripped some kid on the school staircase and sent him tumbling ass over tea-kettle, all the way to the bottom.

Dalton was used to such images. They came and went, not frequently, and over the years the pictures had lost their original impact, become pale as old sepia movie prints. And always they had been of random, anonymous strangers – nobody Dalton knew, certainly no one he had anything against.

And now this vision of stabbing Claudia. So, the question was not *where* it came from, but *why* it had come at all. He let the interrogative syllable float in his mind as he finished chopping the vegetables, put them in the pot, then cleaned and dried the knife and slipped it into its slot in the wooden block.

No answer came as he used a spatula to scrape the seared beef and its fragrant juices from the frying pan into the stew pot and stirred the melange together. Instead, his mind floated up a memory of their buying the knife in a little hole-in-the-wall kitchen shop on Robson Street, before it became trendy, yuppified Robsonstrasse.

That was more than thirty-five years ago now. They had only been a couple for a few months and the eleven-inch Henckel was the first serious purchase they had made together. It had cost more than a hundred dollars, Dalton remembered, which had been, for them in those days, real money – more than they'd paid to furnish the pokey little living room with a couch and two chairs from the Goodwill store.

Buying the knife had been a kind of affirmation. They had invested in something that would stay with them longer than his paperbacks or the things she crocheted while listening to music.

Symbolic? he asked himself. Was the image indicative of some deep-seated sense that their relationship was dead? He looked over at her where she was mixing together the materials for the suet dumplings she would ladle onto the simmering surface of the stew in its last twenty minutes of cooking.

She looked the same as ever. Well, not really ever: all the girlishness was long gone out of her. The figure that had been compact and strong, not particularly feminine thirty years ago, was now rounded—even dumpy.

But worse could be said for Dalton. His once lean and muscular frame was entombed within layers of adipose tissue acquired over decades—dating back to when they discovered that he was a natural cook, indeed, a better cook than Claudia, and he had taken over most of the dinner-making.

He adjusted the seasoning of the stew—he liked a strong taste of basil with beef, red wine and rosemary with lamb— then put the lid on, turned down the gas, and left it to simmer. He poured himself a glass of Shiraz and silently asked his wife with a proffering of the bottle if she wanted one. She signaled no with a flour-dusted hand and kept stirring the dumpling dough.

They ate the stew at the kitchen table and talked about the usual inconsequentials: items in the news, oddments from Facebook. Years ago—decades now—Dalton used to try to talk to Claudia about their relationship. "About us," was how he used to put it. He used the pronoun in the sense that Erich Fromm had meant it in a book called *The Art of Loving* that Dalton had read and been impressed by at nineteen.

But she would not respond. He would lie in bed, turned towards her, propped up on an elbow, trying this or that gambit to generate a conversation. She would lie on her back, looking at the ceiling, saying nothing until finally he gave up. Once she did say something: that he intimidated her and if she expressed her feelings, she knew he would overpower her with words.

It almost rang true: he was good with words. it was how he made a living. But he could be supportive, and he continued to try—for years. Eventually, though, when no amount of gentle encouragement would get her to open up, he stopped trying. He did not stop thinking about what there was between them; he just conducted those discussions within the privacy of his own skull. He could always find someone to talk to there.

In the end, he came to understand that, for Claudia, there had never been an "us." There had only been a "her" and a "him." She had said yes to him, because she liked him and he made her laugh and he was faithful. But underlying the positives was her belief that if she didn't go with him, nobody else would ever ask her.

THE NEXT TIME he picked up the Henckel, to slice diagonally into the fat on the edges of steaks so they wouldn't curl up under the broiler, he remembered the vision. But this time the image lacked punch; it was a memory of the event rather than a recurrence.

Still, there it was, in his mind. He mulled it, considered it, and came to the conclusion that it wasn't a true murderous impulse. Just something that bubbled up from the depths, where some part of him still resented his having to give up the old romantic fantasy of Fromm's "us" and adapt to the mundane reality of Dalton and Claudia, the twain that shall never meet.

Forget it, he told whatever part of him had sent it up to the surface, *not gonna happen*. She would always be a mystery to him, her inner life a dark continent, not to be explored. Her family were much the same; they communicated via freighted silences, a language he had never learned.

They would go through their lives with him not knowing if

her existence was a blessing to her, or a torment, or just a long, tasteless lunch.

He suppressed a sigh, cleaned the knife, and put the steaks under the broiler and thought about other things.

"OR IS IT A WARNING?" he asked himself a few days later while he showered. He had always found the shower a particularly good venue for an internal conversation. He could ask questions out loud without the risk of being overheard. He didn't actually hear replies—he was not afflicted with "voices"—but after he posed such a question very often he would find the answer in his mind; it was as if the knowledge had always been there, along with facts such as what the War of 1812 was or who had flown *The Spirit of St. Louis* across the Atlantic.

No, it was not a warning, he concluded. He was not on the edge of murder and mayhem in their well-ordered kitchen. The vision had been a random *doesn't-count*, his boyhood term for pictures that used to pop into his head for no discernible reason. Often, they were street scenes he would recognize from the many different places where he'd lived, while growing up in a rootless, almost nomadic family.

He would briefly see an image of a particular block of houses or a crosswalk or the old coal-loader in the railroad yards whose buckets on an endless loop of chain he used to climb, to emerge high above the tracks. His mind generated these random scenes and none of them had any emotion or affect attached.

They just came, lasted long enough for Dalton to recognize them, then faded away.

Doesn't count, he told himself in the shower and reached for the shampoo.

A SIMPLE SUPPER: *medaglioni alla quatro formaggio* with a garlic-and-basil *suga di pomodoro,* Rana brand for the pasta, Barilla for the sauce. Dalton was gently stirring the big cheese-stuffed rounds with a wooden spoon to separate stuck pairs and trios, while keeping an eye on the sauce simmering in its small, heavy pot.

Claudia was making a salad. She had already broken up a lettuce and chopped some peppers and green onions, and now she was cutting ripe Italian tomatoes into quarters. When she's started on the peppers she had said the Henckel was not sharp enough so Dalton had given it a few swipes down the length of the fine-grained carborundum stone they had bought in a *ferramenteria* during the year they'd spent housesitting in Italy.

The good German steel sliced evenly through the fleshy tomatoes, the severed pieces falling cleanly away. Claudia's shoulders hunched as she concentrated on the work. She had only ever once cut herself, and that was long ago, but the lesson had gone deep.

He stirred the pasta so that the *medaglioni* below bubbled up and replaced those on the surface. It didn't make much difference to the cooking, he knew, but it felt like being useful.

The words were in his mouth before he weighed them: "A long time since we talked about . . . us."

Her hands stilled for a few seconds, then she cut through another tomato. Her voice, when she said, "Don't," was flat and toneless, but he had seen her knuckles briefly whiten during the pause.

"No," he said, "I suppose not. Would you put the colander in the sink? The pasta's ready."

HE WAS CUTTING up pieces of cooked lamb left over from the big leg they'd had two nights before, far more meat than they could eat at one sitting but a bargain. Dalton was making a lamb-and-leek pie seasoned with garlic and thyme, using pastry shells he'd bought ready-made and frozen at the supermarket. He couldn't do pastry. He'd thicken the contents with a packet of make-from-mix lamb gravy he's found in a newly opened foodie shop on Robson, only a few doors from the long-gone kitchen shop where they'd bought the Henckel.

Claudia was behind him at the sink, peeling the potatoes, a chore he inexplicably hated – probably something out of his childhood. The water was almost boiling. He finished cutting the lamb into cubes and put the meat aside then turned to the fresh leeks, still wet from having the grit washed out of them.

The knife was becoming dull. He took out the carborundum and gave it a few quick swipes then wiped it on a hand towel. When he held it up, he saw the myriad tiny scratches with which the stone had marked the steel over the years, like tiny comet trails.

He said to Claudia, "Remember when we bought this at that place on Robson Street?"

He was going to tie the memory to his discovery of the foodie shop but he heard the clatter of the vegetable peeler falling into the sink. He turned toward Claudia, found her standing right in front of him. Her face was set in an expression of intent concentration, as if she were about to undertake some complex and difficult handiwork.

She took the Henckel out of his grasp, looked at it for a moment as if weighing its usefulness for the task. Then she thrust it into his middle, angled upward.

It felt like ice and fire together and he knew his heart stopped when the point pierced it. He had time for the thought to form: *So, a warning after all*, then she pulled the blade free, and all the many parts of him tumbled down into darkness.

FISHFACE AND THE LEG

This is the first story I ever wrote and I sold it to the first place I sent it, a weekly newspaper that circulated among farmers on the Canadian prairies. Most of it is not my invention but comes from a tale told to my widowed mother by a retired mortician who swore it had happened when he was a young man in a small Saskatchewan town. I just supplied the ending and the voice of the character telling it.

WE ALWAYS CALLED HIM FISHFACE, though I'm damned if I know why. He used to put me more in mind of a fox—red complexion, sharp inquisitive nose, eyes a little too close together. But, within an hour of when he got off the train to be the new corporal at our one-man RCMP detachment, somebody had hung Fishface on him. I guess if you'd asked around town for the man's real name, you'd be lucky to find a dozen who could tell you.

At first, maybe we resented him a little because he took over from Corporal Matheson, after Bob went on to his just reward as a sergeant down in Regina. Everybody liked Bob Matheson, and nobody hereabouts really thought of him as the town cop.

Sure, Bob was the guy who locked up Ernie Laderoute Friday nights, when Ernie had absorbed all the hooch he could wrap his hands around, but he also coached the kids' softball team through two district championships. Fishface, he was a whole different box of biscuits. He'd slope around town like a lost mutt, tall and stoop-shouldered, and you'd have to be a more charitable soul than the average to call him rangy instead of just skinny. The Mounties couldn't make a collar tight enough or a sleeve long enough to stop Fishface from shooting out of his uniform in all directions.

He would have qualified as pitiable if you hadn't always felt that he was just waiting for you to do something that would allow him to pounce. Fishface took a personal interest in the law. Throwing Ernie in the jug once a week wasn't meat enough for him; he itched for some real crime to test his mettle. But in the mid 1930s, there just weren't too many desperadoes lurking around Hubble, Saskatchewan, population 915 and dwindling.

I'm long retired now, but back then I ran the Hubble Funeral Home. Now, a lot of folks will tell me, "Stop right there; we don't want to hear about that," but I was not a bad mortician, and took pride in my work. I'd inherited the business from my father, and he had it from Grandad. I mention my line of work because it led to what happened to Fishface.

Pretty regular, I used to take the hearse over to the regional hospital—I won't mention the name of the town—and pick up bodies from the morgue. Often as not, I'd pass Fishface lurking in his official car behind some roadside blind, waiting to nab a speeder.

He might sit there for hours, and I suppose he occupied his mind with dreams of how someday John Dillinger or Alvin Creepy Karpis could come roaring by, and he would catch them and be a hero. But, given the condition of the highway, and the placement of Hubble pretty far away from most bandits' preferred haunts, the best he ever got was some hapless commercial traveler or maybe a lost tourist. It'd only be a two-dollar ticket, but the recipients would get their money's worth, what with Fishface barreling after them and practically running them into a ditch, siren shrieking and red light blazing, while his hopes and ambitions were inflamed.

Fishface had been among us a little more than three years when he thought he'd finally got his chance to be a major league crime-fighter. It was late winter, and I had driven over to the hospital to pick up old Mrs. Ellis, who had passed away. From my frequent visits, I'd gotten to know one of the interns pretty well, and we'd usually sit and have coffee before I made the run back to Hubble.

Well, this day, he told me he had a problem. "It's the incinerator," he said. "Damn thing's broke down—it'll be a week before we get the replacement part—and meanwhile, we've got this leg."

It seemed some poor woman had been flown down from way up north with a bad case of frostbite, and they'd had to take her leg off to save her. With the incinerator out, they couldn't dispose of the leg and they had no place to store it.

"You've got a cooler," the intern said. "How about you take the leg back with you and keep it until we get the incinerator fixed? You can bring it back next trip."

I guess I don't have to tell you, I wasn't totally pleased with the arrangement. But a friend in need . . . We wrapped up the leg in some newspaper—it sounds gruesome, I know, but that's what we did—and I put it in the hearse with Mrs. Ellis.

When I got back to Hubble, though, I'd had some second thoughts and decided I didn't want it lying in the cooler. So, I put it in the trunk of my Studebaker. It was late February and well below zero day and night, so I thought it would keep just as well there as anywhere.

It was a couple of weeks before I had to go back down to the hospital again. I took the leg with me in the hearse. I remember passing Fishface along the way, which gave me a little twinge. When I got to the hospital, I looked for the intern, but a nurse told me he was down with the flu.

I suppose I should have brought the leg out right then and there, but there had been something decidedly informal about the way we had handled the matter, and I was concerned it might make trouble for my friend. So the leg returned with me to Hubble, and went back into the Studebaker.

I thought about telephoning the young doctor and getting things settled, but we were all on party lines then, and even if none of your neighbors was listening, Mary Haggerty, the operator, almost always kept her earphones plugged in. So, it was a good three weeks before business next called me to the hospital. There was no body to pick up this time, so I went in the Studebaker, with something in the trunk that I didn't intend to bring back.

I asked for the intern.

"He's gone," they told me.

"What?"

"Gone to Saskatoon to work with the public health."

And he wasn't coming back.

Now, it seemed to me that there were only so many ways to handle this situation. I could march into the hospital administrator's office and turn over the leg. I wasn't too sure what the ramifications of that option might be, but I figured they wouldn't reflect too creditably on my professionalism.

Or I could just slip the thing into somebody else's coffin, hoping that the pallbearers would not notice the extra weight. Or I could dispose of it some other way.

One thing I could not do for much longer was to keep the leg in the trunk of my Studebaker. It was already getting up to April, with warm weather about to roll in. In the end, I did what many a young man has done when faced with a thorny dilemma—I went and bought a drink, and when that was of no immediate help, I bought several more.

By the time I was driving home along the empty back roads, the answer was no clearer, and I was not in too sharp a focus myself. But I recognized that the time of decision had come. About ten miles outside of Hubble, there was an old concrete bridge over the river. There the leg and I parted company. The ice was just breaking up, and the water was flowing fast with snow melt. The leg shot out of sight under the bridge, and I went home.

A couple of days later, some kids found it washed up a few miles downstream. Fishface was on the case.

Madge Schmidt, who did the typing and filing down at the detachment office, said it was just like Christmas and his birthday all rolled into one. He was down to the river taking photographs and measurements. He was on the phone to Regina and district headquarters. He brought in tracking dogs and hired an airplane, and the sub-inspector in charge of general investigations came to see him personally. It was Hubble's crime of the century—a murderer who dismembered his victim—and Fishface had come to glory.

He had every able-bodied man out searching for more pieces of the body. He formed us into squads, and we spent days slogging through muddy fields, poking into culverts and among the roots of trees. Fishface ordered schools closed and stopped cars all over in a one-man roving roadblock.

He was having the time of his life. But he wasn't having much luck finding a murderer or any more evidence.

After a couple of weeks, the fuss started to die down. The extra constables who had been seconded to Fishface's detach-ment were withdrawn. The newspapers went on to new sensa-tions. No one on the missing persons list checked out as a likely victim, so the Mounties wrote it up as an unsolved case, and went back to catching bank robbers and bootleggers, business as usual.

Fishface couldn't do that. He couldn't let it go. He tacked up this big aerial survey map on his office wall, all marked off in grids. The thing must have covered fifty square miles, and Fishface meant to search every square foot.

Week after week, Madge typed up his reports to headquarters, telling them where he'd looked and what he'd found. One time, he turned up an old axe out by the Kellerman farm, but it had been lying there a good ten years. And he did find Jerry Harnock's still and busted it up, which was a great disappointment to some.

But it got so that Fishface wasn't doing anything but look for clues to the leg murder. He even stopped throwing Ernie Laderoute in jail, and that brought a sharp complaint from Ernie's neighbors. Eventually, the RCMP pulled Fishface out of Hubble and transferred him somewhere else. Nobody shed a tear, and it turned out that the next corporal the Mounties sent us was pretty keen on softball.

But it's funny how one thing can pop up in a man's path, and spin him off in another direction, for good or for ill. I think about that now when I see Fishface, trudging through some field on his old, arthritic legs, that big map rolled up under his arm.

It's not much of a retirement for him, living in a ramshackle, flat-tired trailer, spending his last days trying to solve a murder that never happened.

Sometimes, I wonder if he lies awake at night, listening to the wind rustling through the grass, looking back on the mess that leg made of his life.

He wasn't completely wrong. Somebody did get killed. I wonder if Fishface ever realizes that it was him.

THE GIFT OF GABBY

I occasionally drop in on a writers mutual-aid site, Scri-bophile.com, to give what I hope is useful advice on the craft and the business of fictioneering. One of the leading members was putting together an anthology, Welcome to Pacific City, *with contributions from the Scribophiliacs. All the stories were to be set in a fictional Oregon metropolis that had beaten out San Francisco, back in the 1860s, to become the terminus of the transcontinental railway and in our time was richly populated by superheroes. The editor asked me to write an origin tale for the city. I shamelessly poached from the real-life story of Gassy Jack Deighton, a saloon keeper who founded Gastown, which would become Vancouver, BC. The "Gassy" nickname came from Deighton's ability to talk your leg off. It was said to be a superpower: he could talk anybody into anything.*

NOBODY KNEW where he came from or how he got here. Some used to say he'd come down the Willamette by canoe after jumping ship off a lumber carrier on the Columbia. Some said he'd lowered a boat off a side-wheeler steaming up the coast, taking nugget hunters to the Cariboo gold streams. And some said he'd come overland from back east, but most discounted that one, because he'd have needed a team and a wagon, or how else could he have brought a barrel of whiskey all that way?

Because that's the part there could be no doubt about. One Sunday morning, those of us who worked at Captain Odlum's sawmill woke up to find this big-bellied, short-legged, red-faced Englishman—"Yorkshireman," he would correct us, though that never stuck—sitting on a barrel just the other side of the Captain's property.

I was one of the dozen of us who went down from the bunkhouse to see what was what, so I remember the conversation.

Tucker, the foreman, said, "Who might you be?"

"I might be anybody," the man said, "but the name's Dunham, David Dunham."

Tucker was set to ask the next question, which might have been, "What are you doing here?" though my money would have been on, "What's in the barrel?"

But he didn't get the chance because Dunham kept right on talking. "I was sitting here enjoying the morning and wondering if there might be a saloon in the vicinity."

I stepped into the discussion at that point. "There is not," I said, "and there can't be because Captain Odlum is a true-blue teetotaler and won't allow strong drink on his property."

"Is that so?" said Dunham. He indicated the white stake pounded into the ground near where he was sitting on the barrel. "And would that be the limit of the Captain's property?"

"It would."

"And does anyone hold title to where I am sitting?"

"Nobody," I said.

"But no saloon?"

Tucker told him there was a trading post a few miles up the river where you could get a bottle, though it was a long walk or an equally long paddle. But there wasn't a saloon anywhere on this part of the Oregon coast.

"Then we have a problem," Dunham said. "Because the barrel I'm sitting on contains rye whiskey and if it were only in a saloon, I could tap it and stand you all to a drink."

There was a long moment of silence during which he looked at us and we looked at the barrel and then we all looked at each other, until Tucker said, "Right."

Tools fell from heaven and a certain number of planks and beams found their way down from the sawmill, along with the rest of the crew. The building we put up would not have won prizes but it was sturdy enough to contain twenty men, one barrel, and a freshly minted saloon keeper.

It was better whiskey than it needed to be, and each man got a mugful on the house. After that it was five cents a shot, which all agreed was fair. Joseph Biddlecomb went up to the bunkhouse and came back down with his fiddle, and his drinks remained on the house as long as he kept playing.

It was a good-humored crowd, for the most part, except for a couple of sourpusses, like you'll find in any crew. One of them was Walter Mathers, and once he'd put a few under his belt he began to bitch and moan and stir the pot. Before it got out of hand, I picked him up by his britches and collar and threw him out the door, which was not the first time I'd served him so.

Dunham called me over to where he was standing behind the plank-and-trestle bar. "What do they call you?" he said.

"Hiram Bassington."

He took a good look at me and said, "That cauliflower you call an ear, you got that prizefighting?"

I admitted as much. I used to tour with a traveling medicine show and I would take on farm boys and such like who thought they could last three rounds with me.

He asked me, "Hiram, how much is Captain Odlum paying you to saw timber?"

I told him and he said he'd double it if I came to work for him. "Plus meals and a reasonable daily allowance of drink."

I took his offer and thus I entered into my new career as what Dave Dunham called "his minder."

THAT EVENING, Captain Odlum and his missus returned from church services up the river where a lay preacher had pitched up by Mr. Woods's lumber camp. He was not happy about the state in which he found his men and come morning he arrived at the saloon, now christened Gabby Dave's. He brought a bull-whip and I thought I might have to demonstrate my loyalty to the new employer by dealing with the old one.

But it didn't happen that way. Instead, I got to see the strange quality for which Dave Dunham had earned his nick-name. I suppose I had seen it the day before when he had talked twenty men into building him a saloon for free, but that had not been much of a challenge. Captain Odlum, he was a different box of biscuits altogether.

Yet when they sat down on a bench the boys had made outside the front door of Gabby Dave's—the Captain having sworn on the Bible he would never enter such an establishment —something happened. The easiest way to describe it is that Dunham had the gift of the gab, that he could charm a fish out of the sea if he had mind to do it. But that would only be saying he could do it, without saying how it was done.

And the truth is, though I heard him do it many's the time, afterwards I couldn't remember much at all of what he had said. There was just this rolling tide of words, like the rip tides that made the beaches so dangerous along this stretch of coast. One minute you're standing in the sea, watching the waves come at you; the next, your feet are swept out from under, and you're being carried along under the water, going deeper and deeper, farther and farther from the light. That happened to me once, and I'm lucky to be here to tell the tale.

But there was one thing. When Gabby Dave started to talk, the people he was talking to would get a kinda dreamy-eyed look to them. It was like they weren't seeing this stubby little fellow in front of them, with the comical accent and the checkered vest. They were seeing pictures in their heads, pictures that made them happy, and even after he stopped talking, they would still have that look, as if the spell hung on and on.

I asked him once if it was some kind of magic. Back in the hill country I came from, there were folks who could lay a hex or tell you the right place to dig your well. He studied me for a while, then he said, "Hiram, didn't you ever hear that bullshit baffles brains?"

So, I can't tell you what Gabby Dave said to the Captain, though I was standing in the doorway the whole time. But the man went back to his sawmill with that kinda blank look on his face, like he was half sleepwalking. And Dunham turned to me and said, "Let's get busy."

We spent the working hours of the day with stakes and strings, pacing off sections of land, dividing them into lots. And he talked all the while through, saying as how he was homesteading the place according to the laws governing the Oregon Territory. Having marked off the land, put up a building, and "established domicile"—he did know a passel of fine and fancy words—the property was now his "in fee simple."

"This will be a city, Hiram," he told me. "One day, a great city full of men doing great deeds and women of great beauty. The grandeur of Rome, the topless towers of Troy, the Big Smoke of London will be as mere villages to the metropolis we are founding here on this auspicious day."

And, do you know, when he was saying it I could almost see

it: buildings rising into the sky, eight, ten stories high; wide and shady boulevards; men in top hats and ladies in furs stepping down from carriages; gaslights in the evening.

"By gar," I said, "I believe you."

"You keep on believing," he told me. "Believing is what makes it happen."

WE HAD THE SALOON, and we had the sawmill, and we had the men who came down the river from Mr. Woods's camp. And it turned out there were others in the area: trappers, homesteaders, some prospectors, a couple of brothers who were making salt out of seawater a little ways up the coast, using the same methods the Salish used to. They all came to Gabby Dave's, and it was a lively place, for sure.

I don't know how he arranged it, but long before the barrel of whiskey was tapped dry, a schooner came up from San Francisco and stopped in the bay. It unloaded fresh supplies: more whiskey and several barrels of beer and even some bottles of wine in wooden cases. And once the cargo was stacked on the wharf, the ship's barge made its last delivery.

Her name was Gertie Gladwell and her girls were Flo, Edie, and Mary Anne. They'd brought a tent, some cots, a few tables and chairs, plus a piano and a man who played it. His name was Walter and he and I became good friends.

Gertie and Gabby Dave had a conversation and a deal was soon struck. He rented her the plot next door to the saloon and would supply her with beer and liquor at reasonable prices. And I would be available to resolve any disputes, for which I would be paid on a piecework basis. Or I could take my payment in kind which, as Gertie put it, would be another kind of piecework.

A month or so later, the trading post upriver relocated to

another plot rented by Gabby Dave. Trade with the Salish tribes had petered out, owing to the smallpox, so the trading post became our general store. And just like that, we had a town. We took to calling it Gabtown, although I'm told Mrs. Odlum refused to let that word pass her pursed lips.

The paddle-wheelers that went between San Francisco and New Westminster had used to stop in our bay occasionally to take on firewood. Now those visits became a regular occurrence. While the cutwood was being taken on board, passengers would come ashore for a drink and to stretch their legs. Gertie's place also drew quite a few interested parties. One of them, a prospector who'd done well out of a placer claim in the Cariboo, took to Gertie and she took to him. He elected to stay on when the steamer continued on south.

MORE PEOPLE CAME: a blacksmith, a barber, a man who repaired shoes and harness, another who knew how to build boats. Another come-by-chance who stepped off a steamer for a drink went back and got his trunk and set up as a doctor, though his skills were more like those of a vet. Every one of them rented not only a lot from Gabby Dave but a building to live and work in. Dunham now had a crew of six men who worked full time putting up new premises. He had two more fellows building boardwalks along the streets he'd laid out. The place was getting to look like a regular town.

The thing was, except for Captain Odlum, who was happy to be selling lumber straight out of the sawmill, every square foot of space in Gabtown was owned by David Dunham, Esquire. That was how his name appeared on the letters that came up from San Francisco, each one of them certifying that he had title to this lot or that one because he had staked it and put a building on it.

As the town grew, I kind of grew with it. My responsibilities as Gabby Dave's minder and Gertie's bouncer expanded until one day they called a meeting of the townsfolk, and I was elected sheriff. Ozzie the blacksmith made me a star and Gabby's crew built me a jail where I could let raucous drunks sleep it off.

There were even women and kids now. The barber and the cobbler had families that came out to join them once they knew they would be staying. Ozzie sent for a mail-order bride from back east, a big strapping woman who spoke only Swedish, but somehow they got along. There was talk about putting up a school if we could find someone to teach in it, at which point Mrs. Odlum surprised us all by volunteering.

"We got us a town," I said to Walter, who still played the piano at Gertie's. We were standing at the bar in Gabby Dave's —a real bar, mahogany with a brass rail, shipped up from San Francisco—and enjoying a beer.

"We do at that," he agreed. "And when the railroad comes .. ." He spread his hands in a way that said, *you ain't seen nothing yet.*

That was a funny thing, him mentioning the railroad. It was the first time I'd heard anybody say anything about a railroad, but within a few days it was all anybody was talking about. People would go down and look at the bay and talk about was it deep enough for four-masted clipper ships to come in and how there was plenty of space for docks and warehouses and the like. Pretty much everybody was talking about "the terminus."

You see, this was just before the war between the states, and the railroads back east were reaching out into the western territories. Everybody knew that soon someone would start building a line from the west coast that would meet up with the one building from the east. They would meet up somewhere and we'd have ourselves a transcontinental railroad.

There were three possible routes across the mountains: a

northern, a southern, and one in the middle. Nobody put much stock in the southerly route because part of it would have to go through Mexico and it wasn't all that long since the USA had been at war with them folks. The middle route would come out at San Francisco, and that was a strong contender. But as everybody kept saying, it was all a matter of the snows in the mountain passes.

It wasn't but a dozen years since the Donner Party had got snowed in on their way to California and people had ended up chawing on each other. For the railroad to succeed, the surveyors had to pick a route that would have the least snow. There were plenty of people arguing for coming through Nebraska into Oregon – the northern route – and if that was so, they'd need to terminate at a harbor that could hold a lot of shipping.

We had that harbor. That's why things went loco.

It was in May of 1859, a little more than a year since Gabby Dave had pitched up with that barrel of whiskey. We were now a town of maybe three hundred people – nobody was taking a census, but you saw new faces all the time. There was even a second saloon over on Third Street, though it took in only those who liked to mix their drinking and dancing with card games and faro.

The town was populous enough that there were men who loafed around on the docks—there were two wharves now—in case any boat came in that needed muscle to load or unload cargo. As part of my regular routine as sheriff, I would go down to the harbor once or twice a day, just to remind those idlers that if they took advantage of any new arrivals, they'd get the benefit of my lead-weighted Billy club and spend a few days sawing firewood in the fenced yard behind the jail.

When I passed along the docks this spring morning, a couple of them wharf rats were arguing with each other whether the boat out in the bay was a ketch or a yawl. I don't think either knew one from the other, and neither did I, but once they drew my attention to the vessel I stopped and took a long look at it.

It was a two-masted yacht with a low-roofed cabin between the masts, and it was tacking back and forth from one end of the bay to another. A man in the bow would swing a weighted line out into the water ahead of the bow then when the boat came level with it, he would haul it out, look at it, then shout something to another man back by the cabin. This fellow would make a mark on a big piece of paper spread on the cabin roof. Then the lead man would swing out his line again and repeat the process.

This went on for some time. At first I thought it might be some kind of fishing technique—there were salmon for the taking in the bay—until I asked one of the idlers what was going on.

"That man in the bow is taking soundings," he told me. "And the one aft is making a chart of the bay."

I didn't hesitate. I was paid to keep an eye on the town, but my pay came from one particular individual. I gave the idler two bits and told him, "Get up to Gabby's and tell Dave Dunham there's something he needs to see down here."

Five minutes later, my employer was standing beside me. He took a long look at the operation out on the water and said, "When the man who's making the chart comes ashore, bring him to me."

"What if he doesn't want to be brought?" I said.

"He will."

The man's name turned out to be Phineas Wetherspoon, and he had come on that boat from San Francisco. He was a slick customer for sure, wore a top hat and some kind of necktie he called a cravat with a big pearl-headed pin stuck through it. He left his yacht out in the harbor and came ashore in a dinghy rowed by the man who'd slung the lead line. I met him, made sure he saw my star, and told him there was a man who wanted to see him.

He looked past me to the town and then to the sawmill camp beyond it. "The mill owner?" he said.

"The mayor," I said. It wasn't an official rank—we'd never held an election—but people had taken to calling Gabby Dave by that title, and it sounded right on this occasion.

"Fine," said Wetherspoon.

I took him to the saloon. Dilly Buncombe was behind the bar, and he cocked his head toward the door in the back that led through to the extra room Gabby had had built onto the original saloon once business had picked up.

Everybody else in the place turned to take in Phineas Wetherspoon because he was a sight to see, what with his little round spectacles and his ivory-headed cane. For his part, he looked like he hadn't a care in the world as we arrived at Dave's door, and I knocked.

"Come in."

I opened it and there was my boss sitting at the desk he'd had brought up from the south. It had a leather top with a big green blotter in the middle of it. Standing in the middle of the green square was a bottle of the house's best whiskey and a couple of glasses.

I looked at Wetherspoon and saw a small smile come and go on his hard-featured face. He stepped past me and into the office.

"You need me?" I asked Gabby Dave.

"Not now," he said.

I shut the door and went and got a beer from Dilly. The guys at the bar wanted to know what was what, so I told them about the boat and the chart. We all knew it meant something, but we didn't know what. And nobody knew what Dunham and Wetherspoon said to each other behind that closed door, but there was no doubt that meeting was what started what some later came to call "the bubble" and others called "the frenzy."

One thing that struck me, though, was that when Wetherspoon came out of his session with Dave Dunham, he didn't have that dreamy-eyed look folks tended to show when they'd been on the receiving end of the gab. He looked just as sharp-eyed and bushy-tailed as when he went in.

I CAN'T SAY I ever understood exactly what happened. After all, Dave used to say to me, "Hiram, I didn't hire you for your brains." But it seemed that, all this time the town had been building, Dave Dunham had owned all the land from the bay right up to Captain Odlum's property line, and somehow he'd managed to get what he called "an option" to buy that piece too, though the price was ridiculous.

Everybody who had a house or a business in the town had got a lease from Gabby Dave. When he found out I could write my name, he had me witness a lot of those leases. I'm not too good at reading, but I know numbers and those leases were dirt cheap – I'd heard people saying that over the year. I figured Gabby rented them cheap because more people in the town meant more customers for Gabby's. But now it started to get crazy.

Phineas Wetherspoon came up from San Francisco again and this time he brought with him a strongbox full of money: bank notes and leather sacks full of ten- and twenty-dollar gold pieces. Him and Dave, they told me to empty out the jail and put that trunk in one of the cells. And I wasn't to leave the jail –

not even for the outhouse – except when Dave was there to spell me off.

I spent three days more locked in than any of my prisoners had ever been, while a crew built Wetherspoon a building. It wasn't frame-and-slab siding like everything else in town. It was solid logs held in place with ten-inch spikes. The windows were small and had strong iron bars set in them and I don't reckon you could have stove in that front door with a battering ram.

When the walls were up and the roof was on, Phineas Wetherspoon moved in and I made sure he and his box of money made the journey unmolested, walking him and it every step of the way with a double-barreled shotgun in my hands, cocked and ready to cut loose.

Later, people asked me if I'd looked in that strongbox while I was guarding it. And the answer is, I never did, cause it was locked and wrapped with chains. But it was heavy as gold and it clinked when he moved it.

Anyway, it didn't matter, because that box of money was just the match that lit the fuse.

IT GOT to be a regular occurrence. Dave would say, "Come with me, and bring your shotgun," and I would accompany him from the saloon over to what folks were calling "Fort Wetherspoon." Dave would go in and I'd wait inside, then when he came out I'd cover him again until we were back at the saloon, when he would disappear into the back room for a while. Over the next few days he made that trip several times. He went carrying papers. He returned carrying stuffed envelopes and bags whose contents clinked.

The rumor went around that Gabby was selling the leases on all the lots he'd rented out to people as they arrived and got settled into Gabtown. After working hours, one evening, the saloon filled up with anxious townsfolk who wanted to know where they stood. Dave got up on a chair and kinda patted the air to quiet them down.

"You've got nothing to worry about," he said. "Those are unbreakable five-year leases and they're renewable for five more years if you want to renew. By the time the second five years is up, you'll have had practically free accommodation for ten years and you'll be able to afford a fair market rent. There's even a clause in there that lets you buy the property."

And then he started to talk about the town and all its promise, and the money that would come rolling in once the railroad came over the mountains from back east. I can't tell you what he said, word for word, because I got caught up in the pictures, like always happened when Dave got to gabbing.

So, things settled down and people paid their little bits of rent to Phineas Wetherspoon instead of Dave Dunham, and life went on same as always.

Until a side-paddle steamer came into the bay and unloaded a whole crowd of men in sharp suits and fancy waistcoats, carrying carpetbags. And they descended on Fort Wetherspoon like locusts on croplands.

Those carpet bags turned out to be full of money. I seen it myself, this time, because Dave sent me over to stand behind Wetherspoon with my shotgun on full display, right next to the big chart of the harbor that showed where deep-water ships could come in and anchor.

These folks had come to buy the leases and they weren't going to take no for an answer. They were offering thousands of dollars for the paper on a single lot, but Wetherspoon he just looked at them with his beady-eyed stare through his little round glasses and faced them down.

"No leases are for sale," he said, "and won't be for ten years." That caused an uproar, but he waited for it to die down.

Then he said, "But I will sell options to buy those leases, ten years from now."

That brought some mutterings and fussbudgeting, but then he said, "Gentlemen, the railroad won't get here before ten years."

And that set off the uproar again. One man dug into his carpetbag and said, "A thousand dollars for an option on any lot within a hundred feet of the docks. He waved a wad of cash under Wetherspoon's pointy nose.

"Two thousand!" said a man farther back in the crowd, pushing forward and slapping his own wad down on the desk. And so it went, with the offers climbing. Wetherspoon stood and spoke to me over his shoulder. I set my shotgun down and drew my leaded Billy club. When I rapped it on the desk, things settled down sharp like.

"Five thousand a lot," said Wetherspoon, "take it or leave it."

They took it. Right then and there, Phineas Wetherspoon sold options on more than seventy lots, stamping each document with a notary's stamp while I signed as a witness. Like I say, I can figure numbers and that amounted to a lot of money. The next day, another raft of speculators arrived, and they bought options on all the rest of the leases in town, so that more than a hundred options were sold. Which was even more money.

It all went into Wetherspoon's strongbox, which was empty when the sale started but full to bursting when it ended. But that wasn't the end of it. That was only the beginning. More carpetbaggers arrived in the following days and if you think they went away disappointed, you have never seen a land-sale bubble. They infested Gabby Dave's saloon so badly the usual customers couldn't drink in peace. And all they did was sell each other options then resell them to a new bidder.

The ones who'd got in early sold their five thousand-dollar pieces of paper to newcomers for ten thousand, fifteen, twenty.

There were men who made a hundred thousand-dollar profit in three days and departed on the southbound steamer, smoking cigars and smiling.

Wetherspoon was smiling, too, though Gabby Dave was looking a little down in the mouth. Folks reckoned Phineas Wetherspoon had been one too many for our town's founder, and some sympathy came Dave's way. But while the carpetbaggers were in town, everybody who sold anything raised their prices and earned a year's rent in a week or so.

Everybody was happy. New buildings were going up, more ships were coming into the port, business was good. The carpetbaggers left, taking their money with them, but having left quite a lot of it behind. And most were glad to see them go, because they'd also brought with them men they'd hired for protection, men who bristled with pistols and knives and made a lot of us mighty nervous—particularly the sheriff.

AND THEN CAME THE FIRE.

It started on a day that the wind was strong and in the north. Near as anyone could figure it, the wind fired up some smoldering embers of a slash fire in the woods where they were cutting cedar for Captain Odlum's sawmill. It was summer and pretty dry and with all those trimmed branches on the ground, it was like somebody had laid a bonfire and put a match to it.

Thank goodness it came in the afternoon and not the night. The first we knew of it was when the smoke from the slash burning suddenly started piling up on the horizon and the first sparks came flying into town. Ozzie the blacksmith had made an iron triangle to beat on if anyone spotted a fire in town and before too long somebody was beating on it with an iron bar.

The whole town came out, as happens when someone sounds a fire alarm in a place built of wood. By then it was already too late to do anything. The fire to the north was a wall of flame and the wind was driving it down on us as fast as a man could walk. As we watched, it came down on Captain Odlum's mill, and his roofs started to burn.

Him and his wife were already running down the road into town carrying nothing but Mrs. Odlum's family Bible, and with his crew coming after them. By the time they got to where we were standing and looking, you could already feel the heat of the fire front. The smoke was thickening, and it wasn't sparks landing now, it was flaming pieces of trees and sawmill settling on roofs and setting the town ablaze.

We ran. There was nothing else to do.

We ran to the tidal flats south of town, struggling through the mud and out into the shallow part of the bay. We could still feel the heat as the town went up, and burning stuff fell on us so we were all busy throwing hatfuls of water onto anybody who was unlucky enough to get touched by the fire.

We watched our town burn, along with everything we owned. It all went up quick, and by nightfall the fire had swept inland when the wind came off the sea. We went and poked among the ashes and called out people's names, dreading that we might not get an answer.

But everybody was accounted for. Everybody except Dave Dunham and Phineas Wetherspoon. There was nothing left of the saloon or Fort Wetherspoon but gray ash and blackened stumps of timbers. People looked but found no shriveled up corpses. And no strongboxes, for that matter.

And then somebody thought to go down to the harbor and look for Wetherspoon's yacht. It had been anchored well out in the bay since the day he arrived. It wasn't there now. We never saw either of them again.

That was it for Gabtown, and that could have been it for Pacific City. But the fire had burned only wood and cloth. The steam-powered saws at Captain Odlum's mill could still be put back to use. The harbor was still there.

So, we rebuilt. I would even say we built it better than before. And when the railroad finally came through, which was a hard poke in the eye to San Francisco, Pacific City became a going concern, and we never looked back.

Now I'm an old man and we're going into the twentieth century as a real city – tall buildings, concrete sidewalks, gaslights up and down every street, even some automobiles. But I've often wondered, as the years have piled up, whether Dave Dunham and Phineas Wetherspoon ever really believed we'd be the terminal city for the transcontinental railroad.

Sometimes I've told my grandchildren, "Pacific City is a magical city because it was founded on a magical lie. But the really magical part was when the lie became truth."

MODIE

Back in the mid-1980s, I augmented my freelance speechwriting income by reading scripts and giving notes on screenplays being considered for funding by the Canadian federal agency that did that kind of thing. I got interested in the format and later wrote a few screenplays of my own. A couple of scripts were actually optioned for real money, though they were never produced.

As Kurt Vonnegut used to say, so it goes.

But my first step was to teach myself the art of screenwriting. So I wrote what might be called "an apprentice piece." I took it easy on myself; instead of putting in the effort to think up a plot, I borrowed one from a classic American novel about a great white whale. And I further indulged myself by adopting the tone of one of my then-favorite TV shows, The Rockford Files. In those days, I used to watch reruns most afternoons—that being one of the benefits of working from home.

I wrote a number of different versions of the script and finally settled on the story as it exists here. At some point, I think at the behest of an agent, I turned the screenplay into a treatment—movie talk for a present-tense, scene-by-scene narrative version that gives *producers a good idea of the story without having to read an entire script.*

Neither the screenplay nor the treatment brought producers knocking on my door, and I decided the movie-writing business was not for me. I was making more progress with genre fiction.

But back in 2003, I found the treatment loitering on my hard drive, read it for the first time in maybe thirty years, and thought, Hey, this is not too bad. And since I self-publish on Amazon, Kobo, and other platforms, I decided to convert the treatment into regular prose. Then I got the thing an ISBN, got it formatted, and offered it to the world at a bargain price of 99 cents.

So, here it is. If you, the person reading this, happen to be producer of major—or even minor—motion pictures, the rights are still available. When I wrote it, the lead roles would have gone to Michael J. Fox, Danny DeVito, and Lou Gossett Jr. I would have liked Rockford Files *tough girl Gretchen Corbett for the love interest, though she was probably too old to play an ingenue, anyway.*

If you're not a Hollywood mogul, then I just hope you enjoy it.

FICTION WRITERS ARE GENERALLY ADVISED NOT to begin a story with a dream sequence. But we're going to do it, regardless.

The same goes for opening with a prologue, but guess what?

The prologuing dream is set on a deserted stretch of San Francisco's docks, many years ago. Imagine a foggy night, with narrow pools of illumination from streetlights spaced far apart. Into view comes a big automobile, an old, tail-finned Cadillac, white with blacked-out windows, only its parking lights showing, moving slowly through one cone of light to the next. It pulls up outside a warehouse and sits there, engine throbbing.

The driver's window rolls silently down. A shadowy figure sits behind the wheel. His name is Amodeus Bick, the child of Mozart enthusiasts who wanted a virtuoso piano player but wound up with a mean little kid who grew up to be a kingpin in the West Coast underworld. If this were a movie, his part would be played by somebody we've seen in a Scorsese film. He hates his name and has always insisted on being called Modie.

He peers at the warehouse entrance then beckons with a finger. Out from the doorway steps Abner H. Abner, whose parents had a sense of humor when it came to naming their offspring. Abner does not share it.

He is wearing a belted trench coat and fedora hat, the brim pulled down so his face is in shadow. If we could see him clearly, he would resemble the actor Danny DeVito: small, round of face, but with a surplus of nervous energy. In his hands is a parcel wrapped in brown paper. He approaches the Cadillac and hands the package to Modie.

The gangster takes it and lays it beside him on the seat. Then he lifts a briefcase from the passenger-side footwell and passes it to Abner.

Modie begins to pry open the package, while Abner opens the briefcase to examine its contents. But he fumbles with it and now banded packs of hundred-dollar bills are falling to the concrete below. He bends to pick them up, but the motion causes the upper part of his trench coat to open. Metal gleams, reflecting the light from a streetlamp.

It's an SFPD badge and Modie realizes instantly that he has been set up for a sting. He throws the package at Abner's feet, slams the Caddie into gear, and stomps on the gas. The rear tires spin in place smoking.

Abner has dropped the briefcase and pulled his service pistol. He points it through the window, but Modie is pressing the control that rolls it up. The edge of the glass jams Abner's pistol against the top of the rim. Abner puts his hand in the little space and tries to force the window down.

Now other cops are coming out of the shadows, including Abner's partner, Henry Queeg, whom we will describe later because Abner is the focus right now, as the Caddie's tires get a grip and the car rockets forward. Abner is yanked off his feet and carried along.

"Hold it!" he shouts, and, "Stop!"

Modie snarls a curse and keeps going.

Abner pulls the trigger. Modie screams. The car swerves wildly along the dock, flinging Abner about. His leg hits a bollard, and now it's his term to scream. He holds on, pulling the trigger until the cylinder is empty.

The Cadillac reaches the end of the dock and plunges into the cold water of San Francisco Bay, taking Abner with it. He lets go of the pistol and pulls his hand out of the window. The car and Abner hit the water together. He goes under but comes back out, while the Caddie floats nose down, one of its iconic fins sticking up in the air. The tide and currents begin to pull it away from the dock.

Abner is floundering in the water, his hat floating away. The cops arrive and one of them throws him a life preserver. His partner, Henry, tears off his tunic and dives in, swims to Abner, and holds him up, pulling him toward where a wooden ladder descends from the dock.

Now we can take a moment to describe Henry: he's African American, mostly, but with some Cherokee, East Asian, and Samoan ancestry. He looks something like Tiger Woods, but with more muscle.

The car is sinking now, one tailfin still above the surface. Through the water we can just see the vanity license plate: "Modie."

Henry has got Abner to the base of the ladder and another cop is climbing down to help haul him out of the water. But then lights appear, the Caddie's pair of double rounds coming on under the water, and rising toward Abner and Henry, a tailfin cutting the water like a shark's dorsal fin.

Abner struggles to climb the ladder while the sound of a heartbeat swells until it's overwhelming.

AND THAT'S when Abner wakes up, as he always does, from this recurring dream. He is no longer the young patrolman. No longer with the SFPD. He has been sleeping on the couch in his office, the best description for which is somewhere between "seedy" and "run-down."

He sits up, rubs a hand over a face that wears three days of stubble. A near-empty bottle of scotch sits on the floor beside his feet. He reaches for it, empties it in two swallows, and belches.

There is a cane leaning against the couch. He grabs it, levers himself up, and limps over to the window, where the shade is drawn. On the wall, framed behind glass, is a yellowed newspaper clipping with the headline: *Shootout on the Docks—Heroic Patrolman Nails Racketeer*. Next to it are three other framed documents: a police citation and medal, a discharge from the SFPD, and a California private detective's license. There is also a framed photo of Abner and Henry on their graduation from the police academy, arms around each other's shoulders, smiling.

Abner glances at the photo, but looks away. He rolls up the shade revealing the lettering on the glass: *A.H. Abner*. And underneath: *INVESTIGATIONS*.

He looks out onto the Nantucket Street, lined with commercial buildings, none of them new. It's dawn. An intercity bus is passing below. Abner sighs at the thought of another day.

AS NOTED EARLIER, experienced authors warn against starting a story with a dream sequence, or opening with a prologue. The main reason why: many editors and literary agents, having had so many clumsy, lumpy prologues inflicted upon them, will simply stop reading if the P-word appears on the first page of a manuscript. And there goes the chance of a deal.

But many readers don't mind a prologue, if it sets up the basis of the story, as the tale of Abner's dream will be shown to have done. So now, having come through the opening, we segue to the interior of the bus that Abner watched go past his office window. And there, in a window seat, fast asleep, we meet the actual protagonist of this story, Michael Ishmael.

Picture a fresh-faced, all-American boy of about twenty. He could be played by Michael J. Fox in his *Back to the Future* days, or the young actor who plays Sheldon Cooper's older brother. Here he comes to San Francisco to launch himself into a career he has long dreamed of.

And speaking of dreams, Mike is apparently lost in one at the moment, the book he had been reading—Dashiell Hammett's *The Maltese Falcon*— open on his lap. He twitches and mutters something about a "fat man" and a "black bird."

In the seat next to him, Sue Ellen Vanderhog watches him in fascination. She is an Iowa farmgirl, even more fresh-faced than Mike, come to the libertinous city by the bay on a mission that we won't go into detail about just yet. She could be played by any number of blonde, blue-eyed ingénues who hide a core of steel beneath the surface beauty. Maybe Reese Witherspoon or Charlize Theron in their earlier days.

Now Mike starts again, and his head comes to rest on her shoulder. She gently eases his head away. It flops over, hits the window, and he wakes up, groggy.

"That musta been some dream," Sue Ellen says.

Mike's vision clears. He blinks and gets a good look at her. "This one's better."

That wins him a shy smile from Sue Ellen. It might be going too far to call it love at first sight, but the mutual attraction is definite.

He looks around and says, "Where are we?"

She cranes to look down the aisle and through the bus's windshield. "End of the line, I think."

Mike sits up and his book drops to the floor. The dream has given him a noticeable erection. Sue Ellen notices. She reaches for the book and hands it to him.

She says, "My momma says you can tell the size of a man by the size of his dream."

Mike is embarrassed and uses the book to cover things up. But she's amused. She offers him her hand. "I'm Sue Ellen Vanderhog. You were sleeping when I got on."

"Mike Ishmael. Call me Ish."

"Is your home in San Francisco, Mike? Do you know your way around?"

"I will," he says. "I start a new job tomorrow. What about you?"

She says she's from Swift Current, Idaho. "That's up near Bonner's Ferry?"

Mike's shrug says he's never heard of it, but he wants to keep the conversation going. "I'm thinking . . . potatoes?"

"Mostly logging," she says.

Mike is anxious to please. "Logging is good. I mean, I've never hugged a tree."

"My folks, they're farmers. That's why I had to come to the city." When she sees that he's not following, she says, "I have to find my brother Duane."

She sees that they're approaching the bus depot. "Never mind, it's a long story."

Mike recognizes that the conversation has wound down and he wants it to continue. "If you need to find somebody, I might be able to help you."

She frowns a little frown. "I thought you didn't live in San Francisco."

"I don't, but I'm a private investigator—well, I mean I've got my license, and I've got a job with a detective agency." He pulls a folded letter from his inside jacket pocket, unfolds it and shows it to her. "See? A.H. Abner Investigations. It says I'm hired if I can start right away. So maybe I could help find your brother. You could be my first case."

The frown is still there but easing up. "Gee, I never thought about getting a detective. I got the address of the place Duane used to pick up his mail so I figured I'd go there and they could tell me where to find him. How much do you charge?

"I don't know. I haven't started work yet."

It sounds a little iffy to Sue Ellen. "Well . . . ."

Mike really doesn't want to let this go, doesn't want to let *her* go. "But it can't be too much. I mean, all the movies and TV shows, you don't see P.I.'s living in palaces."

"Then why do you want to be one?"

It's a question Mike loves to answer. His workmates back at the brewery in Seattle used to ask him the same thing, and he told them what he now tells Sue Ellen.

"Cause it's the best thing to be in the whole world. It's what I've always wanted to do. You know, mystery, figuring out who done it. It's like you're working out a little piece of the really big mystery—like life, the universe, and everything."

She thinks she's catching on. "Like how come suddenly everybody's growing weird long beards and buying AR-15s."

Mike is not sure how to respond to that, but he's certainly not going to give her any trouble. "So, anyway," he says, "I took this mail-order course from the Professor Ernest Hardaker Academy of Investigative Science. Straight A's and B's. I got my transcripts, you wanna see them."

The bus's airbrakes *whoosh* as it pulls into the depot.

Sue Ellen says, "Oh, gosh, we're here."

Mike can't keep the disappointment out of his tone. "Oh. Yeah."

They get up and Mike retrieves a backpack from the over-head rack. Sue Ellen brings down an old-fashioned suitcase.

The aisle fills with jostling passengers waiting for the driver to shut off the motor and open the front door.

Sue Ellen says, "Well, it was nice meeting you, Mike."

Mike doesn't want this to end. "Likewise. Um, listen, where are you staying?"

"I don't know if I am. If I find Duane, I guess I'll just catch a bus home."

Mike knows his face is showing his disappointment. "Oh?" But Mike was born to optimism, so he brightens. "Well, maybe you won't—I mean, I hope you do—but say you didn't and you had to stay around a few days, maybe . . . ."

Sue Ellen catches the dropped ball. ". . . maybe I could call you."

The door opens and other passengers start to squeeze past them to get off the bus.

"Yeah, and that would be like, really. . . Oops, sorry." That was to a large lady with a raffia bag who's having trouble getting past the pair of them.

Sue Ellen picks up the ball again and runs with it "That would be, really. . . ?"

"Really nice," Mike says. "You know, we could, I dunno, do whatever they do in San Francisco, I mean they got to do something, it's a big town, what's the use of building it, if people aren't gonna get together and do things?" He realizes he is babbling but she does seem to be hanging on his every word. That smile is amazing.

"Good things," he rattles on, "that is, nice things that we could maybe do, you and me, together."

He stops and takes a breath. "Am I making any sense at all?"

A middle-aged man, balding, with a well-worn face, has been waiting for them to move. Now he squeezes by, and in passing, says, "No."

"Yes," says Sue Ellen, sticking out her tongue. To Mike, she says, "I could call you when I know what I'm doing."

"Great!" Then he realizes he has a problem. "Except I don't have a phone number yet. I don't have one of those fancy phones."

She doesn't have to think long to solve his problem. "What about the one on the letter?"

"Wow! You're pretty smart, aren't you? Here." He hands her the letter in its envelope.

She opens the envelope, looking for the number, but then stops to say, "I'm not smart. You think I'm smart?"

"Absolutely. And not just pretty smart—not that there's anything wrong with being just pretty smart, cause pretty smart is great all by itself—but you're also equally so... so very..."

He trails off, afraid he's babbling again.

"What?" she says. "So very what?"

"So very..." He swallows. "... pretty."

Sue Ellen looks away. "I'm not pretty." Her gaze falls upon a large woman impatiently trying to squeeze by. "I'm not pretty."

"Sure, you are," the woman says, "and, also, you're in the way."

Mike says, "See? Independent confirmation."

Sue Ellen turns back to Mike, and now it's her turn to be shy. "I'm pretty?"

The large woman sighs. "You are totally pretty. What you are not is *moving*! Could you two maybe fall in love somewheres else, let a person by?"

Two more passengers chime in from the rear of the bus. Mike and Sue Ellen, embarrassed, let themselves be forced down the aisle to the door, and out into the bus depot, where the driver has the cargo door open and is unloading suitcases for the passengers to pick up. The pair move out of the way, over to where a coin-operated newspaper box shows the headline: *GUARDS SHOT IN WELLS FARGO ARMORED CAR HEIST*.

Sue Ellen says, "Well, it was nice..."

"*So* nice," says Mike. And now that moment of parting has come he feels a little desperation. "Look, Sue Ellen, I would really like to help you. If money's a problem, I could look for your brother in my spare time."

"Are you allowed to do that?"

"I think so. I guess so. Jim Rockford didn't get paid half the time."

"You think it's like that in real life?"

The idea has never occurred to him. While he's considering it, the driver nudges a battered old suitcase toward him. "This yours, buddy?"

Mike comes back to the moment. "Uh, yeah." He stoops and picks up the case, slings his backpack strap over one shoulder.

Sue Ellen half turns away. "Well, I'd better . . ."

"Right."

She offers him her hand. "It's been really . . ."

Mike takes her hand and holds on. "Nice."

"So nice."

Mike says, "I would say this is textbook-definition nice."

"And I can call you if I need help finding Duane?"

"Oh, yeah. Or even if you just wanna . . . you know."

Sue Ellen reluctantly withdraws her hand. "Okay. Guess I'd better go find a hotel."

"Yeah. Find a good one."

There is a cab stand out by the street. She walks toward it, looks back, sees him watching her go. She smiles one last smile for Mike. A cabbie who is leaning against his vehicle opens the rear door for her, and she gets in. A moment later, the cab pulls away.

Mike drops his suitcase and runs after her, bangs on the trunk of the cab until it stops. Sue Ellen opens the door.

"What?"

But Mike doesn't have a reason for why he stopped her,

other than he just doesn't want to lose sight of her. "Just call me."

Sue Ellen holds up envelope. "I will." She closes the door and the cab pulls away.

Mike watches her go, sighs, and trudges back to where he left his suitcase. "So nice," he says.

LATER THAT MORNING, a gold, late-seventies vintage Firebird comes down Nantucket Street outside Abner's building. The engine is rough and there is black smoke coming from the exhaust. On the windshield the outlines of soaped letters – *RUNS GOOD*—are still visible. It stops in front of the building and Mike gets out.

He closes the door and stands for a moment looking at the car, shaking his head in happy disbelief. "Wow."

He is holding a page torn from the Yellow Pages. He checks an ad against the number on the front door of the building— and the lettering above the main doors that says, *Pequod Building*—and nods a confirmation. Now he goes to pop the vehicle's trunk, from which he extracts a trench coat and a wide-brimmed fedora. He puts them on, belts the coat, pulls down the hat. He hitches his shoulders the way Bogey used to, then enters the building.

UPSTAIRS, Abner comes out of his office, limping on his cane, with his mouth tasting like a used litterbox and painful thunder in his head. He heads to a washroom down the corridor and steps into it just as Mike opens the door from the fire stairs. It takes only a moment for him to find the half-glassed door that has A.H. Abner – INVESTIGATIONS in somewhat tarnished lettering. Mike knocks but gets no answer. He tries the door, finds it open, and peeks in.

He sees an empty private detective's office that hasn't been renovated since the 1950s, with two beat-up wooden desks, some filing cabinets, and even a hat rack.

"All right!" he says, softly, and steps inside, closing the door after him. He moves to where the certificates and photos hang on the wall and examines them, again nodding in approval.

"All right, all right, all right," he says, and flips his fedora to make it land on the hatrack. Then he goes to Abner's desk, sits in the chair, leans back. He eyes the hatrack and the mood comes over him.

Mike thinks he does a good Bogart. Few agree. But no one is here. He gets up, approaches his hat, hitches his shoulders again and says, "So, fat man, this is it. Play me for a sucker, wouldja? Thought I'd take the rap for you. Guess you never figured I'd find the dame, didja? Yeah, well I found her, fat man, and she spilled the beans, see. Blew the whistle on you. Yeah, and right now she's walking into the DA's office, and she's opening her mouth to say . . ."

At which point, Abner says, "Move one inch, you get an extra asshole."

Mike freezes, turns slowly to see Abner framed in the doorway, in a combat crouch, his cane hung over his arm, aiming a large handgun at Mike.

"Keep your hands where I can see 'em."

Mike raises his hands, his face lit up with appreciation. "Oh, wow!"

Abner begins to suspect he's caught a loony. "What?"

"It's just so obvious. You're a real professional, aren't you?"

"What?"

Mike nods knowingly. "The ordinary guy, he wouldn't see it. But to a fellow pro, well, it's all there in your stance."

Abner edges toward the old rotary phone on Henry's desk. "My stance. I see."

Mike says, "Oh, yeah, perfect balance. But... you don't mind if I ask you one question?"

Abner leaves the gun in one hand, reaches for the handset. "Why would I?"

"Well, when you're using the two-handed combat grip, shouldn't the left hand be underneath and at a 90 degree angle to the axis of the right?"

He begins to lower his hands to demonstrate. Abner cocks the pistol. "Get your hands back up."

Mike raises his hands again. "Oh, yeah, sorry, sorry." He shakes his head. "Give me a chance to talk shop, and away I go. What can I tell you?"

He gestures with hands again. Abner says, "Those hands come down again, you'll be telling it to the coroner."

"Sorry, I just . . ."

Abner gropes for the handset, finds it. "Shut up."

"I just shut up."

Abner briefly takes his eyes off Mike, looks around the room. "Who was you talkin' to?"

Mike keeps his hands up but cocks his head toward the hatrack. "Hatrack."

Abner's expression says he has now decidedly put Mike in the fruitcake category. He gestures with the gun. "Hands onna desk, assume the position. Now!"

Mike quickly goes to the desk, puts his hands flat on top, and spreads his legs. Abner puts down the phone, approaches, touches the gun to the back of Mike's head, kicks his feet apart, frisks him quickly and expertly.

"Very smooth," Mike says. "You ever thought about teaching?"

"Shut up." He steps back toward Henry's desk, uncocks the

gun, but keeps it trained on Mike. "Okay, the hell you doin' here?"

Mike, still leaning on the desk, turns to look at Abner. "I work here."

Abner makes a rude sound with tongue and lips. "Try again."

"It's true. I got a letter offering me a job."

Abner's face says, *Yeah, right*, but his voice says, "Show me."

Mike straightens up and slowly reaches toward his inside breast pocket. Then he hesitates. "I'm just going for the letter."

Abner sighs. "I already patted you down."

"That's right, you did. I noticed you kept the gun right here." He points to the back of his neck. "At Professor Ernest Hardaker's Academy of Investigative Science, they recommend . . ."

"I recommend you shut up. It's a final recommendation. You were gonna show me a letter?"

Mike reaches into his pocket, and now he remembers. "I gave it to somebody."

Abner has had enough. "Brilliant. Okay, face down on the floor, hands behind your neck."

Mike carefully gets down on the floor. "What are you going to do?"

Abner picks up the handset, dials a number. "I'm gonna have the desk man at the precinct book you a suite at the Hotel Hilarious."

He cradles phone against his jaw, but hears a busy signal. "Crap."

Mike says, "Look, Mr . . .?"

"Abner. It's on the door."

Mike levers himself up, extends a hand. "Pleased to meet you. I'm Mike Ishmael. Call me Ish."

Abner is dialing again. "I'll call you the dearly departed, you don't lay down and stay down."

Mike goes prone again. "Okay. But I do work here. And I am a bona fide graduate of the Professor Ernest Hardaker Academy of Investigative Science."

Abner hangs up, then dials again.

Mike says, "I wrote to a lot of agencies looking for work, and I got a letter saying I had a job with A.H. Abner Investigations."

Abner hangs up the phone. "You can never get these guys. Look, kid, I don't know nothin' about no letter. This place, it's just me and my partner, and we ain't hirin'. Specially, we ain't hirin' people wander in, engage the furniture in conversation. It's kind of a policy."

Mike is mystified. "Well, then who sent me the letter?"

Which is when a voice says, "I did."

The voice belongs to Henry Queeg. He has weathered the years better than his hard-drinking partner, though there is definite frosting to his hair and some crinkles around his eyes. He bears a startling resemblance to Lou Gossett Junior. He is wearing a neatly pressed suit, white shirt, sober tie. He looks down at Mike, then at Abner.

"It's a different kind of approach to employee orientation, Abner."

"What employee? You hire this yo-yo?"

"Yes."

Mike gets up on one elbow "Could I get up now?"

"Yeah, kid, you get up. Then you take a hike." He looks at Henry. "Cause we ain't hirin'."

Henry meets Abner's stare. He's not backing down. Mike realizes he needs to sell himself and sell hard. He gets to his feet, straightens his trench coat. "Mr. Abner," He looks at Henry. "Mister . . .?

Henry offers his hand. "Queeg. Henry Queeg."

Mike shakes Henry's hand, offers his own to Abner, who turns away. Mike turns to Henry. "Mr. Queeg. I think I need to talk to your partner."

Abner shakes his head, winces a little because he is still hungover.

Mike bears in. "Well, sir, Mr. Abner, I'm hoping you're going to reconsider your initial position. Because I believe—no, I know—that I can make a genuine contribution to your dynamic investigative agency."

He sees the look on Abner's face "Of course, I'd be willing to start at the bottom and work my way up."

Abner makes a sound that could almost be a laugh. "Kid, look around—this *is* the bottom, and we've been workin' our way down to it the past twenty years."

"Well, maybe you need some fresh blood, new talent, new ideas, the modern, scientific approach to investigation. I mean, sure, there's a lot to be said for the old methods—tried and true —get out on the streets, pick up the skinny, trust your intuition and a carefully developed network of underworld informants. But then there's all the rest, the new stuff, DNA, psychographic profiling, the Internet . . ."

Abner can't believe this. While Mike speaks, he goes to his desk, opens a drawer, takes out a full bottle of whiskey, sits down, and pours a shot. He grimaces as the liquor hits the back of his throat and belches loudly.

Henry holds up a hand to stop the flow of Mike's sales pitch. "No need to beat it to death, son. We know you need the job."

Mike is deadly serious. "No, sir, no, no, I *want* the job, want it like I've never wanted anything before. I mean, I've had jobs, lots of jobs. Some of them were okay. The last one, it was . . ." He gestures with both hands and makes little noise with his lips that expresses his disgust. "But I could have stayed on there. Well maybe not, not after the explosion—only a little explosion, mind, no big deal really, well except for . . ."

He realizes he's babbling, takes a pause, and pulls it back together. "Anyway, I *want* to be a private detective. I've *just gotta* be a private eye. That's all I ever wanted to do—get out there in the mean streets, pit my brains against a complex web of facts and suppositions, looking for that golden thread of logic that unravels the mystery."

He shakes his head in awe of the prospect. Abner shakes his head, winces again, and pours another shot. He downs it and says, "I take it you don't have a whole lot of experience in our line of work."

"Well, no, not actual experience. But I am a graduate—with honors—from the Professor Ernest Hardaker Academy . . ."

Abner shakes his head again, winces, says to himself, "I gotta stop doing that."

Mike is pulling papers out of his pocket. "I brought my diploma and a transcript of my marks."

He offers them to Abner who waves them away, but Henry takes the papers, looks through them.

"Well, I'll be dingled. Fingerprints, an A; surreptitious entry, B plus; inductive reasoning A plus."

Mike swells a little. "Professor Hardaker says I have a logical mind."

Abner pours another shot. "Oh yeah, you a regular junior G-man." he throws back the whiskey. "But we still ain't hirin'."

Henry clears his throat. "It's Mike, right?"

"Yes, sir. But you can call me—"

Henry hands back the papers. "I'll call you Mike. Would you mind stepping into the hall while I have a word with Mr. Abner?"

Mike sees he has had his shot, that now it's all up to Henry. But the detective smiles at him and he keeps his hopes up.

"Sure, no problem."

He goes out into the hallway, but leaves the door ajar so he can listen, whispering to himself, "Passive Surveillance 101."

Mike hears Abner say, "Dammit, Henry, where you get off writin' letters an' offerin' jobs?"

"Abner, we need the help."

"*That's* help?"

"He'll be okay," Henry says. "I'll show him the ropes."

Abner snorts. "I'd show him a six-pack of Thorazine."

"We need somebody."

Mike hears the sound of Abner's whiskey glass touching down on the table from a shaky hand. "Since when?" Abner says.

Up until this moment, Henry has been the voice of reason. But now his tone hardens. "Since you started putting in 24-hour days investigating the bottom of a bottle."

"Jesus, Henry."

"I'm sorry, Abner, but I can't keep carrying the load for the both of us. I've been waiting for you to snap out of it, like the other times, but you're not snapping."

A silence falls and stretches several heartbeats then Abner says, "You know what day it is, Henry?"

"I know."

"It was twenty-five years ago tonight."

"That's right, Abner. That's how long it's been over—twenty-five years."

Mike hears Abner's fist slamming the desk. "No! Cause it *ain't* over! And it's never *gonna* be over! You know why? Cause it's *right now, right here!*" Mike hears the sound of Abner slapping his bad leg.

"And *here!*" Mike peeks through the door, sees Abner touching his temple. "Yeah, I been hittin' the bottle!" He jabs his finger into his temple, and winces at the hangover pain. "Cause of in here! The past two weeks, every night, the same dream! An' I know it's not ever gonna stop till I see Modie dead! *Dead*, Henry!"

Henry goes to Abner and puts a hand on his partner's shoulder. "Abner, Modie *is* dead. You emptied your piece into him. He went into the water. He never came up."

Abner's eyes lose focus. "We never found the body. Hell, we

couldn't find the *car*! Goddam bullet-proof Caddie, like he was the president! And Modie, he was *bad*! Modie Bick was what I joined the force for, to get rid of his kinda trash! Instead, he broke my leg and screwed up my life! And now I got to *see* him dead, Henry! Or I don't never rest easy."

Henry gently shakes Abner's shoulder. "Partner, you got to get through this. They're never going to find Modie. The harbor police, coast guard, they all searched. That *National Enquirer* rag, they had divers down there for a week. They got zip. There's all kinds of crazy currents, and bottom ooze twelve feet deep. Next time anybody sees Modie, they'll be looking at a fossil."

"Sure," Abner says and taps his head, gently, "up here, I know that. But in here . . ."—he puts a hand to his chest—". . . the bastard's still eating me alive."

"Ease up. Look, I gotta talk to the kid, get him set up to start work." Henry takes away the whiskey bottle. "Why don't you take a shave, go and get some breakfast?"

Abner stands, takes a big breath, lets it out. "Yeah, maybe so." He lightly punches Henry's arm. "Hey, partner. I yelled at you."

"It's okay."

"You always been a good partner, Henry. Hell, you saved my life when I was in the water. That's somethin' else I'm never gonna forget. You're one of the good ones."

Henry makes a sound that's not quite a chuckle. "I guess that's why they gave me you."

"Get outta here."

Mike steps back from the door as Henry comes out of the office, closing the door behind him. He hands Mike his fedora.

"Get good marks in eavesdropping?"

"Passive surveillance. I got an A."

Henry nods. "Uh huh. You got a place to stay?"

"Not yet. I came in last night and hung around the bus

depot till morning. Then I went and got a car. I figured I'd need one."

Henry nods again. "Okay. Go get a room somewhere. And be back here eight o'clock tomorrow. We'll see what kind of private investigators your Professor Whoosis is turning out these days."

"That's great, Mr. Queeg."

"Henry."

Mike's turn to nod. "Henry. Listen, Henry, you might find this hard to believe, but I think I might already have got us a case."

Henry's eyebrows go up. "Why wouldn't I find that hard to believe?" He turns Mike toward the stairwell. "Tell you what, let's talk about that tomorrow. I've got to get down to the courthouse."

Mike lights up. "Courthouse? All right! Testifying, right? Surprise witness, expert testimony?"

"Not quite. Now, you run along. I'll see you back here tomorrow morning."

"You bet. And don't worry, I'll be ready for anything. You won't be disappointed. " He exits down the stairs, scat-singing the theme from *The Rockford Files*.

Henry says, "I'm sure I won't." He turns back to office, then stops, remembers. "Explosion?"

But Mike is gone.

LET'S leave Mike to get on with finding a room so we can see what Sue Ellen is doing. She is walking into a small store that caters to survivalists. It's packed with camping gear, camouflage suits, knives of all sizes, crossbows, bumper stickers denouncing the New World Order, Confederate battle flags, and posters featuring muscular guys toting automatic weapons.

Behind a display case whose shelves support a wide range of pistols stands the store's manager. His name is Klassen, and he is big, young, and blond. When Sue Ellen comes in, he is reassembling a field-stripped old Army Colt pistol. She is not fazed by the store's inventory. She has seen all this kind of equipment before.

She says, "Hi, I'm trying to find my brother, Duane Vanderhog."

Klassen keeps assembling the gun. "Never heard of him."

"This is where he gets his mail."

Klassen finishes putting the gun back together. He works the slide then tests the trigger and hammer. Without looking at her he says, "Bye, bye."

She is a little set back by his attitude. "But . . ."

Klassen gives her a hard look, but she is not easily deterred. "Okay. Could I use your phone?" That gets her an even harder look. "It's a local call."

Klassen nods, turns to put the pistol in the display case, but keeps his eyes and ears on Sue Ellen. She takes Mike's letter out of her purse and dials the number on the letterhead.

ABNER IS IN HIS OFFICE, drinking coffee and gingerly eating a donut. The phone rings, and he winces at the sound before picking it up.

"Abner Investigations." He listens for a moment then says, "No, no Mike workin' here. Oh, no, hold it, is he a weird kid, talks to furniture? Listen, he ain't here. Call back tomorrow."

Henry comes into the office, hears Abner saying, "Look, sweetheart, I'm his boss, not his answering service. Call tomorrow."

He hangs up.

Henry says, "What?"

"Some broad wanted the boy wonder. You think he's gonna be okay?"

Henry laughs. "Oh yeah. *You're* the one I'm worried about."

BACK IN THE SURVIVALISTS' store, Sue Ellen hangs up the phone, turns to Klassen, and says, "Thanks."

"No problem."

He watches her leave. As the door closes, he goes to the phone and dials. When the phone is answered, he stands to attention.

"Commander Nordling? Squad leader Klassen, sir. I have to report that a girl came here looking for Trooper Vanderhog. Said she was his sister."

He listens, then says, "No, sir. Not a word. Then she made a call to I think it was a private detective, the name was Mike, at an agency called Abner Investigations."

He listens again then says, "Just a kid, sir. If she's anything like Vanderhog, she's dumb as a bag of horseshoes."

ON THE OTHER end of the line is Otto Nordling, a deadly serious, middle-aged man in a tailored suit, could be a Bond villain played by Christopher Walken. He wears a pin shaped like a lightning bolt in his left lapel. He's standing beside a big, ornate desk in a ground-floor office that overlooks the garden of his seaside mansion.

He says, "Good work, Squad Leader. Probably nothing to it, but let me know if she comes back, or anyone else. I'll send over some back-up. Dismissed."

He hangs up and stands for a moment in thought. Then he

picks up a swagger stick and paces about the office. He goes to look at two large maps tacked to one wall.

One map is of the San Francisco Bay Area, the other is a detailed map of the waterfront. The dockland map has one block circled. Within the circle is the building that houses the San Francisco office of the U.S. Customs Agency.

Nordling taps the circle with his swagger stick and says, softly, "Boom."

He turns to look out the window, smiling grimly, slapping the stick into his hand a few times. You know, like a villain, Bond-style.

MIKE HAS FOUND himself a low-rent room near the harbor and now he's settling in. Humming the Rockford theme again, he is stacking paperback novels on the dresser top. Some of the spines show the names of best-selling mystery authors: Block, Parker, Hammett, Chandler. When the books are arranged to his satisfaction, he pulls a cardboard tube from his suitcase. In the tube is a rolled-up poster showing Humphrey Bogart as Sam Spade in *The Maltese Falcon.*

He finds some thumbtacks in the case and pins the poster to the wall. He does the Bogart shoulder hitch again. "Here's looking at you, kid."

Next to the paperbacks he puts he puts a well-used loose-leaf binder. The printed label on the front reads *PROFESSOR ERNEST HARDAKER ACADEMY OF INVESTIGATIVE SCIENCE.*

Mike is now all moved in. He puts the suitcase under the bed and turns on a little TV that's bolted to a shelf. It's local news time and the anchor is saying, "Still no arrests in the Wells Fargo armored car robbery that left two guards dead. Police say a well-organized—"

Mike flicks through the channels, coming to rest on one that plays nostalgia. Right now, it's Elliot Gould as Philip Marlowe in Robert Altman's *The Long Goodbye.*

Mike sits on the bed, eyes on the little screen. "Classic."

WE'LL LEAVE Mike happy and relaxed, to take a look out the window. A loaded barge is crossing the harbor. Let's take a closer look.

It's a battered and weather-beaten barge used for hauling waste. Beat-up 45-gallon drums marked *DANGER—BIOCHEM-ICAL WASTE—EXTREME HAZARD* are lined up against a rusty chain railing. Two crewmen are arm-wrestling on top of one of the drums. They struggle, then one pins the other.

The winner says, "Five bucks. Wanna try lefties?"

The loser says, "Nah. This mother's too slippery. You can't get no traction."

The loser kicks the drum, and the rusty chains part. The drum falls into the water. They watch it sink.

"Crap," says the loser.

The other crewman tops him. "Megacrap."

The barge moves on. They look back at bubbles where the drum sank.

"Whatta you think was in it?"

"Trouble."

The winner says, "So whatta you say, lefties?"

The loser shrugs. "I guess."

THE BARGE CHUGS ON. The crewmen are intent on their contest so they don't notice that the water where the drum sank is now bubbling fiercely. Nor do they notice an eerie green glow coming from the harbor bottom. The glow begins to move toward shore. Now two headlights come on underwater, and the old Cadillac, dripping silt and seaweed, drives up a boat-launch ramp onto the shore.

The driver's door opens, letting out a rush of water and a large, flopping fish. When the flow subsides, a skeletal lower jaw drops onto the ground, then a skeletal hand picks it up. The door closes. The car drives onto a dark street.

IT's early morning at A.H. Abner Investigations. Abner, shaved and cleaned up, but still frayed around the edges, stands looking out the window. Henry is at his desk going through some papers.

Abner says, "Here he comes."

Henry checks his watch. "Points for punctuality."

Abner turns toward him. "You know, we really don't need anybody else."

Henry sighs. "We're neither of us getting any younger. Another set of hands and feet, we could do more business. Let's see how the boy does."

Abner snorts. Henry says, "You still look a little thinned out, partner. How about you hang around, watch the phones, take it easy?"

Mike enters, dressed in his detective outfit, still heavily under Bogart's influence.

"I'm here."

Henry gives Abner a "don't start" look as he gets up. "Let's do it."

He takes Mike by the arm. They exit before Abner can speak.

OUT ON THE STREET, Mike and Henry exit the Pequod Building, and walk toward Henry's nondescript sedan. Henry glances at Mike's parked Firebird. "We'll take my car."

They get in and drive off. Further down the block is an alley. Deep in its shadows, the seaweed-draped Cadillac sits, waiting. Neither of them notices it.

Henry drives sedately and carefully, with Mike in the passenger seat.

"Er, Mr. Queeg? Henry?"

"Yeah?"

Mike sneaks a peeks at an index card cupped in his palm. "I just want to express my appreciation for this opportunity. And I'm really going to give it my best shot."

"Uh huh."

Mike reads from the card. "And even though this is my first day on the job, I'm fully confident that I can handle anything you might ask of me. I am motivated to put the interests of Abner Investigations above every other consideration. Excellence is my only standard, and I can assure you . . ."

Henry reaches over, takes the card and reads the rest of the line. ". . . that I will give one hundred and ten per cent." He tosses the card back. "You mind if I ask you something?"

"Yes, sir. I mean, no sir."

"No offense, Mike—I just need to know, do you recognize that there's a line where the bullshit stops and real life takes over?"

"Yes, sir. I mean, I think so."

"And do you know which side of the line you're on?"

Mike ducks his head. "Most of the time."

Henry smiles. "Then we'll get along fine. So, what kinds of work have you done before this?"

Mike stares straight ahead. "Oh, this and that. I kind of had trouble finding my niche."

Henry chuckles. "Oh yeah, those niches can be hard to locate. So, what've you been doing until one comes along?"

"Well, I try to improve myself, take courses. Like the Professor Ernest Hardaker Academy of Investigative Science. Mail order."

"But what did you do for a living, meanwhile."

Mike says something too softly for Henry to catch.

"Say what?"

Mike is reluctant but has to tell the truth. "I was working at this brewery, up in Seattle."

"Yeah? Which one?"

Mike's answer is again inaudible.

"Come again?"

Mike clears his throat. "Vaca Sola."

"Vaca Sola? What's that, Spanish?"

"Uh huh. I looked it up. It means 'Lonely Cow.'"

Henry is puzzled. "So, it's what, some kind of Mexican beer? But made in Seattle?"

Mike really doesn't want to say much more, but he can see that Henry is curious. "Er, Peruvian."

Henry says, "I'm not following this. You were in Seattle, but you were making Peruvian beer?"

Mike hangs his head, ashamed. "Well, it wasn't totally Peruvian. Hell, it wasn't even real beer. These two guys, they make it out of rice and sawdust, I dunno, and sell it to the kind of bars where they drink white wine and bottled water and weird foreign beers."

He's relieved that Henry is quietly laughing. "So, now we know you take correspondence courses, and you work in a bootleg brewery."

"Yeah, but then I got laid off. I guess it was all the late hours studying. I fell asleep, and this batch of beer I was watching, it kind of blew up."

Henry is laughing harder now. "How much kind of?"

"Pretty much totally. The roof mostly ended up in the parking lot. Man, there were suds, I mean, it coulda been Christmas if it didn't stink."

"And that's when you knew you just had to be a private detective."

Mike's pride is touched. "No, sir! I *always* knew that! A detective is what I always wanted to be, ever since I was a kid. I used to watch all those shows—Columbo and Rockford—and I read all the books—Hammett and Chandler. And the movies! Bogart. Mitchum. Elliot Gould—"

"Elliott Gould?"

"I guess I know what you're going to say. A screw-up like me can never make it in this fast-paced, action- oriented profession."

"You guess wrong. Listen, Mike, this business is not exactly—"

Mike interrupts. "That's just what I used to think, until I saw the ad for the Professor Ernest Hardaker Academy of Investigative Science. I took every course they offered, and I was good, really good. Would it surprise you to know that Professor Hardaker wrote me personally to say that I was the best student in the history of the school?"

Henry doesn't want to crush the youngster's dreams, but it's time to re-establish which side of the line between reality and BS they're on. He says, "Would it surprise you to know that I never heard of this Hardaker?"

Mike doesn't get to answer because they have arrived at the courthouse. Henry parks the car halfway into a bus stop and puts on his four-way flashers. "Need to move quick."

They pass through the ornate metal doors on the corner entrance to the gray stone building.

"What are we doing here?" Mike asks.

Henry stops in the entrance hall. "Listen, Mike. I can see you've got some funny ideas about this kind of work. So let me tell you. Forget what you've seen on TV. This business is about paper."

"Paper. Should I write this down?" He starts patting his pockets for pen and paper.

"There's not a whole lot to remember. There's two kinds of paper, court paper and repo paper."

"Okay."

"Now, court paper, that's summonses and subpoenas. What we do is pick 'em up here, find the people whose names are on the paper, identify them, hand them the paper and say: 'You are served.'"

"You are served."

Henry nods. "Right. Then there's repo paper. That's when some guy won't make his payments. We find him, take the car or whatever, and deliver it with the papers to the court impound yard. We average $75 per service on court paper, and a percentage of the return on repo. And that's it."

Mike is confused. "What do you mean, 'that's it?'"

"I mean, that's it. That's the business we're in, me and Abner. And now you."

"Well, what about crime and stake- outs? What about missing persons?"

Henry puts a consoling hand on Mike's arm. "Son, that kind of work is once in a blue moon. And it goes to the suits uptown, who get their jobs from fancy law firms. We do paper and repo —I'm paper, Abner's repo. Only crime we run into is when the finance company stiffs us on the percentage."

He pauses to let the information sink in, then he says, "Now, that's the business. You want to be in it, come on into the court-house and we'll get some paper. The bailiff's office is right this way."

Mike watches him go, and for a long moment his determination almost slips. But he gets it back, hitches his shoulders, and follows Henry.

LET'S look in on Sue Ellen. She still has Mike's letter, with the address of A. H. Abner Investigations, so she's gone there to find him. She enters and finds only Abner, with his head on his folded arms, down on the desk. It's not an encouraging sight, but she comes in anyway, nervous but determined.

"Excuse me?" she says.

Abner looks up at her. He's sober but still shaky and hungover. "What?"

"I'm looking for Mike Ishmael."

Abner spreads his arms. "Do you see him?"

"No."

"Then keep looking. Elsewhere." He lowers his arms and head back onto the desk.

Sue Ellen is not giving up. "He does work here?"

Wearily, Abner raises his head again. "Apparently."

"Could I wait for him?"

"Seriously, do I make you feel welcome?"

"No."

"But yet you still want to wait?"

She thinks about it. "Yes."

Abner has no resources to bring to a confrontation. "Then wait. But do it quietly. I'm having the inside of my head renovated."

Sue Ellen sits at Henry's desk, and regards Abner with disapproval. He puts his head back down on the desk.

She says, "My poppa used to get hangovers, till momma straightened him out. Momma says men who drink too much are limp in all the wrong places."

Abner does not look up. "I'll bet she gets shot at a lot."

The phone rings. Abner winces and groans. Sue Ellen feels sorry for him. "Want me to get that?"

Abner's only response is a grunt. Sue Ellen picks up the handset. "Abner Investigations."

She listens briefly then says, "I'm sorry, he's . . ."—she looks at Abner—"not available at the moment. Can I take a message?"

She reaches for pen and paper, writes something down. "Uh huh. I'll tell him."

She hangs up, peers at the note. "A Mr. Sal Minucci. I think he wants you to repair a car?"

Abner's response is a minimal "Uh huh." But the way his eyes move show that the call was important, though he's not going to tell that to Sue Ellen.

BACK TO MIKE AND HENRY, and "the business we're in."

The two of them are in the front seats of Henry's car, an accordion filing folder between them. Henry takes a manila envelope out of it, checks the name and address on the front, and says, "Here we go."

They get out of the car and go to the front door of a small house. Henry rings the doorbell.

While they're waiting, Henry says to Mike, "You just watch the procedure."

The door opens, revealing a hunch-shouldered little man in a ragged bathrobe. From inside the house we hear the voice of an angry woman screaming abuse.

She is saying "When I think of what I coulda been, what I coulda done . . . Thirty-two dollars you earned last week . . . what am I gonna do with thirty-two dollars?"

The man's shoulders hunch a little deeper. He addresses Henry. "Yes?"

"Mr. Angelo Caprioni?" When the man nods, Henry hands him a manila envelope. "You are served, sir."

The man regards the envelope stoically. "I've been expecting this."

He goes despondently into the house, leaving the door open. Henry and Mike watch him go, then head back to the car. They can still hear the woman shouting.

"Didn't I tell you it would come to this? My friends told me don't you never marry no accordion player! If only I'd listened!"

Mike looks back at the house's open door. "That wasn't so hard."

Henry nods "Usually that way."

They get into the car, Henry starts it up, and they drive away.

We can still hear the angry woman. "You're not even a *good* accordion player! *Lady of Spain*, for god's sake!"

There is a brief pause, then, "What are you doing? Angelo! You put that down, Angelo!"

Now there is a gunshot, followed by silence. Then a scream.

BACK TO THE alley where the Cadillac lurks.

The Caddie is parked in the shadows. A teenage car thief sidles up to the driver's door and raps on the blacked-out window. When there is no response, he signals down the alley. A beat-up panel van swerves around the Caddie and parks in front, and more juvenile car thieves pile out. They quickly jack up the Caddie's front end, while the first thief takes a jimmy from his jacket and slips it down between the window and the door.

The door lock pops, and the first thief pulls it open. We don't see what he sees. But we see him react in horror. He backs stiffly away, and sits down against a wall.

A trickle of muddy water drips from the open door, and a small crab falls onto the pavement. A skeletal hand hooks the arm rest and pulls the door shut. The rear wheels smoke. The thieves jump into the back of their van, and the Caddie lunges forward off the jack and smashes into the van. The Caddie pushes the van forward, down the alley and out into the street where Abner's building stands.

Traffic screeches to a stop as the van surges across the street and crashes into a store. A burglar alarm rings.

Up in Abner's office, he hears the noise. He gets up and looks out of his window. He sees the Caddie and the vanity plate, and his eyes go wide and his mouth drops open. Sue Ellen comes over to look.

She says, "What is it?"

Abner rubs his eyes, looks again. "It's *him*! It *can't* be him." He turns to Sue Ellen. "Slap me."

She does, hard. Abner holds his head, moans in agony, then looks out the window again and, this time, his face is a mask of pure delight. "Still there!"

He limps to his desk, yanks open a door, and brings out a .38-caliber police-special revolver. Then he's gone, his footsteps thundering down the stairs. Moments later, Sue Ellen sees him hobble out onto the street below. She can hear sirens, and a crowd is gathering around the crashed van.

The Caddie spins its wheels in reverse, slews around in a bootlegger's turn, and disappears up the street. As it turns the corner, Abner sees it go. He is desperate to follow, and looks around for transportation.

We now turn toward a pair of minor characters, Flo and Eddy, a long-married couple who make their living as armed robbers. It so happens they are practicing their profession in the liquor store across the street from the Pequod Building. Flo sits in the driver's seat of a small convertible, at the curb, engine running. She is waiting for Eddy to come out of the store with the loot.

Now Eddy appears, a cut-down pump-action shotgun in

one hand and a paper bag full of cash in the other. He vaults into the back seat just as Abner, limping but moving fast, arrives at Flo's side of the car, pistol in hand. He yanks open her door and gets in, pushing her over on the bench seat.

She says, "Hey!"

Abner says, "I need the car!"

He guns the engine, U-turns on squealing tires, and goes after the Caddie. Eddy is thrown backwards, but then he rights himself and points the shotgun at Abner.

"I got a gun!"

"Who doesn't?" says Abner. He cranks the wheel and they screech around a corner.

WE'LL JUST CUT AWAY NOW to see what Mike and Henry are up to.

They've pulled up outside a warehouse loading dock. Henry takes an envelope out of his file folder. He and Mike get out and walk up the stairs into the warehouse.

It's a large and busy space, with cartons stacked high on shelves and workers moving them around. Henry and Mike enter and cross an open space, to where a shifty-eyed middle-aged man is moving several cartons on the prongs of a fork-lift.

Henry looks at the name on the envelope and says, "Mitch Eberhart around?"

Mitch gives him the fish-eye. "Who wants him?"

"We're friends of his."

"No you ain't," says Mitch, gunning the fork-lift and wheeling it around, making the other workers scatter. Henry runs after him. Mike stands frozen for a beat, then follows.

Mitch turns the fork-lift into an aisle between tall stacks of cartons. Henry follows, waving Mike toward the next aisle over.

"We'll box him in!"

Mike gets the message and runs that way.

Mike runs into his aisle. Ahead of him, it stretches to the end of the warehouse, crossed by other aisles at right angles. He runs down his aisle a short way, then stops to listen. He can hear the fork-lift engine. It's getting louder.

Mike runs to the first intersection, looks both ways, sees nothing, so he runs to the next one and stops to listen again. The engine sound is growing louder, but he can't tell which direction it's coming from. He jumps out into the intersection.

The cross-aisle is empty. But now the engine is very loud. Mike spins around, sees two tall cartons bearing down on him on the forks of the machine, almost completely filling the width of the cross-aisle.

There's no room to dodge and he can't outrun the machine while it's going at full speed. The only option is to leap onto the fork tines under the cartons. He reaches up and clings to the top of the uppermost carton, struggling to get a grip on the smooth surface. Now he looks over his shoulder, sees he is heading for a brick wall, and begins to panic.

"Hey, buddy! Hey, stop this thing!"

He gets no answer. The brick wall is coming up fast. There is only one thing to do, and he does it, digging his toes into the cardboard and scrambling up over the cartons. The driver looks up, surprised, as Mike clambers over the cartons toward him. Now Mitch recovers, stands up out of the seat, then vaults over its back, hits the concrete floor, and runs. Mike slides down from the cartons into the seat, follows Mitch as fast as he can.

"Hey! Stop!"

With no foot on the go-pedal, the fork-lift slows, but its momentum carries it forward to smash into the wall.

Mitch rounds a corner of the aisle, moving fast. He runs smack into Henry's elbow, held at chin-height, and falls flat.

Mike comes around the corner to see Henry drop the subpoena onto Mitch's chest.

"You are served."

He turns to Mike. "Piece of cake."

Mike says nothing. He is still shaking from the adrenaline.

NOW BACK TO Abner and the armed robbers.

The Caddie turns a corner, pulls into a gas station's parking lot, stops. The convertible with Abner and the robbers screeches around the corner and stops in the middle of the street. Eddy gets upright again, and points the shotgun at Abner.

"Hey!"

Abner ignores Eddy because he now spots the Cadillac. He snarls.

Eddy jabs the shotgun muzzle into Abner's neck and says, "Get outta the car!"

Abner turns and pushes the barrel away. He points his pistol at Eddy. "You get outta the car!"

Flo pipes up. "We stole it first!"

Then they all react as the Caddie's engine roars. The Caddie's rear wheels lay rubber, standing still amid blue smoke, then it comes screeching and fishtailing out of the gas station toward the convertible.

Abner, Flo and Eddy, in unison, say, "Holy shit!"

Abner reacts. He floors the convertible's gas pedal, and it takes off. But the Cadillac pursues them, rushing up to bump the rear of the convertible. Abner and the robbers are thrown around as their car slews from the impact. Abner aims his gun over the backseat, making Eddy duck.

Abner fires a shot but it bounces off the Caddie's windshield. Then he has to grab the wheel to try to keep the car straight.

Flo has had enough. She reaches over and grabs the wheel.

"The hell you doin'?" says Abner. "You gonna kill us!"

"Pull it over! We're getting out!"

Abner Drops the pistol in his lap and pries her hand off the wheel. "He ain't gonna let us!"

Flo looks back at the Caddie, sees it gaining on them again. "Eddy! Do something!"

But Eddy's not sure what to do. He points the shotgun at Abner, who pays no attention, then at the Cadillac,, which comes and bumps their rear again, knocking Eddy over in the back seat again.

Abner yanks the wheel as they come to an intersection, cars screeching and slewing as the convertible runs a red light and the Caddie comes fishtailing after.

Eddy rights himself in the back seat. He's made up his mind. He pumps a round into the shotgun's chamber and fires at the Caddie. The shot bounces off. He pumps another round.

The Cadillac charges forward and hits the rear of the convertible just as Eddy pulls the trigger. But he's knocked off balance again and the shot goes high into the air.

ANOTHER BRIEF ASIDE: a low-rent apartment where an old man and an old woman sit at a rickety table, eating porridge. The man is peering at *The Racing Times*, but has trouble seeing it because a large plant hanging in the window blocks the light.

He says, "Oh, God, will you get rid of that ugly plant?"

A shotgun blast blows out the window, hurling the plant across the room to smash against the wall. The old man looks up in amazement, then his face lights up with an idea.

He folds his hands and looks piously at the ceiling. "God, will you let Teddy Bear win in the fourth today?"

NOW BACK TO the car chase. The convertible slews around as Abner fights for control.

Flo shouts, "Look out!"

The Caddie bumps them, and the convertible slews sideways toward a sidewalk. Flo grabs the wheel, trying to steer.

Abner says, "Leggo!"

They fight for control of the wheel. Meanwhile, the convertible crosses the parking lot of a bankrupt supermarket that has been converted into a revival hall.

There are only a few rows of chairs, with a wide aisle between them, set up in the empty store, where the shelves have been pushed aside to make enough space for a small crowd—none of them too prosperous-looking—who are listlessly enduring a sermon from a preacher in a worn black suit who stands behind a lectern on an elevated wooden platform. His wife, who has gone heavy on the make-up, is vamping on a small electric organ. Tears streak her mascara.

The preacher whispers to his wife, "Dammit, we're losing them. Start passing the plate."

She gets up and gets a tattered basket with a cardboard cross on it.

The preacher returns to his sermon, upping the volume, "And I say unto you, sinners come unto me! Come wailin' and screamin', come in the haste of your sinnin', but come unto me!"

He throws his arms wide. "Come unto me, *right now!*"

The convertible smashes through the windows, with Abner, Flo, and Eddy all screaming. It rips down the aisle between the chairs, scattering the few people there, and crashes into the preacher's platform, which collapses.

Abner and the robbers are buried under wreckage. The preacher ends up sprawled across the hood of the convertible. His wife sits in the wreckage of the organ, which wheezes sadly at her.

Bills from Eddy's bag of loot float down around them.

Dazed, the preacher looks up at the falling cash. "My god, it works."

Then he faints.

Out on the street, the Cadillac rocks impatiently as it shifts from drive to reverse with the brakes on.

Sirens sound in the distance. After a few seconds the Caddie drives away.

Now we're in another part of the city. A gleaming limousine pulls up in front of a modest building. A chauffeur with a military bearing gets out and opens the rear door for Nordling. The chauffeur snaps to attention. Nordling nods and enters the building.

On an upper floor, Nordling exists an elevator and approaches a door on which is a plaque that reads: *Owen G. Hamlin P.Eng.—Mining Engineer*. He looks up and down the corridor, sees no one, and enters.

Down on the street outside the building we find Henry and Mike walking along the sidewalk and entering the building. In the foyer, Henry checks the directory against a manila envelope, finds Hamlin's name and office number. He crosses to the elevator and presses the button.

He tells Mike, "Done this guy before. Blows his money on booze and horses, then can't pay his alimony. He's going to run the moment he spots me."

"What do we do?"

"Make sure he runs in the right direction."

Up in Hamlin's office, which has seen better days, an empty whiskey bottle sits on a credenza. Hamlin is Nordling's size but sloppy and a little boozy, like Jim Backus after a few too many mai-tais. He is showing Nordling two objects that sit on a copy of *The Racing Times* spread on his desk: a small, black plastic box with a button switch and two electric terminals; and a slim plastic tube with two wires protruding from one end. The word *DANGER* and the symbol for explosives is printed on the tube.

Hamlin picks up the black box. "This is your basic impact switch, same sort of thing makes your airbag go off. You connect it to the detonator here,"—he touches the tube—"then insert the detonator into the main explosive. Set the switch to on, and the next time it registers an impact, it sends a jolt that fires the detonator, and that lights up the big bang."

NORDLING PICKS UP THE TUBE. "Excellent. The plan is now complete. These devices will turn a boatload of ordinary farm fertilizer into the opening shot of the second American Revolution."

Hamlin belches. "The politics are your concern. Where's my fee?"

"Come to my estate tomorrow at two. We'll conclude our arrangement there—after you've installed these. Bring them with you."

Hamlin's face turns red. "Hey, that's not our deal!"

Nordling's expression is remote and full of disdain. "The deal has changed."

Hamlin scoops up the bomb components, holds them to his chest. "Then I want another five grand! And I want it right now!"

Nordling gives the engineer a hard stare. Hamlin almost backs down, but he wants the money. Finally Nordling relents.

"Very well. But when you come, come sober."

He takes out his wallet, counts out bills, tosses them contemptuously onto the desk. He leaves as Hamlin is gathering the money.

NORDLING LEAVES Hamlin's office and walks toward the elevator. It arrives before he reaches it. Mike stands inside, holding down the open-door button. Henry comes out of the fire stairs doorway and sees Nordling, and hurries after him.

"Mr. Hamlin!" Nordling turns and Henry sees it's not the guy he's looking for. "Oh, sorry, sir. My mistake."

Nordling regards him with disdain and walks to the elevator, from which Mike is now emerging, looking from Nordling to Henry. Henry waves both hands at Mike in a gesture that says "forget it."

Mike gets back in the elevator. Nordling enters and gives him a scornful look.

"Ground floor."

Mike pushes the button. He and Nordling ride down together. The lightning bolt pin in Nordling's lapel gleams in the overhead light. Mike notices it.

BACK UPSTAIRS, Hamlin comes out of his office, counting the wad of money Nordling gave him, the racing paper under his arm. He goes to the elevator, pushes the button and waits.

Henry peeks out of the fire stairs door. Hamlin sees him, recognizes him, and takes off down the corridor. Henry rushes in pursuit, noting in passing that the elevator is still several floors below on its way up.

Hamlin throws up a window at the end of the hallway and jumps out onto a fire escape. He begins a rapid descent.

By the time Henry pokes his head out of the window, Hamlin is halfway to the ground. Henry shrugs and gives up.

HENRY DRIVES. He pulls a legal paper from the brown envelope and glances through it, then hands it to Mike. "Last one. You want to try it?"

Mike looks at the envelope. "What is it?"

"Business dispute. Lady runs a store, won't pay her suppliers."

THE PLACE IS an up-market hat store. Some well-to-do elderly women customers are trying on hats. The owner, a grandmotherly type, is behind the counter as Henry's car pulls up outside the window. Mike gets out, holding the envelope.

As he enters the store, the owner smiles and says, "May I help you?"

"Mrs. Louise Ignatieff?"

Her face changes. She spots the envelope. "Yes?"

He offers her the envelope. "This is for you."

She looks at the envelope but makes no move to take it. Then she gasps audibly and steps back from the counter, holding her hands up in the air. The hat-buying ladies look up to see what's going on.

Mike says, "I mean, you are served."

The store owner smiles sweetly and says, softly, "We'll see

about that, dear." Then she screams and cries, "Help! Help me! He's a pervert! Oh my God! Get away! Help!"

Mike's mouth falls open. The customers are in shock. Then they rush Mike and beat him with handbags and umbrellas.

"How awful!"

"Disgusting!"

"How dare you!"

One of them blows a whistle while another brings a can of pepper spray out of her purse. She tries to mace him.

Meanwhile the owner is egging them on. "Oh, you horrible little man! I' m old enough to be your grandmother! You should be ashamed of yourself!"

Still under attack, Mike scrambles to the door, hands over his head. He emerges onto the street and dive's head-first through the passenger-side front window of Henry's car.

Mrs. Ignatieff beams as the car speeds away.

Mike gets himself straight in the passenger seat. Henry looks him over, laughs.

"Guess old Professor Hardaker forgot to cover that one. Maybe we better try some repo work."

Mike is still shaken. "No more little old ladies."

Henry pulls up at a streetside phone booth. "I just need to check in with Abner."

Mike sits in the car, reshaping his battered hat, while Henry uses the phone. Across the street is the closed supermarket-turned-revival hall, where ambulances are taking away the injured. A tow truck hauls away the convertible.

Henry gets connected. "Hello?"

After a pause, he says, "Who is this? Where's Abner?" He listens again, then says, "I see. Well, this is Henry Queeg, his partner."

He starts to say something else but the voice on the other end of the line interrupts him. He responds, "Uh huh. Yes, he's with me. We'll be back in this afternoon."

He's hearing a lot, but he interrupts to say. "We can't do that now. But you're welcome to wait. And if Abner comes in, please tell him we'll be there. Goodbye.

He hangs up, shakes his head, a little bemused, and gets back behind the wheel.

Mike sees the look on Henrys face. "Everything okay?"

"I dunno. You know a girl name of Sue Ellen Vanderhog?"

Mike perks right up. "She's my case!"

"What case?"

"I told you, it's a missing persons caper, her brother . . . I don't have too many details.

"I told *you*, we don't do missing persons."

"But—"

Henry eases up a little. "How about we discuss this after we've finished the paying work? She's waiting for you at the office. She says Abner went out to recover a stolen car or something, and he hasn't come back."

He shakes his head again, looking idly at the ambulances. "I don't know what that man's getting into." He sighs then, "Ah hell, let's go repo something."

BACK IN ABNER'S OFFICE, Sue Ellen is shocked to see the detective limp through the door, his head wrapped in a bandage and his cane taped up in the middle. But the hangover is forgotten. He's now firing on all cylinders.

"Mr. Abner! Are you all right?"

He gives her a "who the hell are you" look, then remembers. He doesn't answer, waves away the question, and goes to the phone.

She looks at a pad on the desk and says, "A Mr. Queeg called." Abner grunts. "He'll be in this afternoon."

Abner grunts, dialing a number. When it answers, he says. "Lemme talk to Jerry . . . Well, go get him."

He waits impatiently, then says, "Jerry? Abner. I want you to put the word out on the street. A 1960 Cadillac, white with blacked-out windows, vanity plate says Modie." He gets interrupted and shouts down the phone, "Yeah, *that* Modie."

More interruption, more shouting. "I dunno how, but I *seen* it."

He takes a wad of bills from his pocket. "Listen, I been to the bank, got ten brand new C-notes. You hear that?" He crinkles money near the phone's mouthpiece. "They go to the guy leads me to that car. Yeah, so get lookin'."

He hangs up, dials another number, and when it connects, he says, "Tina? Abner. I want you to do somethin', put the word out."

HENRY'S CAR is out front of a rickety frame house. Henry and Mike are further up the street. Henry is hot-wiring a Mercedes, while Mike, nervous, stands look-out by the open driver's door. The engine starts, and Henry gets out.

He says, "Bet the good professor didn't teach you that one either."

"It wasn't part of the curriculum."

Henry says, "Now, you get in. Lock the doors. The man comes, you drive slowly away. Keep him running, a block or two, then take off. Meet me over at Pine and Ellis."

Mike is confused. "What man? What's he look like?"

Henry smiles. "You'll know him when he gets here. He'll be the one wants to kill you."

That doesn't reassure Mike but he gets into the car and shuts and locks the door. Henry walks back to the rickety house, goes up the steps and stops at the screen door. From inside the house there is the sound of rap turned up loud. He bangs on the door and waits.

A young man dressed gangsta style comes to the door. "Yeah?"

"Pardon me, sir, but is that your Mercedes Benz down the block?"

The man opens the screen door, sticks his head out to looks. "What?"

Henry says, "I think somebody's stealing it.

The man reacts. He vaults down the front steps and runs toward his car, shouting, "Hey, shithead! That's my ride!"

The Mercedes moves slowly away, the owner chasing it. Henry, still on the porch, watches the man go. Then he peeks into the house and enters. The sound of the rap stops. Henry comes out of the house carrying a stereo. He puts it on the back seat of his car, gets in and drives off.

The man comes running back down the street. "Hey, man! My tunes!" He has to jump out of the car's path then can only watch it go, furious. "Shee-it!"

AT THE INTERSECTION of Pine and Ellis, Mike stops the Mercedes at the curb near the corner, rolls down the window and looks out and back, pleased with himself. Henry drives up beside Mike, and leans across the front seat.

"Follow me to the impound yard."

He drives on, and Mike follows.

A few moments later, the Caddie cruises to the stop sign, turns the corner and drives on. A scruffy little man is in a phone booth, watching the Caddie and talking excitedly on the phone.

BACK IN ABNER'S OFFICE, Sue Ellen enters with paper sacks of take-out food. Abner is on the phone, taking notes, slips of paper all over his desk.

"Gimme that again. Yeah. Bleecker and Nineteenth. Okay, okay. But this doesn't help me. I need to know when he *stops*. Yeah, right, later."

He hangs up and notices Sue Ellen. She offers one of the sacks. "I brought you a sandwich and coffee."

Abner waves her away. "No time for coffee."

He gathers up the slips of paper and goes to look a city street map tacked to the wall. He checks his notes and pushes colored pins into various places the map. They tend to cluster in one neighborhood. He stares at the map, his brow wrinkled.

Sue Ellen puts a cup of coffee under his nose, and he takes it and sips automatically. She nods in approval, takes back the cup, and replaces it with a sandwich. He bites and chews, mechanically, eyes on the map. When he speaks, it's to himself. "The hell is he doin'?"

The phone on his desk rings. He doesn't take his eyes off the map.

"Get that, will you?"

HENRY AND MIKE are sitting in Henry's car outside a downtown construction site surrounded by a wooden fence. The project is in the ground-clearing phase. They're just finishing a take-out lunch. Henry checks his watch.

A large flatbed truck comes up the street behind them, passes, and parks in a loading zone a half-block farther on, its engine running. The flat-bed's driver's helper gets out and cranks down a heavy-duty ramp from the back of the trailer, then signals 'thumbs-up' to Henry. Henry and Mike get out of the car.

Mike is a little apprehensive. "Is this gonna work?"

Henry shrugs. "You want to know the future, call a psychic. Now, you know what to do."

Mike walks around the car and gets in the driver's seat. Henry ambles over to the construction site entrance and looks around. Heavy equipment is grading the site, with a small bulldozer in the middle of the action. Near the entrance Henry spots a trailer with a hard-hat and clipboard on its steps. He walks onto the site, puts on the hat and picks up the clipboard. He walks to where the dozer is being operated by a beer-bellied catskinner.

Henry shouts over the diesel noise. "Hey! You Raznowski?"

The catskinner shouts back. "Yeah?"

Henry tilts back the hardhat. "Super wants you!" He gestures over his shoulder with his thumb. "In the office!"

The catskinner climbs down, leaving the engine running.

HENRY PRETENDS to be checking the clipboard until the catskinner moves far enough off. Then he tosses it and the hard-hat away. He climbs up on the dozer, settles into the driver's seat, and yanks at the levers. The machine slews around, engine roaring.

Almost to the office, the catskinner turns and his mouth falls open. "Hey! Hold it!"

Henry is having some difficulty mastering the dozer's controls. He shouts back at the catskinner, "It's okay. All under control."

The catskinner takes a step toward him. "Wait a goddamn minute!"

Henry gets the bulldozer turned around and moving toward the entrance. The catskinner jumps out of the way.

As he passes him, Henry shouts, "Shoulda made your payments!"

The catskinner catches on. He swears and chases after the bulldozer. Henry gets the machine up to speed and heads for the site exit. But a dump truck pulls in from the street and blocks the way out.

The catskinner is running hard to catch him. Henry yanks the control levers, and the bulldozer spins to the right, heading straight for the fence. Out on the street, pedestrians scatter as the fence around the site suddenly collapses and the bulldozer plows through it, flattens a street sign, and crosses the road. Cars skid and screech to a stop.

Henry has the pedal to the floor. He looks back and sees the catskinner stumbling over the wreckage then dodging traffic to cross the street. He shouts to the driver of the flatbed, "Move!"

The truck inches forward, its ramp striking sparks from the street. Henry rounds the corner, and drives the dozer up the ramp. The driver's helper cranks the ramp up and jumps onto the bed, throwing chains over the bulldozer.

Henry kills the engine and drops off the side of the dozer onto the flatbed. Mike drives up close beside the truck, with the passenger-side window open. Henry slides through the window into the moving car.

"Floor it!"

They drive away, leaving the catskinner to fling his hardhat down onto the pavement. Swearing, he kicks the hat and sends it flying.

Mike drives, the adrenaline pumping through him. Henry says, "Hooee!"

Mike says, "This kind of work, does it often involve being chased by angry people after we've just taken away their most cherished possessions?"

"Now that you mention it," Henry says, "that does seem to crop up pretty regular."

"What happens if they catch us?"

Henry's smile is impish. "Probably best not to find out."

BACK AT THE OFFICE, Mike and Henry find Abner with the phone's handset cradled between his neck and jaw as he sticks another pin in the map. The hundred-dollar bills are pinned to the map. Sue Ellen is on the other phone, taking notes.

Abner, pushing in another pin, says, "Amsterdam and Sixteenth, yeah. Headin' west, an' he passed that way twice in the last ten minutes? Well, if he stops, call me!"

Sue Ellen, meanwhile, is talking into the phone, "Main and Johnston, is that with a 't'?" She sees Mike and smiles, gives him a little wave. Then, "Yes, ma'am, I'll tell him directly. Thank you."

Mike says, "Sue Ellen!" and goes over to her. But when he gets there, he's not sure what to do. Handshake? Kiss?

She solves the dilemma by standing up and giving him a hug and a kiss on the cheek. "I'm really glad to see you."

Henry, meanwhile, has gone to look at Abner's map. "What's with all the pins, partner?"

Abner doesn't answer but looks to Sue Ellen. "Main and Johnston?"

She confirms it, though her attention is now solely focused on Mike. "Uh huh."

Henry takes Abner's arm. "Abner?"

Abner pushes in another pin, then turns to his partner. "It's Modie! He's back!"

Henry sighs, looks around. "Where's the bottle, Abner?"

"No bottle. And no shit! He was right out there! Totaled the Gypsy Boys' strip-and-rip van, then he took off. I grabbed some asshole's car and chased him, but the bastard ran me off the road!"

He sees the disbelief in Henry's face and says, "I'm not shittin ya, Henry! Ask whatsername, she saw him too!"

Henry looks to Sue Ellen.

"It was a big old Cadillac, all white. Had some green stuff on it, like seaweed."

Henry is skeptical. "They made a lot of those white Caddies."

Abner is exasperated. "I'm tellin ya, it was Modie! An' he tried to kill me!"

Henry is still not buying it. "You ever think somebody might be playing a joke on you, Abner?"

"Joke, my ass! That thing was armored, it bounced a slug from my 38 and a load of double-ought off the windshield! Pointblank!"

Henry rubs a hand over his face. "This is nuts, Abner. You recognize it as nuts, right? I mean, your average dead hoodlums don't pop up in their cars after twenty-five years at the bottom of the harbor, and start trying to run down middle-aged private detectives. It kind of sticks out from the daily routine."

Abner is deadly serious. "Hey, Henry, you wanna laugh, laugh. If he's got Jimmy Hoffa ridin' shotgun and the Loch Ness Monster in the trunk, I don't give a rat's ass! That's Modie, he's tryin' to kill me, and I'm gonna get him. Don't know where he's been all these years, but I know where he's *gonna* be! He's gonna be *dead*, an' he's gonna *stay* dead!"

Henry struggles to get his head around it. "But, what the hell? I mean why, after all these years, is he back?"

Abner takes hold of Henry's arms and looks him right in the eye. "Henry, who cares? For me, it's enough he's back and I got a shot at him. Dead or alive"—he slaps his bad leg— "I owe that bastard."

Abner turns back to his map.

Mike clears his throat. "Er, Henry?" When Henry turns to him and Sue Ellen, still a little foggy, Mike says, "Am I done for the day?"

He doesn't get an answer so he presses on. "It's just that I'd like to follow up with Sue Ellen. She's my, er, missing persons case."

Henry's brows contract. "I told you, we don't—"

"I'll do it on my own time."

Henry looks back at Abner, his partner intent on the map, and shrugs. "What the hell, go ahead."

Mike "Great!" He turns to Sue Ellen. "Come on!"

But Abner says, "Whoa! Wait, wait, wait! You're still on the clock, kid. Here." He limps over to his desk, opens a drawer and pulls out portable radio. "Take this. You see a white Caddie, blacked-out windows, you follow him and call it in. Got it?"

Mike takes the radio, but looks to Henry. "Uh, my missing persons—"

Abner comes up close. "I said, got it?"

Mike slumps a little. "Got it, Mr. Abner."

"Good boy."

Abner immediately forgets Mike and goes back to his map. Mike and Sue Ellen exit. The phone rings and Abner grabs it. "Yeah. Where?" He calls to Henry, "Eighteenth and Howard, southbound, mark it."

Henry sticks a pin in the map and looks at the pattern. Abner comes over and together they study the map.

Abner says, "He don't stop. Just keeps circlin' round this general area." He taps the map.

Henry says, "Yeah. Like he's looking for something."

While they are talking, Sue Ellen comes back, goes to retrieve the purse she left on Henry's desk. "Excuse me, forgot my purse."

She overhears them and, instead of leaving again, she comes up behind Abner and Henry. She examines the map.

After a good look, she says, "Mr. Abner, it's maybe not my place to say anything, but it seems to me if you want to find that car, you should just stand out on the street."

Abner notices her. "What?"

"Well, I don't know San Francisco too well," she says, "but by this map, I'd say that car's been driving around *this* neighborhood all afternoon. Well, bye now."

And she's gone.

Henry says, "She's right, Abner." He takes a deep breath. "Okay. I'm going to just put aside a whole lifetime devoted to reason and rationality, and I'm going to accept that that really is Modie Bick out there."

Abner says, "Why is that so hard to do? I did it first time."

Henry continues, "And then I'm going to accept that you don't need to look for him anymore. Because I think *he's* looking for *you*. You want to find, Modie, just step outside, he'll be by."

Abner sees the light. "Jeez-Louise, you're right!"

He gets his gun out of the desk drawer, loads it, heads for the door. But Henry blocks him.

"Wait a minute! What do you think you're going to do with a .38? On a bulletproof Caddie, you might as well throw popcorn! We've got to get the SFPD in on this."

Abner shakes his head. "Uh uh. This is between Modie and me." He thinks for a moment. "But you're right about the .38. Need more firepower."

He grabs the phone, dials, waits, then says, "Sal? Abner. That piece of goods I heard you were tryin' to sell?" He listens, impatiently. "I ain't got time for you bein' cute. If you still got that thing, and it's here in twenty minutes, I'll give you what you're askin'. An' a hundred more for some clips of armor-piercing."

MIKE's FIREBIRD is parked down the street from Abner's building. Mike and Sue Ellen get in. Mike puts the radio on the dash.

Mike says, "Okay, let's see about finding Duane."

"But your boss said . . ."

"He said, drive around and look for a white Caddie. I can do that while we're looking for your brother. Now,"—he gets out notepad and pen—"how 'bout you tell me the background?"

Sue Ellen takes a moment to gather her thoughts, then, "Well Duane left the farm—we have a little corn farm in Iowa —and came here two years ago."

Mike makes a note "Uh huh." He looks at her. "You know, you have the most amazing eyes."

She looks down at her hands as she clasps them in her lap. "Well, like I say, Duane came to the city a couple of years ago, and it was okay—Dad said he needed time to find himself, you know?"

Mike has stopped taking notes. "And your voice, it's got kind of like a musical tone to it—"

"Mike!"

"What?"

She's a little embarrassed. "We could talk like this later."

Mike collects himself. "Yeah, what am I doing? You're all worried about your brother, and I'm . . . Okay, just the facts." He steadies himself and makes another note. "Duane came to find himself. But now he's missing?"

"Mmmm, not _really_ missing. I had this address for him, but last spring, he stopped answering my letters. And I need to get him to come home for a while."

"Why's that?"

She frowns a little. "It's these Sunshiners."

"Sunshiners?"

"Well, that's what folks call them. They're followers of the Reverend Sun. He's that guru, thinks everybody ought to love bugs, or something, I don't know."

Mike says, "I see," though he doesn't.

She continues, "The Sunshiners came in last year, and they

bought a little land, then they bought a little more. Now they own about most of the county, 'cept for our farm and a few other places."

Mike has figured it out. He points the pen at her. "And you want to get your brother back to help stop these Sunshiners from taking over."

He's beginning to imagine going up to Idaho, doing some digging, saving the day. But he's way off, and Sue Ellen sets him straight.

"Why, no, not at all."

"Oh. Then why?"

"Well it's like this. The Reverend Sun made us two offers for the farm. Some cash and preferred stock in one of his holding companies, or a straight trade for a tract of houses in Ames. That's where the cult used to be based, but now there are too many new—what do they call them?—Sunbeams."

"So what's this got to do with Duane?"

"It's 'cause he's the only one in the family who can figure worth a darn—we never had much schooling—Papa wants him to look the deal over and decide what to do."

Mike blinks. "Okay, all right. I think I'm getting it. Now, you had that address where Duane was picking up his mail. Did you go there and ask?"

"Well, yes, I did. Funny thing is, the man there said he'd never heard of Duane. But I just don't think he was telling me the truth."

Mike starts the engine. "Then we'd better check it out."

Sue Ellen gives him the envelope. "This is the address, and I have this photo from when Duane won second place in the League of Rights statewide essay writing contest." She hands him a photo.

The photo of Duane shows a conservative young man in a suit and tie, holding a plaque that bears a lightning bolt symbol identical to the one Nordling wore in his lapel.

Mike studies it. "Essay contest, eh? What was his topic?"

"The history of international conspiracies."

Mike nods, then reacts. "International conspiracies?"

Sue Ellen shakes her head. "Duane's kinda funny, you know?"

Mike looks at the photo again. Something about it bothers him. Then he twigs.

"Hmmm."

"What is it?" Sue Ellen says.

"That lightning bolt thing. I've seen it somewhere, just recently."

But it won't come to him. He shakes his head and drives off. His car moves down the street, turns a corner. Moments later, the Caddie cruises by in another direction.

MIKE'S CAR pulls up to the curb outside the survivalists' store. He looks it over, sees nothing much.

"This the place?"

"Yes."

He opens the door "You wait here, okay?"

She puts a hand on his arm. "Be careful. Some of Duane's friends can be a little . . . peculiar."

Mike gets out, looks the place over, pulls down his fedora, hitches his shoulders, and enters.

Kassen is behind the counter. Three more of Nordling's troopers lounge around. They are all suspicious of Mike.

"The name's Ishmael. I'm a P.I. with Abner Investigations."

Klassen gives him a deadpan stare. "I'm so impressed."

Mike produces the photo of Duane. "His name's Vanderhog. You know him?"

Klassen doesn't even glance at it. "Nope."

"How about you look at it first?"

Klassen looks at the photo. "Nope."

"That's funny, you being his mailbox."

Klassen shakes his head. "Never seen him. What you want him for?"

Mike can do his own deadpan stare. He's practiced it. "What do you care? You don't know him."

Klassen shrugs. Now, the three others crowd around Mike, and the vibe is unfriendly. He notices they all have lightning bolt pins on their shirt collars. So does Klassen. Mike starts to get nervous.

One of the troopers, a big, blond who has spent most of his life in bodybuilder gyms, crowds in on Mike. "What you say your name was?"

"Ishmael. Mike Ishmael."

"Ishmael. What kinda name is that? You one a them New York Jewboys?"

A second trooper, lean and sinewy, with a piece of neck tattoo peeking over his collar, says "I think he's a New York faggot. Got a New York faggot hat."

He tips Mike's fedora brim down over his eyes.

Mike says, "Now, wait a minute, you guys."

The first trooper gets right in Mike's face. "That what you are? A New York Jewboy faggot come around asking a lot of New York Jewboy faggot questions?"

The third trooper wants to get in on this, "I bet he's one of them secular humanist, illuminati-lovin', New World Order, black-helicopter-ridin', flag-burnin', planned parenthood, free-tradin', United Nations, godless-liberal-rat-bastards!"

The others look at him, genuinely impressed. Then Klassen gestures toward the door with his head. The troopers pick Mike up by the shoulders of his coat and carry him out of the store.

"Hey, what is this?" Mike says. "You guys better ease off."

The bodybuilder spots Mike's Firebird. "That your car, faggot?"

"Uh huh."

The lean one opens the car door. The other two up-end Mike and throw him head-first into the car. He lands on top of Sue Ellen.

The big blond kicks the door shut then leans in the window. "Y'all have a nice day."

The three goons laugh and go back into the store.

Mike scrambles into the driver's seat, mortified. He rights his hat and stares through the windshield .

Sue Ellen is sensitive to his feelings. "I think you handled that with dignity, considering. Those are just the kind of jerks Duane always hung out with."

Mike lets out a long breath, looks over at her, looks at the store as if thinking about going back in, then decides it would be dumb. He starts up the car, and drives away.

IN THE STORE, as the troopers come back in, Klassen is on the phone.

"Yes, sir, Vanderhog's sister. This time she brought the guy she called before, a P.I. from that Abner Investigations." He listens, then says, "Yes, sir, will do."

Klassen hangs up the phone, turns to the others. "Saddle up. The Commander wants to talk to that asshole."

"Oh, boy," says the speechmaker.

BACK AT ABNER'S OFFICE, a shifty-eyed hoodlum named Sal Minucci is working the action on an K-47 assault rifle with a folding stock. Abner is watching closely. Henry is not happy.

Sal, says, "This here's your safety, this here's your semi, and this is your full automatic. She pulls up and to the left."

Abner takes the weapon, sights along the barrel. "Where's the ammo?"

Sal reaches into a suitcase by his feet and produces a canvas ammo bag. "Three clips. And, like you said, two clips, armor-piercing. Chew up a concrete wall, these mothers."

Abner takes the bag, hands over the wad of bills. Sal quickly counts and pockets the cash, then reaches into the suit-case. Henry quietly draws a nickel-plated 45 automatic from beneath his jacket.

Henry keeps his voice neutral. "What you got there, Sal?"

Sal comes up with an Uzi-type machine pistol with a long clip. "Thought you might want something else. Three hundred rounds a minute, lightweight, handy for close work."

Abner eyes the weapon. "How much?"

"Nother deuce, throw in three clips of ammo for another C."

Henry says, "At that price, it's hot, Abner."

Abner doesn't care. "I'll take it. Henry, give him the money."

"Put it on the desk, Sal, and stand back."

Sal does, and Henry puts down his automatic long enough to reluctantly counts bills out of his wallet and hand them over. "Now, get outta here, Sal."

Sal says, "I'd like to tell you about our buy-back offer, once you're finished with the goods."

Abner ignores him, working the AK-47 action, sighting along it.

Henry takes Sal's arm. "Sal, maybe you haven't noticed, but we've become crazy people today. I think you'd better leave."

When the hoodlum is gone, Henry says, "Abner . . ."

"Leave it, Henry. I'm doin' this." He puts the ammo clips in his pockets. "Where's that kid? He ain't called in."

Henry sighs. "He's probably looking for clues."

Abner says, "Get him on the radio. Tell him to get back here."

Henry shakes his head. "Let's don't get him mixed up in this."

"We may need somebody to watch the phones, okay?"

"Okay. But that's all, right?"

MIKE'S FIREBIRD is parked at the curb next to a taco truck, Sue Ellen in the passenger seat. Mike gets two tacos from the truck, gets into the car, hands one to her. She bobbles it and it drips.

Mike sees and says, "Sorry. You do like these don't you?"

"I don't think these kinda trucks have made it to Swift Current."

Mike shrugs. "I'm not crazy about 'em, either. Just seems kind of a traditional thing." He takes a bite, chews and swallows. "So, once we find Duane, you'll be going home?"

"We're not having much luck so far."

"Oh, we'll find him."

"How?"

Mike is confident. "I don't know yet, but something will turn up. That's one of the things I always loved about the detective game—just when you need something to keep the action moving, bang, it pops right up."

He sees her skepticism. "You'll see."

The radio on the dash squawks. Henry's voice says, "Mike? This is Henry."

Mike grabs the radio, fiddles with controls. "Yeah, I mean roger, over, ten-four."

"Come on in, Mike. Back to the office."

Mike is enjoying the whole radio thing. "Will do, er, ten-four." He wolfs down the rest of his taco and starts the car. "I bet Henry could help us find Duane."

Sue Ellen is chewing a mouthful. She swallows and says, "I

hope so. I'm starting to worry about him. Duane never had a lick of sense about the people he associated with."

OVER TO THE street outside Abner Investigation. A nondescript sedan pulls up to the curb across from the building. Klassen is driving with his three troopers in the passenger seats. One of them says, "No sign of that old Firebird."

KLASSEN SAYS, "WE'LL WAIT."

The Caddie cruises down the street. Abner, watching from the window, sees it.

"Holy shit!"

He grabs the AK-47and stuffs it under his jacket. He heads for the stairwell. Moments later, he comes out of the building's front doors and limps out into the middle of the street. But the Caddie is out of sight. He hops from foot to foot, frustrated, watching for it. Now Henry comes out of the building, stands on the sidewalk, hesitating about trying to bring Abner back inside when he's in a manic state.

Mike and Sue Ellen drive up in the Firebird and park across the street, right in front of Klassen's car.

Klassen says, "Come on," and the four of them climb out of the car.

Mike and Sue Ellen are still in his car. He hands the radio to Sue Ellen. "Put this under your seat. I don't want it stolen."

Abner's shoulders slump. He turns back toward the building. But just then the Caddie turns a corner. Immediately, it speeds toward him. He sees it, makes no effort to get out of the way. Instead, he pulls out the AK-47 and fires a burst at the car.

The Cadillac's windshield stars, but it keeps on coming.

Klassen and his boys duck behind their car. Klassen

watches the action, then uses hand signals to tell his goons to sneak up beside Mike's car.

Meanwhile, Henry has rushed into the street. He grabs Abner and drags him out of the car's path in the nick of time. The Caddie roars off, rounds a corner, and is gone.

Mike and Sue Ellen are still in the Firebird, stunned at what they've just seen. Mike turns to her. "What the—"

He freezes because he sees Klassen is at Sue Ellen's open window. He is holding a handgun to her head. He says, "Okay 'sister,' in the back."

He pulls open her door.

Mike says, "Wait a minute . . ."

Klassen cocks the pistol and says, "We'll have lots of time to talk later. Move."

Sue Ellen gets out of the car and into the back seat. Klassen gets in beside her, and one of his boys gets into the front seat, holding a gun on Mike.

"Drive."

Mike looks over at Henry and Abner across the street, but they have been too busy to notice the kidnapping. Mike starts up the car and drives away.

Henry is saying, "Abner, we can't shoot up cars in the street. We're not on the force anymore. Let's get out of here before the cops show up."

Abner looks up the street to the corner when the Cadillac turned. "You're right. Get the Uzi and the radio. We'll go look for the bastard."

He hobbles over to Henry's car and gets in the passenger seat.

Henry hesitates, says to himself, "Why do I have a bad feeling about this?"

But he realizes Abner will just go looking for Modie without him. He gives up, goes back into the building, and comes out with the handheld radio and the Uzi.

So, now we go to Nordling's seaside estate, where Mike is turning into a driveway barred by heavy iron gates. The name *KARINHALL* is in gold lettering on the arch above the gates. Mike stops. Klassen's sedan with the two other militiamen pulls up behind. A guard with a machine pistol and walkie-talkie looks at Mike.

The two cars drive through parkland to a 1930s-vintage mansion, lots of stone and ivy, then circle to park at the rear of the house among several dark, unmarked vans. Klassen's car parks directly against Mike's rear bumper, boxing it in.

Mike and Sue Ellen are hustled out of the Firebird and marched toward a rear door of the house. They see that the rear lawn slopes down to a private dock on the seashore, where men in black fatigues are loading cardboard drums into a large motor cruiser.

Inside the mansion, they are pushed along a hallway then through a door and down a flight of steps into a basement corridor. They're brought to a windowless storage room with concrete pillars supporting the ceiling. The room is filled with boxes, lawn furniture, garden tools, and other junk. Thrown on an old wicker chair is a canvas money bag with *WELLS FARGO* printed on it. There are blood stains on the bag.

Mike is looking around. "Say, who are you guys? What kind of place is this?"

Otto Nordling enters the room. Mike recognizes him from their encounter in the elevator. He also recognizes the insignia in Nordling's lapel. The recognition is mutual and Nordling's suspicions are aroused.

Klassen and the others have snapped to attention, but the gun remains on Mike.

"To answer your questions," Nordling says, "my name is Nordling. This is my home. And now I'd like to know who you are. And why are you snooping around where you have no business."

"I'm Mike Ishmael, P.I. This is Miss Sue Ellen Vanderhog, my client. I'm helping her look for her brother."

"That won't wash. I saw you this afternoon in the Krell Building. You've been following me."

"No, we were serving court papers on a man called Hamlin."

Nordling sneers. "And you just happened to wander into Squad Leader Klassen's place of business. No, again, I don't think so." He turns to Klassen. "Secure them."

There is rope hanging on a hook. They tie Mike and Sue Ellen to pillars facing each other. While this is happening, Nordling takes Klassen aside.

"I suppose it's just barely possible the girl *is* Vanderhog's sister. What is his assignment?"

"He should be loading the boat."

Nordling nods. "Let's keep him there." He looks over Mike's trench coat and fedora. "Remarkable costume, but isn't it fundamental to the idea of surveillance that one blends into the passing crowd?"

Mike says, "I don't understand."

Nordling shrugs. "Frankly, neither do I. You're either a complete fool playing some sort of childlike game, or the federal authorities have suddenly developed a sophisticated sense of humor—which I find highly unlikely, now that J. Edgar Hoover's favorite summer frock is hanging in the Smithsonian."

He pauses, thinks, then decides. "Well, either way, not to worry. Whoever or whatever you may be, *we* are very serious people, engaged in a rather delicate operation, which will soon be concluded. At that time, you will pose no danger to our plans, and we shall release you.

Mike struggles against the rope. "Hey, you can't keep us—"

Nordling gestures to Klassen. "Hit him."

The punch in the gut knocks the wind out of Mike. He sags against the ropes.

Sue Ellen cries, "Mike!"

Nordling says, "Until then, we would like you to remain quiet."

He gestures to the others. They leave the room, Nordling following. There is the sound of a bolt being thrown.

In the corridor, Nordling watches Klassen bolt the door. He tells two of the troopers to guard the door and the two others to report to their posts. Then he beckons Klassen to move out of earshot of the door guards.

"I don't like this. I'm advancing the schedule. We'll leave tonight, as soon as the boat is loaded. You go find Hamlin—I gave him money, so he's certain to be at the track. Bring him and his device here."

"Yes, sir." Klassen indicates the door. "What about our two . . . guests?"

Nordling has already decided. "They can join us for a boat ride into San Francisco Harbor. We'll get off this side of Alcatraz Island, but they can go all the way to the Customs Building. And . . ."

His hands mimic the opening of a flower. He finishes by compressing his lips then opening them with an audible *pop*.

Klassen chuckles. "Yes, sir. And Vanderhog?"

Nordling shrugs. "If the girl really is his sister, it could be a complication. He might as well accompany them."

Klassen comes to attention. "Sir."

"Dismissed."

AND NOW BACK TO Abner's pursuit of the white Cadillac. They're in Henry's car, with Henry driving and Abner in the passenger seat, leaning out the window, looking in every direction. The AK-47 rests on his thighs.

"I don't see him," Abner says.

Henry is not happy. "Abner, this is profoundly weird. Why don't we—"

"I don't wanna hear it!"

Henry make a noise between a moan and a sigh. "Well, I'm saying it anyway. I don't know about ghosts or haunted cars or the creature from the black lagoon. All I know is somebody is for real trying to kill you, and you're acting like some hero out of the late movie."

Abner grimaces. "Maybe I caught a dose of whatever's wrong with your, you know, *protégé*, Sam Spade Jr."

Henry wheels them around a corner, sees no sign of the Caddie. "Leave the kid be. Look, whoever's in that old Cadillac, he's down for attempted murder, right now, and we should call in the force."

Abner says, "Nope. Don't need 'em. This is tween me and Modie. You don't feel it, that this is how it's meant to be?"

"Jesus," says Henry.

Abner is scanning the street. Then a thought occurs. "Hey, speaking of dime-novel detectives, what happened to whatsisname?"

"Leave him be, Abner. He's got his own troubles."

"Yeah, I'll bet. Probably dreams of servin' a subpoena on Ming the Merciless." He picks up the handheld radio. "Why can't I remember his name?"

"It's Mike."

Abner pushes down the send button. "Hey, Mike. Mike, come in."

Which Mike can't do, because he's tied to a pillar with a sore tummy.

"He don't answer," Abner says. "How about cruising past our building again?"

Henry sighs and turns the wheel. Traffic has gotten heavier as rush hour builds. That's why neither of the detectives notices the Cadillac is several car lengths behind them, hidden by a truck.

IN THE STORAGE ROOM, Mike has recovered his breath. He's testing the rope that binds him. In the books and shows, private eyes often get into these tight situations, but then they get out of them. He is beginning to think real life won't be so neatly organized.

Sue Ellen is more concerned about Mike than their predicament.

"How do you feel?" she says.

"Like a jerk."

"You were very brave."

He makes a sour face. "I was very dumb." He pushes at the ropes, with no success. "Damn."

Sue Ellen looks around the basement room. "So, how do we get out of here?"

Mike finds the question depressing. "I don't know."

"I thought detectives had special techniques."

Mike says, "Listen, Sue Ellen, I gotta tell you. I'm starting to think I'm not really a detective. I'm thinking I'm just a guy who's always wanted to *be* a detective."

"But you work for a detective agency."

Mike doesn't know it, but he makes the same sound, between a moan and a sigh, that Henry just made on the other side of town. "Some agency. All my life, I dreamed of being a PI. I had all these stupid notions about solving crimes, about being a force for good, about maybe amounting to something. Then I find out all it is is chasing people who don't want to go to court or won't pay their bills. But you walk in, my first day on the job, and I think, well, maybe I can help this one person—this special person."

"I'm special?"

"To me, you are."

He's cheered her up considerably. "I've never been 'special' before."

Mike says, "I was kind of too shy to tell you before, like straight out, but now that we're probably gonna get killed . . ."

That changes her mood. "Killed? Why would they kill us? I'm sure once they talk to Duane—"

Mike hates to say it, but he has to. "These are bad guys, Sue Ellen, real bad guys. That money bag down there is from that Wells Fargo armored car robbery. They killed two guards. They're not gonna let us go. I'm so sorry I got you into this."

"Actually," she says, "I guess I have to say I was the one got *you* into it. If I hadn't been looking for Duane . . ."

"You don't have to try to make me feel better. Whichever way I feel, it's only going to be for a couple more hours."

He's making her angry. "Mike Ishmael, you stop that! You've got what my momma calls a defeatist attitude. Momma says you're never licked until you're dead, and even then you can hit them with a real bastard of a last will and testament. Pardon my language, but that's the way mama talks. Now, you've read all those books. How would one of those book detectives get out of here?"

Mike sighs. "The dream's over, Sue Ellen. This is not a book."

She's not having it. "Well, what about *my* dream? There's still a lot of stuff *I* want to do. Open a little business, maybe real estate, meet a good man, then marriage, children, teach 'em all the things my momma taught me."

"I'm sorry."

"Well, I don't take sorry. Sorry don't get the mare with foal."

"Let me guess. Your momma."

"Yeah, and she's right. Now, you start thinking like a detective in one of those stories. I got things to do with *my* life."

Mike's brow wrinkles under the fedora. "Well, okay, say we set fire to this place, maybe we could escape in the confusion."

Sue Ellen wants to encourage him. "That's a real good start. But do you think we ought to set a fire when we're all tied up like this? We might burn to death before anybody noticed."

Which lets the air out of Mike again. "Yeah, you're right. I don't know. In the books, the hero always gets a lucky break or his sidekick rescues him. Guess I should have got a sidekick."

But Sue Ellen has been thinking. "Wait a minute! I know something that might work! I saw it in a movie about a famous escape artist."

"Houdini?"

"I don't know. But what I remember is this guy did deep breathing, really deep, and the deeper he breathed the looser the ropes got, until he could slip out of them."

"I don't know if that works in real life."

Sue Ellen raises her voice. "Mike Ishmael, I never would've thought I'd hear you say such a thing. Here I was thinking I'd finally found a man who had some real faith in himself, somebody I might be able to share my . . . my *everything* with! And now you won't even try a little deep breathing with me."

Mike swallows. "Your . . . *everything*?"

Sue Ellen turns a little shy. "Well . . . yes."

"When you say everything," Mike wants to know, "would that include, like . . . everything?"

"Momma always says, if you're figuring on giving a man your hand, you got to line up everything else behind it."

"You know, suddenly, heavy breathing sounds like a good plan."

"That's *deep* breathing."

Mike says, "You breathe your way, I'll . . . Let's do it."

They begin breathing deeply, whooshing in and out, and keep it up for several seconds.

Mike says, "I'm getting dizzy, hyperventil . . ." He blows out a long *whoof* of air, eyes rolling.

"Keep it up." She takes several long and deep breaths. "I think it's working. Can you feel anything?"

Mike can't help but notice Sue Ellen's bosom, which is in considerable motion as she breathes in and out. Despite their predicament, the sight is a stimulant. The front of his trench coat tents out.

"Not the best of times for that," says Sue Ellen, "but I'll take it as a compliment."

She continues to breathe, then is able to wriggle in her bonds. "It's working! I'm getting out!"

She wriggles her shoulders and breathes deeply. Mike groans, and looks away. She wriggles some more, and now the ropes around her shoulders are definitely loosening. She ducks her head under them, and begins to free her arms.

A few moments later, she is out. She quickly unties him. He steps free, then briefly turns his back on her and adjusts his pants.

"All right! Now let's find a way out of here."

But the room has no windows.

Sue Ellen looks up the stairs and says, "They locked the door. Looks like the only way out is the way in."

Mike finds a spade, hefts it, then flicks off the light. "So, we wait."

MIKE IS NOT right about a sidekick always getting the sleuth out of trouble. Sometimes it's a wild card, and the wild card in this case is Kermit Sherman, an undercover Treasury Department agent from the Bureau of Alcohol, Tobacco, and

Firearms. He has been an inside man, spying on Nordling's militia for seven months and has been promoted to Senior Squad Leader.

He now comes down the corridor to where the two guards flank the door. He tells them to get to their assignments. "I'll take over here."

As soon as the two are out of sight, he unbolts the door and pokes his head in.

"Psst!" he hisses, then, "Where are you? I'm—"

Mike bashes Sherman over the head with the spade. The agent drops to the floor, unconscious. Mike and Sue Ellen step over him, and exit. Mike is still carrying the spade.

They come out into the corridor, now empty. They tiptoe along it in the same direction the guards went. When they get to a corner, they peek around it, and see another corridor. This one has a flight of stairs leading up. But when they get to the bottom of the stairs, they hear voices from above. Someone is coming down.

They spot a door nearby and open it, to find themselves in a small room that is bare except for two wooden chairs. There is a small window high in the wall. Mike shuts the door behind them and looks around.

He says, "We've got to find a phone and call the police."

Sue Ellen says, "The window."

Mike agrees. He leans his spade against the wall, carries a chair over to the window, and climbs on it to peek out. There are low shrubs spaced along the wall. Through a gap, he sees a portion of the estate's back lawn. Unfortunately, a dozen troopers are on the grass, practicing unarmed combat.

Mike gets down from the chair, tells Sue Ellen, "Trouble."

"What kind of trouble?"

Before he can answer, they hear shouts, followed by a blast from a whistle.

Mike says, "Big trouble."

He braces the second chair against the doorknob, climbs back up to the window, and opens it. "Come on."

THE WHISTLE SOUNDS AGAIN, as Mike crawls out of the window, then reaches back in to pull Sue Ellen out. They inch along behind the shrubs on their bellies. The troopers who had been practicing hand-to-hand fighting are just rounding the corner, going away.

Mike gets up on one knee and peers around. He takes Sue Ellen's hand and they run along the side of the house in the opposite direction. They come to a corner, and peek around it to see the parking area, with his car still hemmed in.

Beyond the vehicles, he can see dozens of Nordling's men forming up into squads. But there's nothing between him and the vehicles.

"Stay here," Mike says, "I'll go see if one of them has keys."

He scuttles to the cars and vans and looks in the windows, one after another, but finds no keys. Finally, he ducks down beside the passenger door on his own car and looks around, scared and frantic. He can hear shouted orders and knows that the bad guys are about to do a search.

Then he hears Abner's voice, very faint, coming from inside his car. Only then does he remember the radio Sue Ellen put under the passenger seat. He opens the door and takes it out, frantically fiddling with the volume control. He presses the call button, and whispers into the mic.

"Mr. Abner! This is Mike."

Abner is the front passenger-side seat of Henry's car. He sets down the assault rifle and puts the radio to his mouth.

"Yeah, yeah, Mike! Where are you?"

Mike keeps his voice low. "I'm at some place up the coast called Karinhall."

This is not what Abner wants to hear. "The hell are you doin' way out there, for chrissake?"

"I don't have time to explain. Listen, there are guys out here with guns. There's something weird goin' on. Can you call the—"

Abner says to Henry, "What's he talkin' about, guys with guns?"

Henry shrugs. "Maybe he's tracked down the Purple Gang." To himself, he say, "I'm surrounded by people with unusual enthusiasms."

Abner is shouting into the radio. "The hell with guys with guns! You're lookin' for a white Caddie!"

Mike hears the sound of tires on gravel. He peeks over the back of his car, sees Klassen's car drive up. The squad leader and Hamlin get out. Hamlin is carrying a small cardboard box. Mike ducks down behind the car again, whispers into the radio, "Please, Mr. Abner—"

"The Caddie, kid!"

Mike hears footsteps approaching. He ducks, desperate, and then he gets an inspiration.

"Yeah, the Caddie! It's here, Mr. Abner! I've seen it! But there's all these hard-looking guys. Better call the—"

Abner cuts him off. "Stay put! We'll be right there!" To Henry, he says, "The old Karinhall estate! Step on it!"

Henry is beyond argument. He turns the wheel hard over. Horns honk and someone cries, "Asshole!" as the car cuts across traffic and turns a corner.

The Caddie is blocked from following by traffic. Its engine revs and it rocks back and forth in frustration. A taxi cab is stopped right beside the Caddie's driver's side. Now the Caddie tries to change lanes, trying to nudge in front of the cab.

The cab driver leans on his horn. "The hell you think you're doin'?" He creeps the cab forward. "Get back in there, asshole!"

The driver's window on the Cadillac slowly rolls down a

couple of inches down. It's too dark for the cabbie to see anything inside. But a terrible stench comes through the cab's open window.

"Whoa, man!" says the cabbie. "Smells like something crawled up your tailpipe and died in there!"

Now the Cadillac's window rolls down a little more and the cab driver can just make out the shape of a head. Then he sees two glowing red eyes open and glare at him. The window continues to roll down.

The cabbie has had enough. He yanks the wheel hard, stomps on the gas, and pulls out into oncoming traffic, scattering cars amid a screech of brakes and more horns and curses. The Caddie follows, races to the intersection where Henry turned, and follows Henry's car.

BACK AT THE MANSION, Mike frantically pushes the call button, trying to get Abner back. But he hears shouts and running footsteps. They're coming closer.

He hears Nordling's voice from around the corner. "You men, check those cars."

Mike knows he can't stay where he is. He slips the radio back under the passenger seat of his car and quietly closes the door then turns, meaning to sneak back toward where he left Sue Ellen.

But a shadow suddenly blocks the sun. He looks up to see Klassen and Hamlin standing over him, with two troopers aiming assault rifles. He puts his hands up and slowly rises.

Meanwhile, Sue Ellen is crouching by the wall. She is about to peek around the corner, then she feels the muzzle of a pistol pressed against the back of her neck.

Her brother Duane, quite excited at having caught one of the escapees, says, "Hold it right there, little lady!"

Sue Ellen turns around and it's a toss-up which one of them is more shocked. Duane lowers the gun, and crouches down with her.

Sue Ellen whispers, "Duane! Thank God."

Duane is not good at figuring things out. He is often surprised by things that don't surprise those around him. "Sue Ellen? What the Sam Hill are you doing here?"

"Oh, Duane, I was looking for you. I came with this guy, Mike Ishmael—he's a detective, well, sort of—and then a man called Nordling grabbed us and tied us up."

She doesn't see her brother's expression harden. "But we got loose and now we're trying to get away and—"

Duane points the gun at her again and stands up. She says, "Duane! What are you doing?"

He gestures with the gun. "Sorry, sis. Move out."

"Duane! No!"

He elevates his chin. "Someday, when the last slimy tentacle of the New World Order has been pried loose from the fair bosom of American liberty, you'll thank me for this. Now move."

Sue Ellen shakes her head. "Momma was right about you, Duane. She always said you were an asshole."

But she stands up and raises her hands. He pushes her toward the corner of the wall, and when they come around it they find Mike standing with his hands raised while several troopers point their weapons at him. Then Nordling comes out of the house.

He smiles his grim smile. "Get them inside. Klassen, you assemble the men for a briefing. We're pulling out as soon as Mr. Hamlin installs the detonator and impact switch."

"Sir!" Klassen snaps to attention, then runs off.

HAMLIN IS in the forward cabin of the motor cruiser. The space is packed with cardboard barrels of ammonium nitrate fertilizer. There's a strong smell of bunker fuel oil, some of it leaking from the bottoms of the barrel. Hamlin wriggles between the containers to reach the forwardmost one.

Hamlin uses a screwdriver to make a hole in the top of the barrel then inserts a tubular detonator. He places the impact-sensor switch on top of the barrel, double-checks that it is set to *OFF*, then connects it to the wire from the detonator.

He then very carefully backs away. Moments later he comes up a companionway into the aft saloon of the boat. He spots a drinks cabinet and smiles when he opens it and finds it well stocked. He selects a bottle of well-aged single-malt scotch and pours himself a tumblerful.

He downs half of the liquor in one swallow, belches, then raises the glass. "God bless her and all who sail in her."

He downs the rest of the whiskey and reaches for the bottle.

DOWN IN THE basement storage room, troopers are tying Mike and Sue Ellen up again while Duane and Nordling watch. Sherman, the ATF G-man, is off to one side, having his head bandaged by another trooper who wears a red cross armband.

Nordling says, "Make it tight. Vanderhog?"

Duane snaps to attention. "Sir!"

"Good work. Shows the right spirit."

"Thank you, sir. I'm sure Sue Ellen will see the light, once you explain things to her."

"Of course," Nordling says. Why don't you go make sure Mr. Hamlin has things in hand on the boat."

Sue Ellen watches her brother salute and leave. "Asshole."

Nordling says, "I want a guard in this room."

Sherman gets to his feet. "Sir, I wish to volunteer."

Nordling looks him over, then smirks. "Well, you're not fit for action. Just keep it quiet."

NOW LET'S see what Abner and Henry are up to: they're driving by the gate of Nordling's estate, being watched by an armed guard.

Henry drives on about a hundred yards then stops under some trees by the estate wall.

Abner says, "Whaddaya think?"

"I think we should go home."

Abner glares at him and Henry gives in. "Okay, okay. Only one guard, but he's got a gun and a walkie-talkie. We bypass him."

Abner is all in. "Yeah. Let's go."

Henry puts the car in close to the wall, right under a tree. They get out and climb onto the car's roof, from where it's an easy ascent up into the tree. Abner goes first and gets to the top of the wall, where Henry hands him the AK-47 and Uzi then comes up after him.

Meanwhile, the Cadillac passes by the gate, watched by the guard, and continues up the road to where Henry's car is parked. It stops. Its engine whines, a sound of automotive frustration.

Now the Caddie peels off further up the road, slews around in a bootlegger turn, and comes back. It stops for a moment beside Henry's car then drives on. It goes back past the gate, stops about fifty yards down the road, and turns around again.

The gate guard has been watching this, and he now wears a frown of suspicion. He fingers his radio.

HENRY AND ABNER are now moving through the estate's parkland, taking cover behind trees and bushes. Ahead of them, a wide lawn leads to a low-walled patio which runs the length of one side of the house and is surrounded by a waist-high brick wall. This side of the mansion features a row of curtained French windows.

They duck down behind a topiary bush. Henry pulls a small pair of binoculars from his pocket and studies the windows. "I think that's a ballroom."

Two troopers in combat fatigues and carrying assault rifles step out of the house and take up sentry positions at the edge of the patio.

Abner says, "What is this? The goddamn army?"

Henry says, "Uh-uh. Those aren't soldiers. And they aren't the mob. Too clean-cut."

Abner borrows the glasses, takes a look. "Could be Chu-chu Venucci's boys."

"Why Venucci's?"

"He's, you know, light in the loafers. Likes 'em big and blond.

Henry stares at him. "Where do you hear this stuff? Never mind. Question is, what are we going do about this? If that is the mob, and they're holding some kind of convention, I don't think we ought to consider ourselves invited."

Abner is not deterred. "Listen. The kid says Modie's here, an' I want him. I'm goin' in. You wanna come, come. You wanna stay, stay. But I'm goin' in. So whadda we do about the guards?"

Henry takes the glasses back, studies the scene again. "Let me think." After a while, he says, "Okay, listen."

TWO TROOPERS ARE PATROLLING near a stand of evergreens. They come around a large evergreen and find Abner sprawled face down on the ground. They run over to him, and one points his rifle while the other reaches for his walkie-talkie.

Henry steps out of the tree aiming the Uzi. "Ding-dong."

The troopers see him and freeze.

"That's good," Henry says. "We'll just keep this between us, okay?"

He takes their radio and rifles. Abner gets up, says, "Into the trees."

The troopers pass out of sight, followed by Abner and Henry. Two solid *thumps* follow. Then the detectives re-emerge, carrying the assault rifles, which they throw into the bushes.

Abner recovers his AK-47 from behind a tree. "Now let's go find Modie."

OUT ON THE ROAD, the Caddie has been waiting for Abner to reappear, rocking back and forth impatiently near Henry's car. Now it spins around and drives back past the closed gates. The guard watches through the bars of the closed gate.

BACK IN THE basement storage room, troopers have finished tying up Mike and Sue Ellen. This time they used a lot more rope. One of them eyes Sue Ellen, then turns to Sherman.

"Have fun."

The troopers exit and Sherman follows them to the door, where he looks out into the corridor, watching them until they are out of sight.

Mike is depressed. *The Rockford Files* was never this grim. "Well, I guess this is it."

Sue Ellen has also lost her spark. "I guess so. Oh, if only Duane wasn't such an—"

"Yeah. Well, I can't say it's been a great life, but I'm glad I had a chance to know you."

She smiles at him. "Me too."

He brightens a little. "It was a nice dream, about the . . . everything."

Sherman closes the door and comes to stand between them. "Okay, you two, I don't have much time—"

Mike strains at the ropes in impotent rage. "You lay a hand on her, I'll bust these ropes and—"

Sherman puts a hand over Mike's mouth, cutting him off. "Shut up and listen. I'm a special agent of the Treasury Department—Alcohol, Firearms, and Tobacco Branch.

Mike is impressed. "No kidding, a T-Man?"

"Special Agent Lance Tiberias Sherman the Third."

Sue Ellen is not so impressed. "Really? You're the *third* Lance Tiberias Sherman?"

Sherman bristles. "Something funny about that? Listen, there's been Shermans in the federal government since—"

She cuts him off. "Can you help us escape?"

Sherman touches the bandage around his head, winces a little. "That's what I was trying to do when you slugged me. But there isn't time now."

He unties them both.

Mike says, "Why not?"

"Because you've spooked Nordling. Now he's moved up the launch of the operation by twenty-four hours. We're not ready for that."

"What operation?" Sue Ellen wants to know. "What's he planning to do?"

"He's going to steam into San Francisco bay with a boatload of explosives. He'll blow up the U.S. customs house on the waterfront. When all the cops rush down to the docks, an assault team will storm the federal building downtown. They'll kill as many government employees as they can, empty the vault in the savings bank on the ground floor, and head for the hills. Start a movement."

Mike says, "What for? Why would they do that?"

"Nordling has a dream," Sherman says. "He thinks people like him ought to be running the country. And when he says, "people like him," he means *just* like him, and he doesn't think anybody could be more like him than he is."

Sue Ellen is aghast. "He wants to overthrow the government?"

"Yep. And then he wants to *be* the government."

She sighs. "Momma always told Duane not to mix with people like that."

Sherman says, Your brother *is* 'people like that.' Anyway, there's a combined ATF-FBI task force all ready to hit them when they move out. The Coast Guard will pick up the ship out at sea."

Mike claps his hands. "That's great!"

"Yeah, well it would have been great, except it was all laid on for tomorrow. Now it's going to happen today. We're not ready."

Sue Ellen says, "Can't you just call your people and have them move up the raid?"

Sherman rolls his eyes. "Have you any idea what it takes to set up a tri-service operation like this? I mean the paperwork alone? Besides, my radio is in my kit on the boat. About the best I can do is try to find a phone and call the local district office. And that means I have to talk to Agent-in-Charge Saunders." He rolls his eyes again.

Mike feels like a schmuck. "Oh."

Sue Ellen says, "We're really very sorry."

"Well, can't be helped." Sherman shrugs then gets down to business. "So listen, I got to get you two out of here. You can hide in the trees. Then I have to figure out some way to get to a phone."

Mike says, "There's a radio hidden in my car."

"What frequencies will it transmit on?"

"I don't know. Lots, I think."

Sherman punches his fist into his palm. "Okay, we'll give her the old college try."

He goes to the door, opens it and looks out, then signals for them to follow him.

REMEMBER the ballroom that Henry spied through the French windows? It's been converted into a military briefing room. The outer wall is lined with French windows, their curtains drawn. Along the other three walls the vaulted ceiling is supported by heavy marble columns. At one end is a knee-high dais where musicians used to play, back when this was a scene of dancing and conviviality.

About forty troopers in combat fatigues with slung assault rifles sit on folding chairs at one end of the room, facing the dais, waiting for a briefing. At the back of the dais are a flag with the lightning-bolt insignia and map boards that display the maps we saw earlier in Nordling's office.

Now Nordling strides in from a door at the back of the room. The troopers snap to attention as he mounts the dais and picks up a pointer.

"At ease. Be seated. Now, you've all been drilled in this exercise. This will be the final briefing before we move out, which will be in . . ."—he checks his watch—"twenty minutes."

The troopers stir in excitement. The word "Hooah" is heard.

OUTSIDE, Henry and Abner are sneaking across the low-walled patio to the French windows. They hear the voices from within and flatten against the wall. They can hear Nordling talking but can't make out the words.

Abner looks for a gap in the curtains, but can't find one. "We're gonna have to go in."

Henry says, "I don't like it. We haven't seen Modie's car. This feels wrong."

THE CADILLAC IS AIMED at the gates now, not far off, rocking back and forth, barely held by the brakes, its engine roaring. The guard pushes the button on his walkie-talkie and opens his mouth to speak.

IN THE BALLROOM, Nordling is completing the briefing.

"We'll hit the customs house at approximately 9:15 a.m. At the sound of the explosion, gun teams will enter the federal building"—he taps the map with a pointer—"here, here and here. Team A will take care of the bank, while Teams B and C will give us a maximum body count. I want everybody clear and back in the vans by ten minutes after the jump-off. Any questions? Good. Then let's move out."

The troopers stand up.

Outside, Abner has his ear to the glass. He says, "I heard a guy talking. Now it's quiet. Let's take a look."

Henry is less than enthusiastic. "Do me a favor. Hide the weaponry until we see what we're getting into." He tucks the Uzi under his suit jacket.

Abner folds up the AK-47 and hides it under his coat. "Okay, okay. Ready?"

"No."

"Come on."

He tries the French window and finds it locked. He steps back and kicks it in, and he and Henry rush into the ballroom. They're at the far end of the space. The troopers are still facing the dais but they spin around fast, unslinging their assault rifles. There is a lot of clicking of bolts.

Abner and Henry stop cold. For a moment, nobody moves or speaks. Then Abner says, "The hell is this, Boy Scouts?"

Henry says, "I would say we made a mistake."

Nordling says, "You certainly have. Klassen, kill them."

Klassen motions to two troopers. The men raise their guns.

Abner and Henry look at each other a moment, then Abner swings up the AK-47 from inside his jacket and Henry draws the Uzi. They both open fire while backing to get behind the marble columns.

The troopers who haven't been hit break ranks and return fire. Nordling ducks and exits through the rear door.

BACK TO THE FRONT GATES. The guard hears the gunfire, and speaks into his radio.

"Hey, what's goin' on up there?"

And then he hears the sound of the Cadillac swerving in from the road. It crashes through the gate, knocking the guard flying. The car disappears up the drive toward the house.

MIKE, Sue Ellen and Sherman are tiptoeing along a corridor in the basement. They hear the firefight upstairs.

Sherman looks puzzled. "That can't be our guys. Not in the schedule."

Mike says, "Maybe somebody else has a dream he's working on."

Sherman shrugs. "Whatever, time we got out, now!"

"This way," Mike says. "There's a window."

THE TROOPERS ARE SPREAD out at their end of the hall, hiding behind chairs and columns. Some are dead or wounded. Nordling puts his head through door.

"Klassen!"

Klassen is crouching behind the dais, ducking fire from Henry and Abner. He gets down on his belly and slithers over to Nordling.

Several troopers are behind the columns on the inner wall of the room. They try to rush the detectives while others give suppressing fire. But Abner and Henry fire and cut them down. Abner looks over at Henry.

"You see Modie 'fore we ducked?"

Henry fires a burst. "For Christ's sake, Abner!"

Nordling tells Klassen, "We're wasting too many men. Take a squad around the side of the house and hit them from the rear."

Klassen beckons to five men behind the columns. "With me, the back door."

They scuttle out.

THE CADDIE PULLS UP outside the front of the mansion, revs its engine, then drives around the side.

Meanwhile, Sherman, Mike, and Sue Ellen have come out the basement window. They run down the side of the house toward the rear where the cars are parked. They make it to Mike's car. He gets the radio and gives it to Sherman, who resets it.

BACK IN THE ballroom Henry is putting a new magazine into the Uzi. He sees Klassen and his squad leave.

"They're going to flank us! Let's get the hell out of here!"

"You sure you didn't see Modie?"

"Abner!"

"Okay, okay! Cover me!"

Henry blasts away with the Uzi, and Abner scuttles through the French windows, then ducks down and gives covering fire while Henry scuttles out.

ABNER AND HENRY run to the low brick wall between the lawn and the patio. Abner raises his head to look out. Suddenly, bullets chew up the wall and he ducks down.

Klassen and his squad are running across the lawn toward them, firing.

Henry says to Abner, "Gimme that!" He seizes the AK-47, quickly resets it to single-round fire, rises up and fires four quick shots. Four troopers drop. Klassen and the lone survivor dive to the ground.

Abner says, "Nice shooting, Henry."

"You forget I was Department champion?"

Behind them, glass blows out as troopers in the ballroom shoot through the French windows. Abner picks up the Uzi and returns fire into the mansion.

Meanwhile, Klassen and the remaining trooper have scrambled for cover behind some decorative bushes and now they fire at Abner and Henry. Henry returns fire. Abner continues to fire short bursts into the ballroom.

And then the Cadillac comes around a corner of the house and onto the side lawn.

Now let's go into the haunted car and see what its occupant sees: Abner on the patio, ducked down behind the low wall, shooting into the mansion.

The Caddie's engine inches its way across the lawn toward the patio, like a cat stalking a mouse.

Henry is focused on Klassen and his trooper. He tells Abner, "Give me more another clip."

Abner feels in his pockets. "All I got's the AP."

"That'll have to do." Henry reloads the AK-47. Pops up above the wall, and ducks as bullets hit close. "We're too exposed here! This way!"

He points down the side of the house, past the remaining French windows. Abner fires one last burst into the ballroom, and turns to run. Henry fires to keep Klassen's head down, then runs after Abner.

And now we really should look in on Mike and Sue Ellen, crouched beside parked cars at the rear of the mansion. Sherman is finally getting through on the radio.

"Highball, this is Gin Fizz. Highball, this is Gin Fizz, copy?"

"Gin Fizz?" says Mike.

Sherman looks a little abashed. "Alcohol, Tobacco and Firearms humor."

Mike says, "Sheesh."

The radio squawks. A voice says, "This is Highball. Go ahead."

Sherman talks fast. "Listen, you got to hit this place now, repeat now! All hell's breaking loose here!"

There is a pause, then the radio voice says, "Copy, Gin Fizz. Cavalry's on the way."

ABNER AND HENRY, running in a bent-over crouch, are just about to pass the last of the French windows.

Now the Caddie accelerates across the lawn toward the patio.

Abner looks back and sees the Caddie coming toward him. With a look of quiet joy, he stops, turns, and raises the Uzi.

Henry looks at him. "The hell are you doing? Keep moving!"

Abner says, "I knew he was here somewhere."

Klassen and the other trooper have scooted forward to the other side of the low wall. They pop up and fire at Abner. Henry returns fire and shoots them both. The armor-piercing rounds do massive damage to the bodies.

Abner pays no attention. He stands up, coaxes the Caddie toward him. "Come on, bring it on."

WHILE THE FIREFIGHT was going on, Nordling had hidden in a corridor beyond the rear door of the ballroom, uncertain which way to flee. Now that the firing stops, he steps back through the door, sees the dead and dying, but focuses on those troopers still available to be commanded.

Some of them are warily approaching the shot-out French windows. Now they look to Nordling for orders.

"Klassen must have got them. The rest of you, move out. I'm going to the boat!" He sees a trooper stoop to help a wounded man. "Leave him!"

He departs through the door behind the dais.

OUT ON THE PATIO, the Cadillac crosses the last stretch of lawn and crashes through the side wall, scattering chunks of brick and smashing its grill and bumper. Abner aims and opens fire with the Uzi, to no discernible effect.

But Henry has the AK-47 loaded with armor-piercing rounds. He flicks the setting switch to full automatic and opens fire on the onrushing vehicle. Several rounds penetrate the busted front. Smoke and steam rise from under the wrinkled hood.

The car's steering is wrecked. It slews sideways and crashes through the French windows. Abner, ecstatic, follows it in, firing.

IN ACTION SCENES, details count. So now we go inside the Cadillac and see a skeletal hand dropping the column shift into first gear, while a rotted shoe, with spats and a bony big toe protruding, stomps on the gas pedal.

The Caddie fishtails on the smooth floor. The last of the troopers scatter for the exits.

Abner, screaming, chases the Caddie, firing. More details as the car's headlights explode, the side mirrors are torn off, and the chromium Vee on the hood spins away. The license plate dangles by a single screw. Abner keeps firing, until he runs out of ammunition.

Smoke billows from the shattered engine, which sputters and then dies.

Abner lowers the Uzi. "Now come outta there."

Henry enters through the French windows as Abner limps toward the Caddie.

The Caddie's door stays closed. Abner advances on the car.

Some more details: The red eyes glow in bony sockets. The skeletal hand clears seaweed from the ignition key and cranks it.

The Caddie's engine grinds and sputters, making a tortured sound, then some of the cylinders catch. The car lurches toward Abner. Abner raises the Uzi and pulls the trigger, but it fires only one shot before the magazine is empty.

He turns and limps at his maximum speed toward the other end of the ballroom.

The Caddie, skidding and pouring out smoke, chases him.

Just before it reaches him, he skids on a pool of blood and falls to one side, fetching up against the dead trooper who supplied the blood.

The car just misses Abner. It screeches to a halt, backs in a turn and points itself at him again.

Abner is worn out from all the running and shooting. "This is getting' ridiculous," he pants.

Henry has come to help him up. "I told you. Would you listen?"

Henry takes aim, and fires at the Caddie. Both front tires blow, and the car skids more wildly.

Abner's gaze falls upon the dead trooper, and specifically on a concussion grenade clipped to the man's belt. He stoops and seizes the grenade, as the Caddie slews in another attempt to run him down.

Henry aims the assault rifle but he is out of ammo. He calls to Abner, "I'm out of ammo! Throw me a clip!"

But Abner has another plan. He limps over to one of the marble columns and gets behind it. "Stay there, Henry. I gotta do this alone!"

Henry looks around for another weapon. "I'm coming to help you, partner!

Abner shakes his head. "No, Henry. Just me, this time."

The Caddie lumbers across the floor to hit the column Abner s behind, but it slews and crashes into the column sideways. Its passenger door is crushed and flies open.

Abner sees the open door. He pulls the pin on the grenade, clutching it tightly.

The Caddie's wheels spin on the ballroom floor as it tries to set itself for another go at Abner. But Abner is not trying to get away now.

"Modie Bick!" he shouts. "Twenty-five years is enough! You're goin' out of my dreams for good!"

Henry shouts, "Abner, no!"

But Abner screams, with the grenade held high, and launches himself at the open door. He dives into the front seat, holding the grenade in one hand, and seizing Modie by the neck with the other. Then he sees what he's holding.

More details: Twenty-five years at the bottom of the harbor have not been good to Modie. He is mostly slimy bone and tattered cloth. The only thing lively about him is the red glow in his eye sockets.

Abner gags at the sight—and particularly the smell—of Modie.

"Oh, shit!"

He releases the corpse and turns to get out of the car. Modie's jaws open. A small sea snail crawls out of one corner of his mouth.

The dead man's voice is appropriately deep and sepulchral. "Whyncha stay awhile, Abner? For old times sake."

The door slams closed. Abner looks at the door, the corpse, and the live grenade.

"I changed my mind."

He clutches the grenade with both hands, and kicks at the door with his feet. It begins to open.

Modie says, "Nuh-uh, Abner. We got business."

SMOKING AND SLEWING, she Caddie heads smoking for an undamaged set of French windows. On the way it sideswipes another column. The passenger door is jammed closed.

Henry jumps out of the way, then chases after the car. He follows it outside, where it crosses the patio and crashes through the wall Henry and Abner had hid behind.

ABNER WRESTLES with the steering wheel and tries to step on the brake pedal. But Modie's corpse is in the way, and he needs to keep one hand firmly holding the pin-pulled grenade.

"What kinda business?" Abner feels he has to say, even though he doesn't want an answer.

Modie says, "I'm takin' you for a ride, Abner! Your turn to sleep with the fishes!"

Abner says, "You always were a walkin' cliché."

The corpse laughs. Its lower jaw drops off again.

BACK AT THE rear of the mansion, Mike, Sue Ellen, and Sherman are still hunkered down beside Mike's car. They see troopers running from the house and piling into vans in the parking lot. Then Nordling staggers out of the house and heads for the dock.

Distant sirens are sounding, lots of them and coming closer.

Sherman gets up. "I gotta stop that guy!" He chases after Nordling.

Mike tells Sue Ellen, "Stay here. I'm going to help. The feds are on the way."

He follows Sherman. Sue Ellen gets to her feet. "Mike! Be careful! This is real!"

After a moment's hesitation, she follows him.

SLEWING AND FISHTAILING, billowing smoke, the Caddie has got around to the rear of the mansion, where the lawn slopes down toward a dock jutting out into the sea, with the motor cruiser tied up beside it. With gravity's help, the car picks up speed.

Through the starred windshield, Abner sees where they are headed. He tries to crank the wheel around, one handed.

Modie growls, "Leave it be, Abner!"

MEANWHILE, the boat is now under power, the water gently churning at its stern. Hamlin, the engineer, slightly drunk, staggers onto the deck and casts off a bow line. Duane is with him, looking uncertain.

He says, "Shouldn't we wait for the Commander?"

Hamlin draws himself up. "Son, I am a trained engineer. I can describe for you with mathematical precision exactly what happens when shit impacts a fan. You heard the gunshots and now you hear the sirens. But if you want, you can get your ass back on the dock and find out for yourself, along with your beloved Commander."

Duane may not be bright, but he does have a sense of survival. "What do I do?"

"Go below, and bring me that damned switch. Carefully."

Nordling runs shakily down the dock as Hamlin finishes casting off and goes to the bridge. "Wait! Hamlin, wait!"

Hamlin is at the controls. He hears Nordling's voice over the chugging of the engines. Hamlin looks over his shoulder and sees Nordling running toward the boat.

Hamlin turns to look forward and reaches for the throttle. "Anchors away, my boys, anchors away."

The boat engine roars and the boat begins to move.

Nordling is running but Sherman is gaining on him, with Mike coming up behind them on the dock.

Sherman shouts, "Nordling! Federal agent! You're under arrest!"

Nordling stops and turns. He draws a military .45 from a holster and fires one-handed at Sherman. Sherman goes down, shot in the shoulder. He rolls off the dock into the water.

Nordling now turns his gaze on Mike and he raises his gun to fire again. Mike stops, scared, and raises his hands.

"I'm unarmed. Don't shoot."

Nordling lowers the gun and gives Mike the kind of look you give to an underachieving nephew. "Ah. I almost wish I could keep you around, just to enjoy your charming naivete. However . . ."

He raises the gun again. Then Mike sees the commander's eyes widen and he leaps sideways off the dock. Mike turns to look behind him and sees the Cadillac barreling down to dock toward him, smoke streaming from under its battered hood.

INSIDE THE CAR, Abner is still fighting for control. But Modie has seized the wheel in both skeletal hands, which have surprising strength considering they have no muscle.

Panicked, Abner is shouting, "Goddamn! Goddamn! Goddamn!"

MIKE DIVES into the water after Nordling as the Caddie rockets toward the end of the dock.

On the motor cruiser, Hamlin sees the Caddie coming and puts the wheel hard over while pushing the throttle lever to maximum.

Meanwhile, below decks, Duane is moving heavy containers out of the way, searching for the switch. Finally, he sees it and squeezes forward to reach for it. He touches it, just as the boat heels over and the cargo shifts.

His fingers lose their his grip, but not before his fumbling has set the switch set to *ON*.

THE CADDIE REACHES the end of the dock, hits a bollard, and arcs into the air. Inside, the impact throws Abner and the corpse together. Abner drops the grenade.

Abner says, "Holy Mary and all the angels!"

Modie laughs. "Don't expect you'll be seein' them, Abner. Less they like to swim."

The boat rocks as the Caddie leaves the dock and hits the water a few feet in front of the bow. It wallows in the splash waves.

Down in the forward cabin, Duane scrambles to get his fingers on the switch again, but he's getting pushed around as the barrels shift under the boat's motion.

NOW A FEW THINGS happen in sequence:

Henry runs onto the dock.

The Caddie sinks nose-first to the bottom.

Abner, frantic, searches on the floor for the grenade.

Modie says, "Don't sweat it, Abner. You might like bein' dead."

Abner's fingers touch the grenade. He grabs it, and smiles.

Duane's fingers connect with the switch. He smiles.

The Caddie hits bottom.

The grenade jumps out of Abner's fingers.

Hamlin guns the engine.

The cargo shifts again, and Duane loses his grip on the switch.

Abner says, "Oh shit."

Henry says, "Oh shit."

Duane says, "Oh shit."

And Modie says, "No shit."

He gets the last laugh as the grenade explodes.

The boat is rocked by the underwater explosion. In the forward cabin, a light on the motion-activated switch comes on.

Then the motor cruiser is blown to smithereens.

TREADING WATER NEAR THE DOCK, Mike ducks under the pilings as wreckage from the boat rains down. There he finds Sherman, wounded but not too badly.

Nordling is not so lucky, being farther out. A piece of wreckage, ironically decorated with a lightning bolt, hits him on the head.

Mike helps Sherman to a nearby ladder, where Henry helps him up onto the dock. Mike paddles out, grabs Nordling's collar, and hauls him in to shore. Henry sees him and goes down the ladder to help.

As they get the unconscious militia leader onto the concrete, they hear sirens crescendo, then cut out.

Henry says to Mike, "You okay?"

"Yeah." Mike looks around. "Where's Mr. Abner?"

Henry doesn't answer for a moment, then points at the floating wreckage. "Out there."

Mike doesn't know what to say. But all potential conversation becomes academic as armed federal agents in body armor swarm toward the dock from around the house. Sherman waves to them.

Nordling is regaining consciousness. Two agents haul him to his feet and lead him away.

Sue Ellen comes up to Mike and hugs him. They walk up toward the house with Henry.

Henry says, "Well, is this the kind of detective work you were dreaming of when you were taking that correspondence course?"

"I guess it was," Mike says. "I mean we nailed the bad guys and stopped them blowing up the waterfront."

Henry nods. "And I lost a partner."

Sue Ellen puts a hand on Henry's arm. "I lost a brother." She thinks for a moment, then adds, "Not such a big loss."

Mike says, "I'm starting to think maybe it's better, people don't get their dreams come true."

Henry stops him. "No, son, don't think about it that way. Abner finally got what he always needed." He looks at them sideways. "And maybe I could say the same for you two."

Mike and Sue Ellen look at each other. Clearly, Henry is right.

But Mike says, "All the same, Henry, I'm starting to doubt whether I'm cut out for real-life detective work."

"So you'll be signing up for another one of those correspondence courses?"

Sue Ellen has a suggestion. "Maybe in real estate. I know where you can find your first client."

Mike smiles at her. "I think what I need is a good partner."

"Well Momma always says you give a man what he needs, he'll be too worn out to want anything different."

Says Mike, "I'm kind of looking forward to meeting your mother."

Sherman catches up with them, his shoulder bandaged. "Task force leader's going to want to talk to you folks. You know, there's a twenty thousand dollar federal fugitive reward for Nordling. And Wells Fargo put up another twenty grand."

Henry tells Mike, "That ought to get you started."

When they reach the top of the slope, they stop and look back at the wreckage.

Mike says, "What about you, Henry?"

Henry contemplates the mess down below and sighs. "Abner and I had joint wills. I'll inherit his share of the business. Guess I'll just keep doing what I do. But I'll keep his name on the door."

As for Abner, he is now a ghost. He's sitting, sad and disgusted, on the end of the dock. Modie's ghost, looking like a generic old-time gangster in homburg and spats, comes and sits beside him.

Abner glares at him. "Will you look what you done to me?"

Modie shrugs. "You get used to it."

"I hate your guts, Modie."

Another shrug. "Crabs ate my guts, long time back."

Abner makes a disgusted sound.

"You know, Abner, I wasn't dead when I hit the water. Paralyzed, couldn't move, but there was enough air to keep me alive a while. I spent that time thinkin' of you.

"That's nothin'. I spent twenty-five years thinking of you."

"Look, Abner," Modie says, "we both got what we wanted. You got to kill me twice. And, what the hell, now I'm outta that stinkin' car. What say we let bygones be bygones, go haunt someplace classy?"

Abner doesn't reply for a while. Then he says, "Remember that asshole, McSweeney?"

Modie nods. "Used to run the North Side numbers action? What a piece of crap he was."

"I hear he's retired. Got a big fancy place out inna valley."

"I never liked McSweeney," Modie admits.

"Me neither. Whatta ya say?"

Another admission from the gangster's ghost. "You do a pretty good scream." He offers his hand. Abner's ghost hesitates, then shakes.

"But if there's any drivin', I'm doin' it."

"I never see the inside of a car again," Modie's ghost says, "suits me fine."

Up at the mansion, Mike and Sue Ellen stand with their arms around each other's waists, watching the sun go down. Henry stands a little apart from them.

Two small globes of light lift from the end of the dock and spiral up into the air. Henry sees them and smiles.

Mike and Sue Ellen turn to each other. Of course, you knew this had to end with a kiss.

And it's a good one.

BIBLIOGRAPHY

Fools Errant, Maxwell Macmillan Canada, Toronto, 1994; republished by Warner Aspect, New York, 2001, (304 pages)

Downshift, Doubleday Canada, Toronto, 1997, (256 pages); republished by Five Rivers Press, Neustadt, ON, 2013

Fool Me Twice, Warner Aspect, New York, 2001, (304 pages)

Gullible's Travels, Science Fiction Book Club, New York, (omnibus edition of *Fools Errant* and *Fool Me Twice*), (401 pages)

Black Brillion, Tor, New York, 2004; Science Fiction Book Club, New York, 2005, (272 pages)

The Gist Hunter and Other Stories, (short story collection), Night Shade Books, San Francisco, 2005, (247 pages)

Majestrum, Night Shade Books, San Francisco, 2006, (209 pages)

The Commons, (a Guth Bandar novel), Robert J. Sawyer Books, Toronto, 2007, (311 pages)

Wolverine: Lifeblood, (writing as Hugh Matthews) Pocket Books, New York, 2007, (320 pages)

The Spiral Labyrinth, Night Shade Books, San Francisco, 2007, (256 pages)

Template, PS Publishing, Hornsea, Yorks, UK, 2008, (pages t/c)

Hespira, Night Shade Books, San Francisco, 2008 (pages t/c)

The Other (a Luff Imbry novel), Underland Press, Portland, OR, Spring(?) 2011

To Hell and Back: The Damned Busters, Angry Robot, London, May/June 2011

Song of the Serpent (writing as Hugh Matthews), Paizo Publishing, Bellingham, WA, April 2012

To Hell and Back: Costume Not Included, Angry Robot, London, March 2012

To Hell and Back: Hell to Pay, Angry Robot, London, February 2013

Old Growth, (writing as Matt Hughes) Five Rivers Publishing, Neustadt, ON, 2013

9 Tales of Henghis Hapthorn, self-published collection of backlist stories, 2013

The Meaning of Luff and Other Stories, self-published collection of backlist stories, 2014

The Compleat Guth Bandar, self-published collection of backlist stories, 2014

Devil or Angel and Other Stories, self-published collection of backlist stories, 2015

A Wizard's Henchman, PS Publishing, Hornsea, Yorks, UK, 2016; originally serialized as *The Kaslo Chronicles* in *Lightspeed Magazine*

9 Tales of Raffalon, self-published collection of backlist stories, 2017

One More Kill, PS Publishing, Hornsea, Yorks, UK, 2018

What the Wind Brings, Pulp Literature Press, Vancouver, 2019

A God in Chains, Edge Science Fiction and Fantasy Publishing, Calgary, 2019

Forays of a Fat Man (A Luff Imbry Omnibus), PS Publishing, Hornsea, Yorks, UK, 2019

Barbarians of the Beyond, (a sequel to Jack Vance's *The Demon Princes*), Spatterlight Press, Oakland, CA, USA, 2021

The Emir's Falcon, a YA novella, (Shadowpaw Press, 2022)

Baldemar, a Dying Earth fantasy novel self-published in 2022

Passengers & Perils, a space-opera SF novel self-published in 2022

Ghost Dreams, PS Publishing, Hornsea, Yorks, UK, November 2022; self-published in North America, December 2022

The Ghost-Wrangler, a fantasy novel self-published in 2023

Modie, an urban fantasy novella self-published in 2023

Cascor, a collection of Dying Earth stories, self-published in 2023

A God in Hiding, self-published in 2023

The One, a space opera novel self-published in 2024

Margolyam, a Dying Earth fantasy novel self-published in 2024

A NOTE FROM THE AUTHOR

I put out a monthly newsletter, with news on what I'm writing, forthcoming books, sometimes a brief autobiographical episode, and other goodies.

Anyone who signs up by following the link below gets a free ebook (epub and Kindle) of 9 *Tales of Henghis Hapthorn*, the first of the Hapthorn series.

http://eepurl.com/cyNSA9

www.ingramcontent.com/pod-product-compliance
Lightning Source LLC
Chambersburg PA
CBHW060415180626
46817CB00007B/2587